Part One

Seth Garner

An Early American Story of Wild Adventure, True Love and Unmatched Courage

Front Cover image: "1882 US Great Seal Centennial Medal Obverse" by U.S. Government. Medal made by Charles E. Barber (Chief Engraver of the U.S. Mint). - Extracted from PDF version of Commemorating the Seal poster, part of a State Department exhibition on the Great Seal. Direct PDF URL [1] (33MB). Licensed under Public Domain via Wikimedia Commons –

http://commons.wikimedia.org/wiki/File:1882_US_Great_Seal_Centennial_Medal_Obverse.jpg#/media/File:1882_US_Great_Seal_Centennial_Medal_Obverse.jpg

ISBN: 978-1-511411-26-4

All rights reserved. No part of this publication may be reproduced, stored in a retrieval system, or transmitted in any form or by any means—electronic, mechanical, photocopy, recording, or any other—except for brief quotations in printed reviews, without the prior permission of the author.

*Dedicated to my father-in-law,
Chloe Selden Stewart*

Contents

Part I—Breaking Away

1. Escape from Heathshire 13
2. Trader Jack 29
3. Prudence Nightshade 45
4. Spies Among Us 85
5. The Big Float South 113
6. The Treachery 145
7. Battle in the Bayou 157
8. Two Madams and a Princess 177
9. Into Texas 199
10. A Vile Deed Done 217
11. Two Rangers, a Scout and a Mission 223
12. Judgment in Mexico 231

Preface

Time matters when it's human. That is, the only history we can know is one that has a human face. That is why great writers such as Dickens, Melville, Twain, and London all realized that the story of life can only be the story of people. For them, the varied landscapes of geography, climate, culture, and politics were all, in one way or another, the landscape of humanity. Strong characters wed to equally powerful storylines not only made sense of times past but also gave direction for times yet to come. More recent authors such as Stephen Ambrose (*June 6th 1944 and Undaunted Courage*), David McCullough (*John Adams* and *1776*) and Laura Hillenbrand (*Sea Biscuit* and *Unbroken*) clothed the dry bones of history in the warm flesh of human beings. In so doing, events long dead came to life again and inspired the living to keep going forward.

In some measure, the goal of this present book is to give place to the life-bearing spirit that lay behind the aforementioned works. Indeed, its task is to bring together two great births; the birth of one Seth Garner and the birth of a nation, the United States. Its method is to parallel the growth and experiences of them both, all of the pain and the promise, the fear and the fight to the point that one informs the other, one affects the other, one inspires the other. In this way, the unfolding life of Seth Garner is inseparably bound to the life of young America, so much so, that to truly understand the one is to see deep into the heart of the other.

So the author is indebted to innumerable persons who have taken on an impossible task: to make mere words bear the weight of the human spirit. Moreover, he is indebted to a sea of faceless, nameless souls who failed and succeeded, who lived and died in utter obscurity, and against all odds gave rise to the greatest nation the world has ever known.

Acknowledgements

Sincere thanks to my wife, Lenae C. S. Simmons for designing the cover and formatting the text. I am also grateful for the artistic talent of my father-in-law, Chloe S. Stewart who supplied all of the drawings for *Seth Garner*.

Part One

Breaking Away

You don't know your Latin, do you Master Garner!

Escape from Heathshire

Laudo...Laudās...Laudat....
"Sound out, gentlemen!"
Laudāmus...Laudātis...Laudant....
"Again!"

Like an ancient Gregorian chant, every mouth voiced the by-gone language with mind-numbing repetition...save one. For this one, the present had dimmed, slowly faded and then calmly slipped away. He

13

Seth Garner: Part One

had crossed over into that strange world familiar to all yet understood by none; a land dispossessed of body but fully indwelt by spirit. It is a place where things are heard without a sound and things are seen in total darkness. As the lecture droned on, he plunged deeper into the world of dreams.

Life-giving warmth filtered into the clearing.

Laudo...Laudās...Laudat....

Faltering steps slipped through dew-laden grass as primal darkness closed in from behind. He was in the deep woods now. A few paces further and then. . . the faintest, most unnatural glimmer of light.

Laudāmus...Laudātis...Laudant....

Fearful eyes peered through the gloom. Frantic, straining, desperately trying to add substance to what, just moments before, was only a hint, perhaps even an imagined glint on the margins of sight. The light-dappled leaves, normally a welcomed distraction in the dim underbrush, were a nuisance now. They fairly glowed in the deep shade, their dazzling and fluttering presence played havoc with perception. The longer the thing eluded him, the more anxious he became, for he felt deep down inside that somehow his life depended on laying hold of it, casting it aside, doing anything to move it far away. Then, as a specter, like a haunting apparition, it loomed up before him. A thin silver ring, about the size of a half-pence, not twenty yards off, hovered motionlessly in mid-air, still barely visible in the deep shadows, but now it was surely there. Quavering ever so slightly, the shining circle would steady again, coming to rest at the center of his chest. Rising now to full height, squinting to piece it all together, just

Escape from Heathshire

behind the ring, a smooth, steely line appeared, stretching back further into the dark. He was sure that he had seen this before, but maddeningly he couldn't make sense of it now. No matter how hard he pondered, the full meaning of the thing escaped him. Heart racing, beads of sweat streamed down a worried brow as the steely line was traced along to its source. It was then that his blood turned cold. A horror-driven chill ran done his spine. At the far end, a single menacing eye, framed by war paint with wild, ominous lines streaking away, glowered down the rifle barrel, intent on sending deadly harm his way. Belated knowledge can be costly and he reckoned that the highest price was about to be paid. The command to run went unheeded and for some reason a scream, born deep in his gut, hung in his throat. He could feel his mouth open to yell, but not a sound came forth. The young man watched in sheer terror as the hammer of the rifle slowly arched downward signaling his untimely doom. *Crack!*

As his head snapped backward, the cry once caught came free, being dully heard by ears only half awake. With a gasp, the pure unspoiled air of nature left his lungs only to be filled with the stultifying clime of the lecture hall. Groggily peering through the window, struggling to get his bearings, the pristine vision of the forest faded away even as the greasy, gray clods of the schoolyard crowded in. Fully awake now, the sad reality of his present state became clear. He had gone on no adventure; there was no danger. There had been no harrowing journey into the deep woods of the frontier. He had simply filched a mid-class nap and drifted into the nightmare of the wild. He was still at Heathshire, the premiere boarding school of New England.

"Seth Garner! Recite not your Latin paradigms with the brethren?!" barked the schoolmaster. Turning away from the window, Seth stared blankly down at the hickory cane that had so rudely slammed into his desktop only moments before. The coarse grain of the wood contrasted

15

sharply with the white ruffled cuffs of his dress shirt. Steadily raising his gaze, he peered into the stone-cold face of Andreas Krupsteiner, the headmaster at Heathshire. Seth made no reply.

"You don't know your Latin, do you Master Garner!" growled Krupsteiner. Hefting the hickory rod like a dueling sword, Krupsteiner pressed home the attack. "Two months at Heathshire and I'll wager you know not a word of it!" he crowed as a mocking grin spread across his wizen face. Indeed everything about Krupsteiner reflected his narrowness of soul. A spider-work of vessels reddened the tip of his nose, the only color in an otherwise pale gray complexion. Hollowed cheeks betrayed a gaunt frame, famished not by want but stinginess of spirit. Gnarled hands accented by swollen knuckles befit the crooked line of an unsightly body. There was no denying that the headmaster possessed integrity of a darker sort. That is, mind followed body in an unhelpful kind of way. Krupsteiner could read a language long dead, yet had no facility in reading character. So it came as no surprise that he totally misread Seth Garner. For sure, compared to the welcoming voice of Nature, Latin weighed heavy upon Seth's mind. The rote repetition of grammatical nonsense was poison to his active, ever-searching spirit. But Seth was no slacker in study. He read constantly, often throughout the night, taking in the collective wisdom of the ancients and reliving as it were, the rise and fall of world empires in his mind. Learning for Seth was not parroting Latin paradigms. For him learning was life. The dismal nature of Krupsteiner discerned none of this in Seth and so grossly misjudged his person.

"You see! Just as I thought! No answer! Ignorance is as ignorance does!" snarled the headmaster as he turned his back on Seth, welcoming a pattering of giggles that rippled throughout the class.

Escape from Heathshire

"Dixitque Deus fiat lux et facta est lux." Seth's voice was clear and strong; his elocution... flawless. "What was that?!" snapped Krupsteiner as he whirled to face Seth once again. "Never heard such gibberish." "No doubt," deadpanned Seth. "No! Not in my class! Not once in the twenty years since I've been headmaster at Heathshire has anything of the sort ever entered my class!" the teacher roared on. "Again, undoubtedly true," quipped Seth. Krupsteiner glared at Seth, raising the hickory staff once again, this time more like a club than a sword. Seth glared on, unflinching. Awkward moments passed. Finally Seth broke the silence. "It's from the Bible," he sniffed, looking off as if supremely disinterested. "Meaning!?" the old man bellowed. "Let there be light, and there was light," Seth interpreted for his nonplussed professor. There was dead silence for just a moment, only to be shattered by an explosion of laughter from the class. They had pieced together that Seth, in one stoke, had forced Krupsteiner to admit that neither light nor divine truth had ever entered his class for over two decades. Fuming and raging, Krupsteiner wheeled one direction and then the next until the entire class was cowed into submission. "Don't get smart with me, young man!" he howled brandishing the hickory stick above his head, this time more like a lariat than a club. "Small chance of that or anyone else getting smart with you!" Seth sniped to yet another raucous wave of guffaws.

Stammering incomprehensibles choked in Krupsteiner's throat. Stuttering starts of non-words squeaked through purpled pursed lips until at long last he howled, "You're dismissed, boy! Go to your quarters! And don't forget to report early tomorrow for disciplinary chores. Your father! I know your father! It was a favor to him....A letter's on the way to Rev. Garner. He'll find out about what happened today! That he will!" As the door

17

closed behind Seth, something also closed in his heart. Somehow Seth knew that this may be his last day at Heathshire.

On the long, lonely walk back to the commons, Seth rehearsed the events that had led him to Heathsire. The fact was that his presence in Boston was due more to the good intensions of a loving father than to any aspirations of his own. Too young to fight in the Revolutionary War, but old enough to clearly remember the signing of the Declaration of Independence, Seth's father, Nathaniel Adam Garner, mirrored the birth of the nation. Born to humble circumstances but not content to stay there, Nathaniel worked hard to improve his lot in life. His fateful opportunity was literally heaven sent when, like many others, he had been swept away by the Second Great Awakening of 1800. This momentous spiritual revival reached out to the unchurched, called for personal repentance and offered salvation to anyone who would call upon the name of the Lord. Imbued with the purest spiritual fervor, Nathaniel answered the call and acquired the best theological training he could afford. Remaining true to his roots, the reverend spurned a more cosmopolitan post and instead headed into the wilds of young America. He became a pioneer Methodist missionary, working hard to bring the Good News to the Ohio Territory, the first officially organized territory of the United States. There was no shortage of work to do, for his parish numbered upwards to 100,000 souls and was increasing daily. Yet even though the land was people rich, it was penny poor, each family struggling to eke out an existence on the frontier. These facts bore down hard on the Garner family. The Lord indeed had provided but just barely. The Rev. Garner was determined that his only child and son, Seth, would have a better future.

As fate would have it, it was education that brought Seth's father into contact with Andreas Krupsteiner. As "a man of the cloth," Rev. Garner was numbered among the intellectuals of the newly founded nation. As such, on occasion he met with and befriended persons of the upper echelons of society. One such person was Master Krupsteiner. From the start the pastor sensed that this harsh and difficult man was Seth's best hope for the future. To that end, he carefully cultivated a longstanding relationship with Krupsteiner so that Seth might gain a coveted seat at Heathshire. For Rev. Garner, a stint at Heathshire was but the first step to an even more impressive career. From there Seth would continue his studies at Harvard and become one of the finest lawyers in the land. Following that, he would no doubt ride the favor of the people to Congress. And then....who knows... perhaps Seth would follow in the footsteps of that great farmer turned statesman, Thomas Jefferson, and become the next president of the United States!

Yet the truly redeeming quality of his life was to be found in his mother. Born Elizabeth Anne Henderson, she came from one of the most respected families in all of Boston. Nevertheless for Elizabeth, grace won over pretension and an easygoing civility colored all of her ways. She possessed an inherent sense of dignity, yet was never condescending to others, regardless of their station in life. Moreover, Elizabeth was the embodiment of natural beauty and physical strength. Ever modest but never prudish, she attracted many suitors in her time. In courtship, force of character was more important for her than social class. Thus to those who truly knew her, it proved as no surprise when she settled on Nathaniel Garner to be her mate. Even her marriage to this hardscrabble farmer turned preacher could not negate the respect she held in the community. And finally, her faith was as winsome as her person. Hers was a spirituality of an authentic kind, one not born of religion or ritual, but of an unbroken communion with her Maker. All of these elements had come together to form a person who was calm yet confident, and able to rise above every crisis. How dearly Seth wished she could be with him now.

All of these remembrances pained Seth to the core. The life goals of his father, not to mention the selfless commitment of his mother, had come to an end with his verbal free-for-all with Krupsteiner. And to make matters worse, if in fact they could be worse, was his own experience at Heathshire. From the start, things had not gone well for Seth. It was not that he was a homely boy or a dullard; quite the opposite. In body he was a commanding figure, standing head and shoulders above his classmates. He was built like a pyramid turned upside down. Broad, muscular shoulders melded into overpowering arms that tapered down to strong, outsized hands. Atypically, his brawn was outmatched by his brain. He evidenced a penetrating intelligence, one never satisfied with the facts at hand but ever curious about the substance of things. Thus for Seth the "What?" in life was only the beginning of a journey that quickly led to the "How?" and didn't stop questioning until he arrived at the "Why?" of the matter at hand. Those who claimed he didn't study were both right and wrong at the same time. The fact was that he really didn't need to study for he rarely forgot anything that he read, could recall most everything that he had heard and could repeat nearly every word he had ever said. Yet the most striking feature of his presence was his eyes. Crystal blue, framed by straw-blonde hair, Seth's eyes were windows on his soul. They emanated a kindness born of confidence that in turn graced Seth with an air of self-assurance. Yet as was the case with his mother, there was not the slightest hint of arrogance about his person, for he possessed a native humility, one that sensed the pure giftedness of every good thing.

The oddment here is that all of these qualities were wrapped about a young man who was not yet sixteen years of age. Indeed it was precisely here, that is on the untested field of youth, that Krupsteiner's attack had its ill effect. Seth was convinced, naively so, that his entire future, moreover his whole world, was in the hands of this mean-spirited, cruel little man. So in spite of his cool demeanor in the classroom, Seth was truly shaken on the inside. The old crone's tirade had rattled him; had unhinged Seth's heart, so much so that there was no one to help him now.

Such was the grim state of affairs as Seth prepared to enter the commons. His keen mind had worked quickly to draw together the salient facts and come to a clear but sobering conclusion: he was very different from his peers and nothing short of an aping insincerity could change this. Yet at the same time he realized too….that if he yielded to the ever-present pressure to blend in…to become invisible in a crowd of persons of no real distinction….in that very moment… he would cease being that person he was meant to be. He would cease to be Seth Garner. What lay before him now was not a palette of choices but rather the stark mandate of a single choice. He must quit Heathshire.

That night he slept little. His thoughts were plagued by expectations and feelings, all of which eventually came to rest on the only two things that really mattered right now: his family and his future. With regard to family, he knew that his father and mother were committed to him, but in very different ways. Elizabeth was unconditionally devoted to him. Her heart was always toward him…regardless. He was *her* Seth. In light of the prospects that lay before him, it was her desire for his happiness that weighed heavily on his mind. His father was totally dedicated to Seth's development as a man, as a professional, as a contributor to society at large. He dearly cared for Seth, yet ardently believed that Seth's route to happiness would be conventional, prescribed and professional. Seth reckoned that the difference between how his mother related to him and what his father had planned for him was due to their makeup. Nathaniel's personality was directed outward toward the public. He *engaged* life and viewed the world as his congregation. His mother, on the other hand, possessed a spiritual power that was rooted deep within her heart. Inwardly contemplative, her thoughts were concerned for the welfare of others, especially for Seth.

Seth's father, Nathaniel Adam Garner

As Seth stared at the clapboard ceiling, he sensed that a harrowing journey had just begun. The soft glow of the Franklin stove brought no warmth to his soul. Normally comforting on a cold New England night, now claw-like flames leapt against the grate, threatened to break the confines of the hearth and to do harm. Ominous dark shadows cast about the room while even darker thoughts raced within, ignoring every effort to bring them under control. Sleep fled before fears. Hours wore on. His breathing became labored, shorter. Seth felt oddly heavy.

An unseen something was bearing down upon him, pressing him deeper into the feather bed, as if to drive him through the floor. He was well aware that a battle of a strange kind was raging inside and sensed that in this fight, neither hands nor head could help. As an unkind night wore on, Seth felt that strength of every kind was ebbing away. Somehow the savage hounds of dread and fear had slipped their reins and backed him into a corner, even as the pale light of dawn crept into the room. And so it was that a much diminished Seth prepared himself for "discipline day" at Heathshire.

Like Seth, Tim Larken had been misplaced at the school, but for different reasons. Tim was a kind yet dim-witted soul. He cared nothing for true learning and had no mind for it if he did care. Yet he was a simple, good-natured, no-harm-done kind of young man. His red hair, freckled face and wide girth befit his character. Making friends came easy for Tim. So in the stilted world of Heathshire, it was just these kinds of traits that required his presence this morning.

As Seth walked up, Tim held out his hand with a smile. He looked as if he were ready to embark on a fine outing rather than to slave away on discipline day. As they split long logs into rails, Tim prattled on about things of no consequence. Seth hewed away in silence. The spell that had seized him the night before had not left him, but instead grew worse. So he didn't answer the many questions posed to him by Tim, nor did he need too, for in an instant Tim answered them for himself. As they were ordered here and there by the school's provost, Seth couldn't help but notice how artificial it all seemed. Their task was to extend the fencing around the school grounds. But for Seth it was not a fencing in but a closing in. As they zigzagged the split rails along carefully laid lines, the contrived purpose of their labor came crashing in with

23

Seth Garner: Part One

horrifying clarity. Construct a clear boundary between all things human and the wild expanse of nature. But to what purpose? What good thing could come from being so narrowly fenced in? Seth's mouth grew dry. As the heavy mall thumped down again and again, Seth stared at the tin-toy fashion of Tim's work. Mechanical. Mindless. Incessantly talking. The maddening monotony of it all continued to bear down on Seth as the day wore on. He felt ill. The palms of his hands sweated profusely and that on a cool autumn day. More than once the maul slipped from his grip, only to have Tim cheerfully heft it up again, hand it to Seth, and ramble on as if nothing had happened. Things grew worse for Seth. He could hear his own pulse now, throbbing in his head, keeping time with the dull "*thump. . . thump. . . thump*" of Tim's mall. He was having difficulty swallowing now and the blood coursed through his veins like streams of fire. He grew faint as things appeared to move in slow motion. Seth was shaken when he noticed that Tim's voice had become distant and garbled. It trailed off to a high whine and thinned out to a "pinging" sound, more metallic than human. Seth's breathing became labored still. He felt that he was being smothered even while he heaved in great blocks of air. Panic had finally won out. Looking wildly about, he vaguely noticed that Tim had left off pounding dead wood. He looked blankly at Seth, mouthing something but making no sound at all now. "It's closing in!" Seth shouted. "The rails...they're crowding in!" With that Tim gained his voice and yelled,. "Ye say what?!" Seth's eyes darted this way and that as if beset by some unseen foe. He took on the demeanor of a panicked animal, hemmed in, desperately looking for a way of escape. Again the weight rumbled onto him, driving his boots as it were into the soil. Chest heaving for air that wouldn't come, Seth let the mall slip from his hand one last time and then. . . he was on the

24

move. His steps were measured at first, but his pace soon quickened as he burst through the barrier they had just erected. The "Now hold to!" of the provost had no more weight than the leaves that raced past him as he blundered on. It faintly registered that some of his classmates had tried to hail him as he sprinted toward the commons, but their calls were of no consequence now. Having made it back to the sleeping quarters, he burst through the door even as the tumult was gathering without. He quickly grappled together some books, cast his dress clothes on the bunk next to the door, and was gone.

Instinctively, he took the lane that lead away from Heathshire. Persons ran behind shouting and waving their arms as if to catch a panicked horse. Spying a rider ahead, Seth dove into the woods, branches lashing at his face and hands. Tripping over an unseen something, he crashed headlong into a cold stream. The frigid jolt did nothing to loose the madness that so gripped his soul. Springing up in an instant, he drove on, running on pure instinct now. Without thinking, he lunged back toward Heathshire, plowing through the cloying underbrush, back toward his pursuers, taking refuge in the upturned roots of a massive chestnut tree. The ploy worked. Krupsteiner, together with a passel of classmates in tow, overshot Seth's location, entering the wood much further down the road. Flailing about and hollering at the top of their lungs, the group stumbled along working ever farther away from Seth. Seth stayed put, peering through the brush, pulse racing, barely able to control his breathing, yet determined to remain hidden. Tiring of the search, Krupsteiner clambered up the steep bank and menacingly trudged back toward Heathshire. When they were dead even with his hiding place, Seth could hear the anger and frustration in their voices. Those that counted Seth as a friend lamented the odd spell that had so suddenly taken hold of him. Others, who cared little for him, asserted that Seth had been an odd one from the first day he had arrived at Heathshire and that sooner or later something like this was bound to happen. Krupsteiner droned on and on that Seth's father would be duly notified *in writing*. As the group moved past, Seth knew that his life would never be the same again.

As soon as the last glimmer of evening light had faded, Seth cut a path through the forest, intersected the main road and ran on toward Boston, the largest city of the young democracy. Why he chose to go into town, he did not know. In any case, at fifteen years of age he soon stood before the old North Church, the very place that had signaled to Paul Revere not many years before. Thoughts of that famous ride lightened Seth's heart. For him, Revere's ride was about wild, unbridled movement into the future. It was about freedom. Seth felt that was what he was about too, about moving and traveling, about freedom, but to what purpose he had no idea. For now, though, he was cold, tired and hungry, but worst of all, terribly lonely. Stepping into a narrow alley way, he slumped down between two oak barrels. Pulling his wool coat up around his ears to ward off the chill of a late fall night, he curled up as best he could and fell fast asleep.

For a time he entertained the fool's notion of just staying there.

Trader Jack

A timid sun struggled to birth an uncertain dawn. Its pale, gray light warmed neither soil nor soul. For some time, Seth remained in a cramped curl, fighting to ward off the cold. But his mind was awake long before his body. In the stillness, he entertained the fool's notion of just staying put. Little trouble could reach him here, hunkered down amidst the rotting rope and lumber that filled the alley. Thinking better of it, he mustered enough courage to stiffly stand to his feet and look about. Indeed, the sights and sounds of old Boston harbor coming to life worked like a tonic. He might not know where he was going, but there were a lot of people who did. He held fast to that thought.

As for him, what was done could not be undone. The disaster of Heathshire was now in the past and Seth stood before a new day. This was his chance to make a fresh start. Shaking off the ill will of Krupsteiner and the troubles of the day before, his decisive will cut the cords that bound him to the past. In a moment, the whole of him...his mind...his heart...his strength...was thrust into the future. Picking his way through the clutter that crowded the alleyway, Seth cleanly stepped into the street.

As Seth took stock of the city, he took stock of himself as well. To be sure, he had been cast adrift, but he was not a drifter. He was taught to believe that each person, regardless of how weak and problem-ridden they may be, when compared to the lifeless void of space and the mute wastelands of this present world, every person was a thing of incredible beauty and power. So in spite of the gloom that threatened to bury him once again, Seth dared to believe that he still mattered. He held out the hope that he was a person of destiny. So as unpromising as this day dawned, for Seth, it was a morning of pure intention. He was determined to turn it to his advantage.

As he worked his way along the boardwalk, the squeak of well-worn pulleys met his ears. Weathered sailors were outfitting whaling ships, preparing for voyages that could last for years on end. Without thinking, Seth turned his back on the gathering noise of the fleet. A life at sea held no interest for him. Stiffly shuffling further down the street, he heard the slap of harness leather and the creaking of wagon wheels. Trail masters shouted commands to swarthy hands that were busy loading gear into heavy freight wagons. Seth eased closer to take in the scene. At that moment, a thickly built trail boss wheeled about, nearly knocking Seth to the ground, as he lunged toward his next task.

"Gang way, lad!" he bellowed. "Round cheer ya' either haul freight, pay up or get out of da' way!" he barked as Seth scrambled to step aside. Even as he strode away, Seth could tell that this was a man in charge. Everything about him spoke "command." His chest was as big around and sturdy as the oaken barrels that he wheeled about. Seth noticed that he could in no wise hold his arms flat against his sides; he was as solid as a keg of nails. His buckskins were trail worn and the rawhide fringe was missing here and there, granting an irregular, rumpled appearance to his frame. This was not due to slovenliness on his part. His focus was on the task at hand and he simply had little time for fashion. He was a man of business through and through.

As the foreman charged on, Seth said weakly, "Excuse me, sir." The man froze in his tracks with arms arched at his sides as if he were about to fetch something from both pockets at once. The foreman's eyes were clamped shut, his teeth were clinched and his brows furrowed. The "Excuse me, sir" had cut off the path to progress, and so he

Trader Jack

stood there trembling, a living monument to frustration. "I'm...I'm...looking for work." At the word "work" the foreman's features began to soften. Like flint turned flesh, Jack Taylor repeated the present point at hand. "'Work', say ye?" "Yes, sir..." Swooping low to within a few inches of Seth's nose, Jack forwarded, "Where're ya' headin', son?" "I'm going where you're going," Seth replied. "How long kin ya' stay on?" Jack hollered. "Till the job is done," Seth said with confidence. "You're a'hired! Ma' name's Jonathan Taylor, but prit' near ever' one 'round cheer calls me 'Jack'." "Thank you, Mr. Jack..." "No 'mister' and no 'sir.' Jus' Jack. Anything more an' ya know ya ain't workin' fur ol' Trader Jack!" he shouted with as a big grin spread across his whiskered face. "Well...I'm..." "I know! Don't tell me! Yur a' hungered!" "Powerfully hungry, and I... "An' ya ain't got no money!" Jack yelled before Seth could explain. "Ya go an' chow down at the diner and tell 'em to charge it to Trader Jack. Dare used ta dat." "And what I'm..." "What'cha wearin's no good, too! Won't do fur da' trail. A coupla doors down is da' tanner. Hab'em fix ya up wit' some buckskins. Charge dat too! He knows me. Oh! Da' tanner! Do I ever give'em trubble! He's used to dat too! Now, son...dese wagons will be a'rollin' by 8:30!" "Where we're going?" "Sout an' den wes! Furs ta New York, an den on to Philadelphiyeh! Wid' some luck, on to Pittsburgh by winter!" Jack hollered as he waved him off toward the diner. Seth raised a finger, but it was no use. Before he could ask another question, Jack had completed two tasks and was on his way to a third.

Soon after finishing a hasty breakfast, Seth found himself at the tanner's shop. The name of "Trader Jack" was all that was needed to get things under way. In no time Seth was outfitted in soft, supple, yet durable buckskins. He felt reborn, as well he should, for he was about to embark on a life unplanned. As he strode toward Jack's

Seth Garner: Part One

buckboard, the wagoner hollered out, "Now ya' look da' part! An' a sight better, if ya' don't mine me a' sayin'!" So in less than a day, Seth had gone from an aspiring student in Boston to an apprentice on a wagon train headed for the west. Whereas he wore a white ruffled shirt before, he wore tanned leather now. And most importantly, Seth was at peace with the whole affair.

Whereas he wore a white ruffled shirt before, he wore tanned leather now.

As they lumbered out of the city, they struck the Boston Post Road travelling south toward New York. The road was originally an Indian trail but became widened as the colonists rode horses along its length. As early settlements developed into towns, wagon traffic called for more improvements. Yet it was the creative vision of Benjamin Franklin, who over fifty years prior, realized that a well-maintained road was necessary to link the colonies together. Such a road would not only make way for the mail, but would also be of strategic military importance. Moreover, the Post Road would serve as a veritable highway of commerce, allowing the many rural farms to carry their goods to market. And to it was, as Jack led his wagon train through the Connecticut valley, they joined a large caravan of wagons, stage coaches and smaller rigs, all caught up in the business of the new nation.

From the start, Seth was mightily impressed with the wheel stock. German immigrants of the Conestoga Valley had built these wagons to withstand the rigors of the trail. They were nearly sixteen feet in length and their frames curved up at both ends, like the keel of a ship. This shape added great strength to these wagons. Indeed, these "Conestogas" would in time become known as "Prairie Schooners" due to their ship-like appearance. There was no suspension to these rigs either, for a wagon equipped with springs would easily be tipped over by the many pot holes and boulders along the way. Yet the most interesting feature for Seth was the wheels. They were nearly five feet tall and their steel rims were at least eight inches in width. The height allowed the wagons to ride over the many stumps and hillocks on the road. The wide rims would not sink deeply into the mire after a heavy rain. Moreover, some of these hickory-spoked wheels were painted bright red or yellow. They contrasted nicely with the sky-blue color of the wagons and the tightly stretched canvas canopy overhead. Altogether they struck a lively scene in an oft times drab woodland landscape.

Jack exploited every feature of these well-built rigs. As the wagons winded their way past stately towns like Cambridge, Hartford and New Haven, Jack took on supplies at every stop. Yet, on board everything was neat and clean, and in time each wagon became a veritable traveling dry goods store. Jack opted for teams of oxen over the more common choice of draft horses. Though slower, the oxen were hardier and pulled the heavily laden Conestogas with ease. Also, Jack planned to offload the wagons and teams to

Seth Garner: Part One

settlers travelling further west. The oxen made good plow stock for these pioneers once they reached their homestead. So what the beasts lacked in speed, they made up in strength, patience and utility.

Each step of the journey was an education for Seth. The pageantry of the newly founded nation flowed all around him. The stops along the way informed him of the diversity of the young nation and also of its strength. The nation was growing. The whole thing was of endless fascination for Seth, and he peppered Jack with questions at nearly every turn in the road.

"How does all this work? What we're selling? What's my part? It was then that Jack commenced a lesson on practical economics. "Well Seth, ma' boy, here's how it works. We're a' sellin' all what dey wants, but dey ain't gots." Jack explained. "An' we're a' buyin' what all we needs an' dey don't wants. Can ya' see dat?" "Yes, indeed I can. But way out west, I mean past the mountains, do they have any money?" "Do dey have money?!" (Jack had a way of starting nearly every sentence with what the other person had just said.) "Dat's 'bout all dey gots. An' dat's where we can hep 'em. Ya' ever sell what's ya' got fur more dan what's we paid fur it. Are ya' still with me?" "Indeed...." "Indeed so. Now *how* much more depends. Iffen da' customer buys right off with a smile, den ya' sold too low, an we ain't friends no more. You follow?" "I think..." "Ya' thinkin' right, now. But iffen dey look kinda solemn and hands over da' money anyway, den yur workin' right. So sum' airs 'tween smilin' an' frownin's da right price. It takes time."

The year was 1810 and Seth's fifteenth birthday had come and gone. By this young age, he had seen the pomp and wealth of Boston. But nothing had prepared him for New York. If Boston broadened Seth's horizons concerning the wider world, New York was nothing short of a revelation. Even as the spires of the city came rolling into view, Seth knew that for the rest of his days he would never see anything like New York.

With its nearly 100,000 inhabitants, New York had already surpassed Philadelphia as the most populous city in America. In one day, Seth had the sensation of seeing more people in New York than in the combined total of his life. Moreover, the historic role of the city matched its grandeur. During the fight for independence, New York was of strategic importance for the Americans and the British. It was the "jeweled buckle" of America that joined New England with the rest of the states to the south. If the British could take New York, they would literally split the "colonies" in two. No one was more aware of this than George Washington. He was determined to deny the British of New York. Nevertheless, he doubted that his ragtag army could hold out against the heavy canon fire that was sure to come. In order to "deprive the enemy of aid or comfort," Washington lodged a grim request to Congress. In the face of defeat, Washington sought permission to burn New York to the ground. John Hancock's fateful reply: request denied; do not burn the city. As Seth gazed upon the stately homes of old New York, he was glad that Washington did not get his way. But the British did get their way. On Sept. 15, 1776, the British admiral, Lord Howe, commenced a withering bombardment of the city. The American defenders fled in terror, suffering a humiliating defeat.

In short order, though, New York rose like a phoenix to become the capital of the United States from 1785-1790, and continued to play a decisive role in American politics. Even as Seth observed the construction of a magnificent city hall, some of the greatest statesmen of the Republic walked the streets of New York. He had heard too, that the renowned American orator, John Jay, was busy warning

Seth Garner: Part One

the people of impending war with England. Yes, he argued, America had wrested its independence from Great Britain, but the people should know that the fight for freedom is far from over. He, as well as many other notables in the government, feared renewed conflict with England. So as the city prospered at a riotous pace, rumors of war filled the air.

Although Seth wanted to tarry in New York for some days, Jack was a man of enterprise bound to a schedule. Hundreds of miles of rough, country roads lay ahead of them, and there was little time for socializing. If they were going to make Philadelphia by mid-fall, they could not afford a long stay in New York. So after taking on some bolts of broadcloth, calico and bundles of glass beads for trading, they struck camp and headed for the Pennsylvania Road.

The Pennsylvania Road ran east to west from New York to Pittsburgh. As Jack and Seth rolled along its length, the road had already been in existence for more than fifty years. It was first constructed as a military road during the French and Indian War under the direction of the British generals, Braddock and Forbes. Indeed, the road proved critical for the defeat of the French at Fort Duquesne during this campaign. Once the British were in control, Forbes renamed the stronghold Fort Pitt, after his commanding officer. This settlement eventually grew into the great city of Pittsburgh.

All throughout the trip, Seth pondered Jack's counsel. Indeed as the wagons lumbered along the wilderness trail, pulling further and further away from civilization, Seth began to understand how things worked in life. In a backwoods kind of way, Jack had taught him the rudiments of supply and demand. Seth began to see that the principles of free enterprise placed a lot of stock in the good sense of the individual. No one buys what they don't need, and no one pays more than they absolutely have too; not repeatedly anyway. Then again, if a people are onerously stingy, the wagons of trade will simply roll another way. What's fair is fair. It suddenly dawned on him too why money is called "currency." Everything must balance out for the pulse of commerce to flow in both directions. Seth came to understand that business was a living thing that continued on in all directions, and then in some way, found its way back home again. When this didn't happen, hunger and need were not far behind. It came to him again that he was getting a real education even though he was no longer at Heathshire.

One lesson he learned quick enough was that there was a big difference between "inns" and "taverns." The inns were outfitted for the folks that rode the stage line. Hauled by a team of six horses, three matched pairs in all, a stagecoach could easily cover up to sixty miles in a day. At times, these fancy rigs would overtake and pass their Conestogas like they were standing still. As an inn came into view, the stage master would blow a quavering blast on a festive tin horn to announce their arrival. The inn keeper would then prepare to receive tired and hungry travelers. Some of the better establishments provided their guests with sumptuous fare. There were hams and beef and all kinds of roasted fowl, including wild ducks and geese, as well as domestic hens. All of this was followed by a variety of tarts, pies and puddings, only to be washed down by stout ales, wines and port. The taverns, on the other hand, specialized in the later and seldom dished up the former. But what Trader Jack's team lacked in speed and comfort, he made up with dependability and power. And all of this was by design. Compared to the stagecoaches, their faithful oxen were lucky to make ten miles before sundown. Yet the slow pace meant that a man carrying a pack and rifle could comfortably keep abreast of a freight wagon for nearly the whole day's journey. Also, it took months to traverse the vast unbroken planes of the American west. The flashing hooves of the stage horses would be broken and lame in a week out there. But the ever sure but shuffling gait of the oxen could and would trudge on for weeks and months on end. So the simple fact was, the inns catered to the clientele that could afford the fast transport, while the taverns took in the rest of the folk. The taverns were rustic way stations for the common man. For the most part, they were outsized log cabins with crude livery stables at the rear. They served up beans and beer, and the sleeping quarters differed little from that of the livestock. The redeeming quality of the taverns was the folks who stayed there. The bread might be stale but the company never was. They were a hale and hearty mob. These folks were as honest as the dirt that graced nearly every visible part of their bodies and all of the clothes they wore. All in all, Seth supremely enjoyed their company. Tales of the Revolutionary War and the exploits of those who had crossed the "big river" to the west filled the evening hours. Stories of lonesome, danger-filled watches of the night and the stoic resistance to incredible hardship were told for hours on end. Although the people and places were varied, one theme was common to them all: undefeated. Regardless of what fateful consequence in life, or the depravity of man or the unkind hand of unthinking Nature, one must never give in. Even in the face of relentless trial, if in the end of the day, you just broke even, then that was counted as a victory. This was the unwritten code that was explained by none but understood by all. Individual survival had very little to do with it. There were bigger things at stake. Whether it be a single family, or an entire fortress or even the whole frontier, failure in one point could be the end of it all. And so it was that the stories rolled on and Seth listened. He came to know that he and his family were a "notch above" the likes of those in the tavern. Nevertheless, Seth felt increasingly at ease among these rugged heroes of the wild.

The days on the Pennsylvania Road fairly flew by. Jack filled the time with riveting tales of journeys past and of practical wisdom on how to get along in this new world. Seth also noticed that the further they got from New York, the more interested the people were in the goods they were hauling. Always the mentor, Jack had Seth observe the sales for the first couple of days, and counseled that as the business picked up, Seth would barter his own poke of goods. When that time came, Jack filled a sack with the standard fare of domestic goods. This was the "women's department" so to speak. He then had Seth fetch a small cart lashed to the rear of the Conestoga. Seth then loaded the cart with heavier gear such as steel tomahawks, trade points (that is, steel wrought arrowheads used in trading with the Indians further west) and skinning knives. Jack's last task was to carefully enter each item in a ledger with Seth's name neatly printed at the top. Jack then explained to Seth that he would pocket 10% of the profit, less the breakfast and the buckskins charged back in Boston. Seth suggested that the grub and garb be thrown in for free. At the word "free," Jack launched into a spirited tirade. "Da only thang dats free in dis whole turnin' world is purple unicorns! And I got ma' one an' only look-see after drinkin' ten dollar worth of corn whiskey. Leeswize, dats what dey say hit twuz. So when what's done is done, free ain't worth da money!" From all of this Seth surmised that Jack didn't believe that anything was really free. He thought on this for a long while.

Hefting his sack of domestics while pushing the cart ahead, Seth walked toward a hovel of cabins. Not halfway to the cabins, he was swarmed by a bevy of matrons. "Got any sewing needles, young man?!" As Seth pulled a card of

Seth Garner: Part One

pins from the sack, the woman pressed a quarter into his hand. He hesitated a moment then slowly said, "Two cents a pin? I dunno..." "I'll give you twice as much!" said another. A heavy set woman strode forward, thrust two bits into Seth's hand and then snatched the packet of needles from the first buyer. As Seth returned the quarter to the erstwhile customer, he noticed that both ladies were frowning, yet still eyeing the merchandize. "A good sign," he thought, "things were going well." Digging deeper into the sack, Seth hawked, "I've got buttons!" "Last trip I paid a nickel a piece, and my man gave me down the country for it too!" rasped an old crone. She had worked many a wagon train in her day and no doubt knew what she was doing. A hard sell would be futile. Thinking on his feet, Seth chose the route of appeasement. "Rightly so!" quipped Seth. "Outrageous, true enough! But you can't go to church without 'em. And they're getting scarce here about. Heard something about the quality of thread in these parts too... not like my thread, mind you. . . but a poor lot's been traded about. Buttons popping off all over the frontier!" Peering through squinted eyes, the woman tried to make Seth flinch. He held his ground. "I'll give eight cents a button, or we'll just make our own!" she fired back. "Eight cents it is, ma'am. Can I interest you in some high quality thread?" By the time he pulled out the calico and broadcloth, a crowd had gathered and there was a genuine spending spree. In less than an hour, all the "domestics" were sold.

Even as Seth was counting his money, a man shouted from down the street. "Stand to, boy! I'm a' commin' to ya'!" A real frontiersman was making haste to meet Seth. Even from a distance, Seth could tell that this was a man used to getting his way. A scar ripped around from the corner of his left eye to his chin. He ran with a slight limp but managed to cover ground just the same. Seth braced himself for a tough sell, but softened a little when he spied a money pouch dangling from an outstretched arm. Hauling the cart along side, Seth made his pitch. "I've got..." "Hang fire, son! I knowed what ya' got! I'll take a dozen tommyhawks, six rings of trade points and ten skinning knives." "But that's just about the whole lot." "Ya' got sumptin' agin sellin' ta' me, son?!" growled the man as he glowered at Seth through reddened eyes. "Oh, no sir! Nothing, at all." Even before Seth named his price, the old trapper unloaded all the goods onto the boardwalk. Sensing everything coming his way, Seth dared to bid high. The man grumbled a bit and then loosened the drawstrings of the money pouch. Seth knew then that it was a done deal. As the trapper counted out the tally he muttered, "This is half again what I paid last year, so ole Jack will be pleased. Oh yeah, I knowed ya' wit his outfit. Can tell by what ya' peddlin'." The trapper lit in again, "Don't need your peddlin' cart, but I'll take the buckskins." "What buckskins?" Seth asked. "Why da' ones yur' a'warrin' boy. Get shed of 'em, and I'll pay!" "Wha? I can't. I'll have you know sir that I paid five dollars for these back in Boston!" "Where ya bought'em means nuthin ta me! I'll give ya' seven dollar! Now peel'em and I'll pay!" Backing away Seth stammered, "You don't mean? What will I....? *Good day, sir!*" Jogging back to the wagon, Seth stole fleeting glances over his shoulder even as the mountain man held out folding money. As rattled as the cart clattering after him, Seth took solace in this fact: his sack and cart were empty and his pockets were full *of real money.*

Climbing up beside Jack on the buckboard, the old trader whispered, "What ya' sell?" Still overwhelmed by the whirlwind turn of events of his first sale's trip, Seth said weakly, "Everything." "*Everthang!*" Jack shouted loud enough to be heard four wagons back. Chuckling and shaking his head, Jack continued, "E-v-e-r-t-h-a-n-g!" "I jus' love da sound of hit! But I knowed it. I knowed it all along. Seth, you a natural born trader. A real aunttreepenure! But ya' look a bit flustered, ma' boy. Sumpin ailin' ya'? Why ain't ya happy like ole Tradder Jack?" "Some old trapper wanted to buy my buckskins!" "Wat he offer?" "Seven dollars. What!? *Not you too!*" "Hmmmm....that was a good price," Jack mused as he rubbed a whiskered chin between thumb and forefinger. "You say what, man?! I couldn't sell what I was wearing!" Seth protested. "Well, did he ask fur ya' hat? I wager he didn't, he bein' a Gawd-fearin' man!" Jack protested. Seth looked gap-jawed at Jack and blinked a couple of times in disbelief. "If you'da shucked dem skins, you'da fount a good use for hit, I'll wager! I tell you Seth, on more'n one occasion ma' hat was da only thang standin' 'tween me and woeful mortification! But dat's a nuther lesson for a nuther time. The point being, son, a sale is like taday; once hits gone, it's turned ta yestiday and that won't do fur tamorra'. Ya' understand, Seth?" Looking puzzled, Seth remarked that he needed to think on that for a spell. He gathered that Jack's point was that one must always be mindful of timing and opportunity. Since Jack's lessons usually came in equal parts of good natured humor and serious teaching, Seth wasn't too sure of how things divided up this time. Jack gave Seth a reassuring slap on the back and added, "None ta worry, son...none ta worry. Ya' done good. Ya' done *real* good."

As Seth was taking Jack's praise, he noticed a mail sack being carried out to one of the stage coaches. "Mail runs way out here?" "An' further!" Jack assured. "Thanks to ole Ben Franklin, why dares even letters bein' sent ta' places where dare ain't no people!" Seth wrinkled his nose at that remark, but quickly sifted out the point at hand. Founding father, Ben Franklin, realized early on how critical reliable postal service would be to the young nation. He knew too that the mail would play a major role in unifying the states. Indeed, the Boston Post Road, and many like it, was largely due to Franklin's efforts, and he went on to become the first Postmaster General of the nation. All of this meant that far-flung settlements could still stay connected by way of the mail. It was time for Seth to take advantage of this service. Turning to Jack, he asked if he could climb down and step into the inn for a moment.

After sorting out the necessary details and purchasing parchment and postage, Seth sat in a corner alone. In spite of all of the excitement and business of the last few weeks, Seth had been thinking deeply about the changes that had taken place in his life. Although he was at ease with the way things had gone thus far, there was sadness at the bottom of it all. He had literally turned his back on everything he had known from birth. He had cut that invisible cord that bound him to his parents. Their hopes and aspirations for him were over. They had no idea where he was. He would not be home for the fall harvest festival, and now, their only son, would not grace their table at Christmas. He knew deep down that he had blazed a new trail and that there was no turning back now. After a few moments, he took quill to hand and wrote:

Dear Father and Mother,
It's not that I'm not grateful...

Seth Garner: Part One

As Seth retired to the loft above the press, even the strong odor of the ink and solvent could not distract his thoughts.

Prudence Nightshade

Seth's heart lightened as they worked their way through the Conestoga Valley, the very place that their sturdy wagons were made in the first place. In less than a fortnight, Philadelphia, the veritable heart of American freedom, was upon them.

This "City of Brotherly Love" was founded in freedom for freedom. In the late 1600's, William Penn, the great Quaker pioneer and visionary, established Philadelphia as a beacon of religious liberty and peace. In less than fifty years, the city had become the intellectual and cultural center of the colonies. By 1723 it was the perfect place for a young Benjamin Franklin, just seventeen years of age, to make his home. So it was here that the first true American genius resided for over sixty years. Franklin was a child of the Enlightenment, that wave of intellectual freedom that had energized Europe and was now enlivening America. Early on, Franklin championed freedom of the press, became a publisher and regaled early America in printing *Poor Richard's Almanac*. Nearly everyone was familiar with *Poor Richard's*, including Seth. This practical, down-to-earth paper commented on just about everything from the weather to politics. Yet by far Franklin's most memorable literary creation was "Silence Dogood." This fictitious female was anything but silent. By way of irony and satire, Silence exposed the corruption of the day and extolled the virtues of frugality, hard work and simple honesty. Seth was mightily impressed with the intelligence and political savvy of Silence.

In addition to being a publisher, Franklin was a world-class scientist. His famous experiments with electricity led to the invention of the lightening rod which no doubt saved untold lives. Those who took no stock in such newfangled contraptions might live to benefit from another one of Franklin's firsts: an organized, municipal fire department. His invention of bifocals not only allowed people to see better, but they could continue to read and learn later in life. His establishment of the first lending library allowed the less fortunate to have access to books. So the poor of society could enjoy a good book while being warmed by another one of his inventions: the Franklin Stove. All in all, Franklin was a true American hero, and Seth relished everything about him.

Prudence Nightshade

As Seth stood before Independence Hall, his spirit soared as he celebrated Franklin's greatest contribution of all: *freedom*. It was here that Franklin signed the Declaration of Independence in 1776 and reportedly made his famous quote, "Yes, we must, indeed, all hang together, or most assuredly we shall all hang separately." So in Seth's mind it was perfectly fitting that Philadelphia served as the first capital of young America from 1790-1800.

Publicist....scientist...statesman: all of this was Ben Franklin and it inspired Seth to the core. He knew now that Franklin's passion for freedom, together with his matchless intellect and courage, were, in part, who he was. A love of liberty, the power of great ideas and a willingness to fight for what you believed in, all of this, was what had led him to this point in life. Even though his heart still ached for his frontier home in Ohio, he was more convinced than ever that he had chosen the right course. In fact, if it were not for Trader Jack hurrying him along, he could have stayed in Philadelphia. But winter was pressing in upon them and the wildest part of the trip still remained. Remote and lonely trails led the way to Pittsburg. Reluctantly, Seth clambered onto the buckboard next to Jack and bid farewell to Philadelphia.

The mirth and surplus of Philadelphia quickly faded as the wagon train pressed deeper into "Penn's Woods." As the trail wore on, the wagons grew lighter and the air waxed colder. The first snows of November had already fallen and Seth was glad to spend some of his earnings on an out-sized buffalo robe. Its warmth and earthy smell warded off the frigid air and brightened the gray landscape that descended on Trader Jack's caravan. Now was the time to enjoy the bounty of summer for the full harvest had come in. Many a home was busy with packing and canning and curing all kinds of foodstuffs in preparation for winter. Seth's thoughts turned to those first Pilgrims who, at this season, shared a thanksgiving meal with the Indians. That was nearly two-hundred years ago and many families of young America, including Seth's own family, would express their thanks to God by eating a grand meal at this time of year. Seth knew that he would be missing all of this and it bore down heavy on his heart. Yet Jack was as buoyant as ever and was determined not to let the day past without some form of merriment. Sensing Seth's mood, he offered, "Ah knowed a nice little place up a piece. We kin git some grub, hear some tales and bed down. Hit'll be fine. Yu'll see, Seth." And so it was that just before sunset he and Jack "celebrated" at a ramshackle tavern on the outskirts of Pittsburg.

As Jack reined up, Seth gazed on the scene in dismay. The place was a wreck. A sagging, cedar-shake roof was punctuated at both ends by a pair of crooked chimneys. They were not made of stone but of green logs that were about an arm's width in thickness and a bit less than a yard long. The logs were chinked with clay and plastered with the same to hold them together in a stack and also to prevent them from catching fire. The whole thing spoke of a minimum care in building and even less in maintenance. It was the most uninspiring structure Seth ever saw. Even so, from a distance of twenty yards off, he could hear laughing and clanging and shuffling. Of a fact, there really were people inside.

Climbing down from the buckboard, Seth's first tug on the door went unrewarded. The top hinge was busted and a wide arc gouged in the dirt meant that it had been that way for some time. Glancing nervously back at Jack, Seth heaved upward and outward at the same time and so managed to snatch open the heavy oak-planked door. What he saw within was nothing like the warm, welcoming feast he was accustomed to back home. For sure it was cold without but only marginally less cold within. From

Prudence Nightshade

what he could see, a veil of tobacco smoke wafted about waist high only to be topped off with a mantel of coal smoke just beneath the ceiling. Three feeble lanterns cast a haunting light throughout the tavern. As Seth hesitated, Jack stormed past, slapped him on the back and yelled, "C'mon, Seth! Let's have oursef a time!" When others of his crew filed past, Seth followed suit.

Jack had planned it just right for as they dragged three-legged stools up to a darkened table, "fixins'" were already underway. The yeasty smell of ale filled the room even as fat-packed sausages sailed past on greasy stoneware. A three-tined fork struck home like a whale man's harpoon, hefting a struggling sausage high into the air. Further down the table, barely visible in the shadow, an old trail hand joked, "Dibs on the drumstick!" The room erupted with laughter from a score of partially lit faces. Seth managed a weak smile even as a twinge of pain pierced his heart. With no prayers said, rough cast pewter utensils clinked and scraped against cold metal plates. Once again, Seth's thoughts drifted to what no doubt was occurring around his family's table. Rev. Garner would offer heartfelt thanksgiving for all the gifts that were brought by his grateful congregants. Best of all, they would have a *real* turkey; maybe two. At the close of his father's prayer, his mother's eyes would have moistened, just as they did every year, for all of God's goodness to them. It pained Seth to know that Krupsteiner's poisoned letter would have already done its damage by now. That fact, together with his absence, would have added to his mother's tears as well. Seth felt deeply sorry for this.

A sharp slap on the back jerked Seth back into the smoky tavern. "Where ya' been Seth? Thought we lost ya' this time!" jeered a good-natured but grimy trail hand. Seth looked into a circle of fire-lit faces, smiling yet straining to make some contact with him. How long he stood staring

Seth Garner: Part One

ahead while looking back, he didn't know. Gathering his senses a bit, he quickly realized that the men were in the midst of some kind of toast. "Tiz time ya' downed a wee dram, ma' boy!" rasped an unknown, all the while pressing a cup into his own palm. Still not fully present, Seth quaffed down the contents without thinking. It was as if the fire in the hearth had changed to liquid and flowed across the table then down his throat. The homebrew scorched his inner hide, hit bottom, reversed course, and came up faster than it went down. The hoots and howls of the men shook the tableware as one shoved a lard-filled something or other before his nose in an effort to quench the fire. As Seth stared down at the greasy, by now, cold sausage, his stomach did a slow roll. Weakly standing and turning toward the back of the tavern, he managed to stammer, "I...I...think I'll turn in for the night." A chorus of "No! No! Da' nite's yung!" could not dissuade his path toward a hovel of a room. The creak of the door unnerved him as he held forth a stump of a candle to look in. The mattress mirrored the roof for it sagged like a bowl in the middle. Setting the now nearly spent candle on a stand, Seth climbed in. The bedding was damp and as he pulled up the covers to his chin, he smelled mold. With a sigh, he let his right arm fall into the space between the bed and the wall. As soon as his knuckles hit the floor, he heard something scurry along the wall. Jerking his arm up again, he braided it in with the other, folding them both across his chest. He laid there a long while staring through the dark at an unseen ceiling.

As the laughter and merriment rolled on for hours, Seth's thoughts whirled wildly in his head as the reality of his situation came crashing home. Pittsburg would soon be upon them and the Pennsylvania Road would come to an end. What then? With Jack, there had always been a schedule of sorts; he made sure of that. His incessant barking of orders lent a kind of security to the day. But that was coming to an end as well. Where too now? Sleep came in pieces throughout the night. Between lonely naps, Seth thought hard on problems he could not solve. When he had awakened for what must have been the twelfth time, he could barely make out a dusty window across the room. In short order... the orange glow of dawn met his eyes... and he was glad for the night to be over.

His spirits lifted further still as the smell of hot coffee seeped into his room. The rest of the trail hands were already sopping coarse brown bread into the brew and had saved a place for Seth at the table. That small token of care meant the world to him. It meant that they thought of him as part of their group and he knew that they were all that he had at this time. "Sleep well, young Seth?" "Oh, yes sir! The best ever!" Seth replied as he broke off a hunk of the loaf as it passed by. Regardless of the meager fare set before him, Seth judged that it was one of the best breakfasts he had eaten in a long while. Things were getting better.

The wind blew cold and hard as Seth helped Jack harness up the teams. "Goin' in ta Pittsburg taday, Seth ma' boy! Never seen nuttin like it, ah wager! Not like Bean Town or Philadelphiyeh... no how! Oh! Dares a heap a' folk in Pitt. But hits not all citified like Boston and New York. Oh no! Half wild! Oh yeah hits true! Ole Pitt a' shovin' hard agin the frontier! Why Pitt waz da jumpin off place fur ole Lewis and Clark, doncha know! Cuz' Pitt is smack dab on da Forks a' da Ohio!" As usual, Jack seemed to holler regardless of the time of day or how near the listener was to him. On this last point though, there was no need for hollering. Seth knew all about the Lewis and Clark expedition and the role that Pittsburg played in the success of the mission. Indeed, the great exploration began at the "Forks of the Ohio," that is, at the confluence of the

Seth Garner: Part One

Allegheny and Monongahela rivers, the point at which the mighty Ohio River flows westward to the Mississippi. This all happened nearly a decade earlier when the "Corps of Discovery" had over 2 ½ tons of provisions sent down from Philadelphia to Pittsburg. Keel boats had been built in the nearby town of Elizabeth, and thus the renowned journey began just to the west of the great city of Pittsburg. No, Jack didn't need to tell Seth about the Louis and Clark Expedition. The thought that he was following the same path as the first brave pioneers of the Oregon Trail had been on his mind for some time.

As he climbed up on the buckboard next to Jack, he couldn't help but notice how light the wagons were. Nearly all their stock had been sold on their journey down the Boston Post and Pennsylvania roads. As Seth held onto his hat to keep it from blowing away, he yelled back at Jack to be heard above the wind, "After Pittsburg, then what?" "Den wat wat?!" Jack yelled back. "Then what will you do when you take the wagons into Pittsburg?" "Goin to pick up a load of coal, pig iron, kegs of nails, and such truck and head back da way we cum!" The strong blast of Jack's voice overpowered the chill wind of early winter. Seth looked about at the neatly appointed covered wagons. At points along the trail he noted that Jack had taken pains to keep the wagons clean and undamaged. "That heavy ware will fairly ruin these wagons!" Seth shouted back as a gale nearly stole his voice away. Jack let out a howl of a laugh as a heavy palm slapped Seth on the back. "Can't tote no pig iron an coal in deez rigs! Nosiree! Goin' ta sell em in Pitt to da folk dat's westerin!" Before Seth could ask his next question, Jack bellowed out, "Westerin is a crossin the Big One, da Mizzazip, fur parts naern heerd of! Ain't hit a wonder!" he shouted as he looked dreamily ahead. "Iffen ah wazza youngblood, say like ya'sef, ah'd be a westerin too! Naw, not now! Too long in da toof, ole Trader Jack is!

52

Prudence Nightshade

Ah jus keep makin ma runs up an down these old roads." As Seth lifted a finger to ask his next question, Jack started in again. "We'll sell deese here rigs ta doze wanderin souls, Gawd bless 'em! Den we'll use dat money to buy heavy freight wagons, wide, flat, and open, but day'll get da job done. Jus thow a tarp over em an head back da utter way, tiz'all!" Since Jack had answered all of Seth's questions without him asking, he just sank down in the folds of the big buffalo robe and enjoyed the ride into Pittsburg.

The smoke from hundreds of chimneys could be seen miles away as their wagons drew closer to Pittsburg. Seth knew they were getting nearer to the city as the cabins and houses were bunched closer together. At last they rolled into the city proper, and Seth was fairly overwhelmed with the hustle and bustle of this grand town of young America. Churches and taverns abounded. There were shops of every kind and plenty of them. There was industry, refinement, and hints here and there of the frontier. Pittsburg was a little bit of everything, roots, trunk, and branches altogether, everything that the new democracy is and was becoming. As Seth's eyes nearly popped out of his head, Jack yelled, "Go on! Ah'll take keer of ever thang!" At that, Seth lit off the buckboard and started to make his way to who knows where down a busy street. "Hold on, jus a minute!" Jack hollered before Seth took five steps. Turning back, Jack took hold of Seth's hand and pressed in a number of coins. "This is jis a little bonus fur ya!" he yelled as a smile broke over his whiskered face. Before Seth could thank him, he bolted out, "Naw go on an have yasef a time! Jus be back at Sam Tate's livery in the morning." As Seth held out his arms and looked nonplused about the stable, Jack shooed him away and yelled, "Jis ask anybody an day'll tell ya war Sam Tate's is! Naw go on!" And so he did.

At fifteen years of age, Seth felt both exhilarated and intimidated by the city. The first order of business was

Seth Garner: Part One

food. Even at his young age, he had enough sense not to dine with the parasoled ladies and finely dressed gents who were making their way down well appointed streets. Laying hold of something between a tavern and a restaurant, Seth sat down to the first real steak dinner of his life. Following that, he made his way into a candy shop and wolfed down the best chocolate he had ever eaten and then followed his nose to the mesmerizing aroma of freshly brewed coffee at a shop next door. Taking a room in a hotel, he scrubbed weeks of trail dirt off of his body, and then slumped into a real feather bed. The coal fire in the grate not only warmed the room, but also dried the air, making all the difference from the places that he had bedded down along the Pennsylvania Road. All of this, and he still had money in his pocket. Things were really looking up now.

As the wind howled and drove snow against a real glass window, Seth's mind took stock of his situation. Trader Jack was heading back to east, and soon, before the deep winter snows blocked the road. Somehow Seth felt that there was no future for him back east. On the other hand, there was no place for him to stay in Pittsburg. Once again, he was at a crossroads and hadn't a clue where to turn. But for now, the room was warm and dry, the bed felt like something from another world and Seth fell into a deep sleep.

As gray light forced its way through frosted glass, Seth staggered half asleep across the floor. Jamming a small coal shovel into the box next to the grate, he poured on more fuel and climbed back into bed. Who knows when he would sleep in such quarters again, so he took full advantage of the situation. A couple of hours later, he dined on fried eggs, lean bacon, and biscuits. Once in the street, a few inquiries directed him toward the livery. Half a block away he could hear Jack's voice ring out through the clear, cold mid-morning air. He was auctioning off his wagons, and the "westerin' folk" were starting to come together. "Why, dis rig'll tek ya' into Kintuck and Tennersee! If ya' hankerin' to go on to Massourah, hit'll do dat too!" Young hopeful couples would timidly walk up and have a few words. A few would walk away dejected, but more would proffer a small poke containing their entire life's savings up to that point, then drive away with what would be their home in the months to come. These families were the growing edge of the new nation, and Seth could sense the excitement and the anxiety in their young faces as they drove their teams away. Jack had already lined up the purchase of the freight wagons, as he had done in years past, and it looked like all was going according to plan. As Jack had just closed another deal on one of the few remaining wagons, Seth walked up and tapped him on the shoulder.

"Seth, ma' boy! Did ya have yassef a time!?" "Well...yes..." "I knewed ya' would! Dat's Pitt fur ya!" "Well...Jack....I'm wanting to..." Jack grabbed Seth by the shoulders, furrowed his bushy eyebrows, and peered deeply into his eyes. "Ya' taint cummin' back wit' me, are ya, Seth?" he shouted inches from Seth's nose. "Well...Jack...last night I was thinking...." "I knewed it! I knewed dat too! I says to ma'sef, 'Seth ain't cummin back wit' me in da mornin'!' an now, ain't it so!" "Yes, that's so, Jack. I am sorry..." "Naw! Naw! No cause for dat! But you can't wester now, son! Winter's hard on us! Deeze folks are goin ta hunker down in Pitt. Gradly scrape up a grubstake an' light out first thang in da Sprang. Ya can't wester now!" "I guess I'll have to do the same, Jack. I don't know..." "Thar's a place fur ya in Pitt, Seth! Jus' go on! Sumpin'll turn up!" With that Jack gave him a bear hug, directed him to gather his pack together, and rattled on about how to get along for the next few months. And so

Seth Garner: Part One

Seth walked away from the first real friend he had made since he left his parents some months ago in Ohio. As he hefted his pack and slung his books over a shoulder, he bid farewell to Trader Jack.

The sun shown bright and clear. It turned out to be one of those unusually warm days just before the onset of serious winter. Despite the cheery clime, Seth felt more alone now than when he had fled from Krupsteiner's school. He jostled his way through the crowded boardwalk, envying those who had sweethearts, friends and family. He reasoned it was the price of personal freedom, and if he was going to continue on his own, he would have to get used to it. Lost in his thoughts, he didn't even slow his pace at the "Hey, boy!" shouted his way. Then "Hey, boy!" again turned him about to see a hunchbacked old crone with a grizzly wisp of a beard hobbling his way. His clothes were tailored but tattered. A large gold watch hung from a checkered waist coat, and well-worn but newly pressed wool slacks sported a neat pleat down the center. A frazzled, beaver felt top hat was titled at a smart angle on his head covering a good bit of his snow white hair. Gold spectacles sat askew across his nose and nicely framed a crooked smile. Wrenching his way through the crowd, the man poked a pointed finger at Seth's pack. "Those books there, lad!" "They're not for sale," Seth responded as he started to turn away. A bony hand clasped his shoulder and held him fast. Seth was surprised at the strength of one who looked so frail. "I'm not buying!" snapped the old man. "My point is, my good man, is if in fact you can you read?" rasped out the old soul as he peered intently into Seth's eyes. "Of course I can read. I was trained at Master Krupsteiner's boarding school back in Boston." "Means nothing to me. Tell me now... can you write?" "Good sir, I can both read and write and...." "Good! That's good. But can you spell words rightly?" "Dear man, I am hungry, and

Prudence Nightshade

tired, and I have no place..." "That's the very thing I am about! Shamus Dundee's my name and printing's my trade. Sole owner, editor and distributor of the Pittsburg Herald. I am offering you, right here, in this place, a position in my establishment! A printer, a typesetter, a reporter. Room, board, a few coins a week..." "Mr. Dundee..." "Shamus...Shamus is all." "Well enough, Shamus. I'll be moving on in the Spring..."Long enough...plenty long enough. Cold weather's the time for reading anyway." "Well, if you think I can help..." "I do! I most certainly do! I could see you're a gifted man from half a block away! You walk smartly! A man of destiny, no doubt! Now come this way. The sooner we get started the better!" The old man hooked Seth's elbow and started tugging him down the boardwalk from whence he came. Pausing for a moment and pointing skyward at a weather-worn shingle emblazoned, "The Pittsburg Herald," Shamus smiled from ear to ear and crowed, "That's us! The veritable presence of free speech in this rambling wreck of a town!" That single word...*us*...did more to sell Seth on the job than anything Shamus had said to that point. Pushing through a massive wooden door, a high-pitched bell rang as they entered the room. Turning about, Shamus pointed out the bell, "You've got to know when one passes through that hallowed portal!" Seth nodded knowingly. Taking hold of a cord, the old man pulled down a blind to cover the window, and with a wink added, "Betimes, there's cause for secrecy in this business!" Again Seth nodded as if that made perfect sense, although he hadn't a clue what it was about. As they walked deeper into the press room, the pungent odor of ink and solvent fairly overwhelmed him. "You'll get used to it! That you will! I'll confess that the smell of ink makes me feel at home!" Seth surveyed a dizzying array of metal type, trays, ink mops, and in the center of it all, a solidly built printing press with

57

more gears and levers than he could take in at the moment. He heard a light clatter above just about the time Shamus shouted up the stairs, "Make that two bowls of stew, Penelope, make that two! We've got company today, by crackin'!" Turning again to Seth, "We live, Penelope and I, we live upstairs. That's why I said the smell of ink makes me feel at home!" As the old man laughed and shook his head, quite satisfied with his own humor, a ruddy cheeked, plump woman floated down the stairs with two steaming bowls of beef stew. As Seth took down some of the most glorious stew he had ever tasted, Shamus continued. "Now don't let all of this truck worry you. In the end of the day, it's quite simple. It's the story and the timing of the story...that's the thing." As they ate, Shamus rattled on about accuracy, fairness and developing a feel for what's important.

Seth's apprenticeship began in earnest the next day. As Shamus explained the mechanics of printing and typeset, the lessons of Trader Jack began to kick in for Seth. He sensed that a paper had to strike a fine balance between supplying what the people want to read and reporting what the people need to hear. In any case, a newspaper was a business, and from what he could tell thus far, the Pittsburg Herald was in real need of help. "How do you get sources?" "Sources?" "Who brings you the news?" Seth continued. "Oh we have some standard pieces, sections of *Poor Richard's Almanac*, church announcements, farm reports and the like." "How are sales?" Seth asked. "Profit is not the only thing in journalism and it is certainly not the most important thing! The people are depending on us!" Shamus responded. "What about ads?" "Well Seth, we have lots of ads about egg sales, horse trading, and the like." "And the proceeds from the ads? How much do you take in?" "My ads are a service, Seth. I aim to help the community!" "That's good...to a point," Seth said weakly as he scanned a painfully dull article scrawled on brown paper. Shamus took no notice of Seth's sad tone as he clattered about the shop gathering up small lead letters and arranging them in a frame.

As Seth went out at first light to drop off bundles of papers to a handful of carriers, he saw more papers used to wrap fish than being read. At the same time as he settled into the ebb and flow of city life, he saw children slaving away in wretched conditions rather than going to school. The wealthy showed no regard for the poor. Crooks were swindling the uninformed, crime lurked in the shadow of stately churches and those elected to serve appeared more interested in filling their own pockets than in helping the people who had put them in office. So as the gray pall of winter settled over the city, Seth became increasingly concerned about the relevance of the Pittsburg Herald. Sales were abysmal and a good portion of what was sold ended up in the garbage away. The paper was simply not doing what a paper ought to do. The really important news was falling off the edge of the table and no one even noticed. From Seth's perspective, the Herald should have been the voice of democracy railing against injustice and corruption. Instead it had become the lackluster rag of egg peddlers and folksy tales about the weather. As Seth retired to the loft above the press, even the strong odor of ink and solvent could not distract his thoughts. It was clear that the entire tenor of the paper had to be changed. It was equally clear that Shamus, for all of his goodness, would not be the agent of that change. Hours passed as Seth pondered the problem at hand, even as he studied the pattern of shingles just above his head. What this town needed was a Silence Do...

Suddenly he sat bolt upright in his bed. It came to him all at once, whole cloth, seamlessly streaming into his mind like a sweet aroma. He quickly lit a candle, snatched up a

Seth Garner: Part One

piece of scrap paper and took quill in hand. Words ran ahead of the quill as it feverishly scratched across the paper. He wrote:

> Dear Residents of Pittsburg:
>
> Please grant me the pleasure of introducing myself. I am a woman of means most recently moved to your fair city. Being a person of culture, I take pleasure in the life of the mind, in the cultivation of moral virtue and in the pursuit of that business which leads to fiscal security. Needless to say, I am unattached. Moreover, I have no inclination to alter my station in life, for God's gift is too dear to fritter away in the service of a man.
>
> Leaving my concerns aside, as difficult as that might be, I must confess that my chief aim is to get to know each of you on a more personal level. Although I have been here but for a few days, I am already very impressed with the citizenry of this town. So industrious, so ingenious, so unreservedly committed to the promotion of itself. What I mean to say is that so many of you are not getting the attention you deserve. Much of what you are doing is going unnoticed and I pledge my intellectual talents (which are considerable), my strength and my unspoiled virtue to correct this injustice! To that end I shall devote myself fulltime, having no need to work otherwise, in the judicious observance of all your

Prudence Nightshade

ways and to give public notice of my findings in this selfsame newspaper. Rest assured that my unyielding sense of integrity will report not only the good, but also the less than inspiring, so that we might all profit thereby.

In the meantime, continue about your affairs as usual. Indeed, I would suffer unfeigned sorrow if my unfailing eye should cause you to live otherwise.

Until we meet face to face,

Prudence Nightshade

Seth rolled up the paper, tied it with a length of brown cord and quietly slipped down the stairs to the print shop. Unbolting the front door he nearly made the mistake of pulling it wide open until he remember the bell attached over head. Drawing up a stool he crammed some paper about the clapper to silence it, and proceeded with his plan.

At breakfast the next morning, Seth did his best to look disinterested as Shamus got up from the table. It was his custom to be the first down the stairs to open up the shop below. When he heard the bell signal the opening of the front door, Seth could hardly contain the feelings that welled up inside; excitement, fear, a twinge of guilt, all rolled together. As the minutes wore on and the usual, "Come now, Seth! Let's get to work!" was not forthcoming, Seth nearly cracked under the strain. "Are you alright, Seth?" Penelope asked? "Oh! Yes! Never felt better! Just eager to get to work is all!" The steady, "Clomp! Clomp! Clomp!" of Shamus' boots trudging back up the stairs diverted Penelope's attention from Seth's nervous walk

61

about the room. Shamus came in holding the note that had been wedged in the shop door the night before. With head down he steadily walked back to the table, his lips muttering the words "Prudence Nightshade." Holding up the paper he asked Seth if he knew anything about the note. Shrugging his shoulders and looking perfectly stupid, Penelope took the paper from Shamus' hands. After a quick skim, she pronounced her judgment. "Seems that we have a well-heeled busybody who's trying to stir up trouble around here!" Shamus again looked Seth's way. Again looking perplexed and a bit put out, Seth strode forward and took the note from Penelope. Reading it as if he had never seen it before, he simply said, "Well...I don't know..." The expression meant nothing either way, but it was enough to send Shamus to the window looking pensively out over the city. After a few awkward moments, Seth said, "I am going to cast this rubbish into the fire!" As he made a few measured and loud steps toward the hearth, Shamus' shouted, "Wait!" even as his right arm raised high and a bony finger pointed toward the ceiling. "It's my fault! It's all my fault!" croaked the old man. "I've turned a blind eye to the dark side of this city, the really hard calls, the stuff that keeps you up at night. My age, I guess. But there's no place for it in newspaper work! I can see that now. Why... when I was young man, I...!" "Shamus, what are you saying," interrupted Seth. "I am saying that taking the safe path has forced this young girl...um..um...What's her name, Seth?" "'Prudence', Shamus. She signed her name, 'Prudence'." "Yes...Yes...has forced Prudence, may God bless her, has forced Prudence to write what she has written. That's what I am saying!" "What do you mean, dear?" piped in Penelope. "I mean I owe it to her...What have I done?! I mean, I owe it to her to print her work." "You don't mean it!" exclaimed Seth. "Indeed I do!" "Are you sure, Shamus?" inquired Penelope looking more

Prudence Nightshade

worried than ever. "I am more sure of this than anything in a very long time. Seth, are you up to it? Can you set the type?" "I think I ...." "Good! Get right on it! Prudence is your part. Run it by me first...Oh! What do I have to do with it now at my age? She's all yours, Seth. Prudence is your portion of the newsprint."

And so he did. On the second page, in the place of the usual bit on hog sales and feed, Seth set the piece on Prudence Nightshade. He ran off extra copies, bundled them together and threw them into his push cart. The outward trek of delivering the papers went on as usual, but the return trip was anything but the norm. Here and there he would hear, "Ya gotta read this!" or "Have you read Miss Nightshade yet?" Rather than using the paper to wrap fish, copies were being passed on to those who didn't subscribe. By the time he got back to the print shop, several people had walked in to by surplus copies. Prudence had struck an interesting chord with the public and they were eager to hear the next song. Yet Seth decided to hold off writing the next installment. He did so for a couple of reasons. First, he wanted to whet the appetite of the readership. That worked. Within days he overheard folk ask, "Have you heard anything from Prudence yet?" or "What's the holdup with Miss Nightshade?" Second, he needed to allow a few days for Prudence to collect information as she mentioned she would do in her first open letter to Pittsburg. But on Friday, Shamus "found" another note wedged in the shop door. It read:

Dear Friends of Pittsburg:

My admiration for this fair city has only increased with the passing. So much being done for the public good! Take Mr. Springhauser for example, the man seeking

63

Seth Garner: Part One

to be made sheriff this next election. I do respect his stance against all of the vices that lurk in the shady parts of the city. Why just last night, yes I believe it was about ten, I lost my way and found myself in just such a neighborhood! And who did I see? If it was not Mr. Springhauser entering the Fallen Angels Saloon, a house of ill repute, I do believe. He no doubt was spreading his message of moral reformation. And campaigning so late at that! Now is that not a man given over to the task at hand? Also it was a pleasure to meet Mr. Cornwall of the General Mercantile and Feed on Grassmarket Street. As he was weighing out 5 lbs. of flour for me, one of those little weights for the scale fell to the floor and broke to pieces, like it was made of clay. I guess they don't make lead like they used to. But he felt so awful about it! His face turned so red and he assured me that he would replace it in short order. He had several more just like it in his shop. And I do believe in industry, even for the young. Idle hands are the devil's workshop for sure! Like that young man, I don't know his name, he works at the livery, must be about fifteen. He helped me with my groceries, so nice he was. I gave him a nickel, to which he said, "Ahm goin' ta fetch me sum shugah." And if he didn't stride up to a barrel clearly labeled "SALT" and started ladling it into a poke! I don't know what to make of it. It's like he had not been to school a day in his *life! Oh well, there must be differences between the classes, and those that attend classes are the ones who make the difference.*

I must say that my brief tour of the city has made me want to delve deeper into each and every corner of life here. No...no...there's much more meaning here. I have come to accept that it is my life's calling to know each one of you as I would know an open book. I won't rest until that's done!

Until we meet face to face,
Prudence Nightshade.

As the weeks stretched by, the notoriety of Prudence spread. Sales of the Sunday edition spiked in comparison to the weekday issues, yet circulation expanded overall. The Pittsburg Herald was the thing to read. Moreover, the movers and shakers of the city clamored to have their names in print and that as often as possible. The paper quickly became the place to promote your business or product. Soon the income from ads surpassed subscriptions. All of this meant that Shamus and Penelope were financially solvent for the first time in their lives. No one could doubt that success upon success was due to one person and one person alone: Prudence Nightshade. Her fans were as varied as her readership. Some hailed her as the savior of the city while others branded her a malicious muckraker. Simply put, she was equally loved and hated by all. However each reader shared one thing in common with all other subscribers. Regardless of their opinion of Miss Nightshade, a single burning question was on all of their minds: Who was Prudence Nightshade?

Seth Garner: Part One

Of all the persons who were truly vexed by that one question, there was none more vexed than candidate Springhauser. He was determined to smoke her out and grind her underfoot if given the chance. So at an open air campaign rally, Springhauser climbed upon a stump and lit into a scathing tirade against Prudence. If words could kill his speech was a masacre. "I don't give a dead toad's wart who Miss Nightshade is! For when she is found out... and mark my words... she surely will be found out... she should be whipped like a man, tarred and feathered like a criminal and run out of town like an animal!" With hand over heart and hat in hand, Springhauser pressed on. "Though beneath my station in life, I am more than willing to pay cash money to expose Miss Pretense. Indeed I will! To show my unwavering commitment to truth and character, I am offering a personal reward of $100.00 dollars to anyone with credible information as to the identity of little Miss Muckraker!". At that remark, a pattering of whispers spread throughout the crowd. Donning his hat again, he gestured to the crowd to be silent. "Moreover, I have reliable evidence, the nature of which I shall divulge at the appropriate time, that Miss Pernicious Meddler is not the person she purports to be!" Again, murmuring gasps of surprise erupted here and there. "'Until we meet face to face.' Ha! I promise you that when Miss Busybody comes out of hiding, you're not going to like what you see! What we need, folks, is a free and open society. We can't live in fear of secret informers, the constant tyranny of witch hunts and the general eroding of public trust." In closing, Springhauser summoned all of Pittsburg to join him in rooting out every rumor monger and tale bearer in the city, starting with Prudence Nightshade. When he finally finished his speech, he heroically stepped down off the stump and strode through the crowd, accompanied by rousing applause from all quarters.

Prudence Nightshade

It was now Sheriff Henderson's turn to address the people. He had clearly been put on the defensive by Springhauser. Rather than trying to promote himself or even defame his opponent, Henderson decided to take another route altogether. Staring out over the crowd for a moment, Henderson started right in. "You all have been long on listening so I will be short on talking. Mr. Springhauser is no doubt a learned man and a good speaker. But for some reason, and I think that this is clear to all, his thoughts have come to rest on Miss Nightshade. More directly, he is determined to keep her quiet. In this regard, permit me a word. The reason why we can gather here today and say our piece without fear or dread is because we live in a nation built on freedom of speech. Anybody, be it president or pauper, can express their views openly without apprehension provided they do not disturb the public order or incite to bodily harm. We might not like what people say, but that does not mean they don't have the right to say it! I've got my troubles with Prudence too, just like many of you, but I'll defend her liberty to speak her mind. And what I can make of it, as far as I can tell, a good part of what she's said is the truth! And I don't care where this goes, that is, as far as the election is concerned. I am for common sense freedom regardless of whether it wears a bonnet or spurs! Now folks, I'm done." Once again cheers erupted from the crowd, the larger part coming from the ladies that were present. As Henderson was just about to jump down, someone shouted, "Speak on, sheriff!" Straightening up again, Henderson took a deep breath and addressed the people. "I want you all to know this. I don't only believe in upholding the civil law, I also believe in the law of being civil. What I mean is, whether it be Springhauser, or Prudence, or a lout I am about to throw in the slammer, I aim not to speak mean of any person." Looking sternly at Springhauser, the sheriff took

Seth Garner: Part One

hold of the brim of his hat and with quick tip said, "Now...again...I'm done." The crowd clapped wildly as Henderson hopped down from the stump. As he sauntered back to his office, Springhauser glared menacingly at him and at the people.

So as it was, in her single person, Prudence became a lightning rod for all that was right and wrong in Pittsburg. She was at once a saint and a sinner, a savior and a scoundrel, but in the end of it all, she remained a deep mystery.

It didn't take long for the public to realize that the connection between Prudence and the Pittsburg Herald was a close one. What she wrote, the paper printed. So on more than one occasion Shamus and Seth were questioned about her identity. Shamus rightly claimed he had never even met the woman and that he didn't work with that part of the newsprint. Seth handled the situation a bit differently: he lied. While acknowledging that he did have written contact with Prudence, he added that he had never met her personally and wouldn't recognize her if they met on the street. All of this was technically true but substantially false. His main response was that as long as her stories checked out, and so far they all had, he had no trouble with not knowing her true identity. Seth also added that Miss Nightshade always included a peculiar trademark in all of her correspondence, a sign that he had vowed never to divulge. So it was futile to try and foist one's opinion in the name of Prudence. As assistant editor of the paper, he could tell the difference between Prudence and a pretender and would immediately scrap all forgeries. In this way Seth deflected suspicions concerning himself and effectively closed the door on forgeries and fakes. However, what happened next took him totally by surprise.

Prudence Nightshade

As Seth crept down to plant another message from Prudence, he noticed a folded note already wedged in the shop door. The anonymous letter was addressed "To Prudence Nightshade." Not long after this first message, he began to find similar notes so addressed or simply labeled: "Please get this to Prudence." The messages invariably contained a report by some concerned citizen about an injustice or scam. However, a few contained threats promising bodily harm to Prudence if she should continue to abuse the good citizenry of Pittsburg. Thus for better or worse, Miss Nightshade had become the moral conscience of the city. She welcomed the increase in civic mindedness, and in her next open letter, she expressed her delight.

> Dear Friends of Pittsburg:
>
> I now feel as one among you for I am now, indeed, one of you. Also I can tell that many of you feel the same towards me. Together we have come to learn what has always been surely true: we the citizenry of Pittsburg are Pittsburgh. That is to say, you (excepting the immature and unenlightened), have come to identify with my unfeigned character and also to embrace my sterling vision of justice. In short, I can sense a collective endorsement of the virtuous path I have chosen in life. So I cherish this sweet spirit of fellowship and rest in the secure knowledge that I am not alone on this journey.
>
> And now to the point at hand – As of late, the newspaper has conveyed to me, by secure channels,

69

Seth Garner: Part One

letters deserving my expert counsel. In the main, apart from the cowardly threats to my person, allow me to say this: they are welcome. They represent the concerted soul of our great city! Furthermore, the veracity of these selfsame reports I have no reason to question. On these bases, I invite you to read on.

 It has been reported to me that the local miller has committed adultery of such a nature that affects us all. I am not a baker or even a homemaker, but I don't figure that a loaf of bread should be the first cousin to the board that it is sliced on! That is to say the miller is commingling the grist at a rate of one measure of sawdust to ten of flour. May our indignation rise higher than our doughy white buns!

 Leaving that aside, allow me to renew a former concern. Far be it from me to sully my hands in the surly world of local politics, but allow me this once to cast my bonnet into the ring. When Master Springhauser bawled out his stump speech recently I was there in the midst of you, as always. So again, against my good judgment, permit me to speak more directly to this person. Sir Springhauser, I am certainly not a man so I can't be whipped like one, if one should be ever whipped at all. Also I am not an animal, though they have many sound lessons to teach us, as the Good Book tells. So the tar you intend

Prudence Nightshade

for me would be better used to fix the rooftops of the poor and the feathers for the pillows of the aged. And finally, if anyone can indict me of a crime, no...moreover...if anyone can convict me of a misstatement, (Master Springhauser notwithstanding), I will hew down the rail myself to be run out of town on!

But alas! I sense the ebbing of that sublime state of grace so inherent to my soul, therefore I bid you all...adieu.

Until we meet face to face,

Prudence Nightshade.

With her dalliance into the realm of local politics "Nightshade Fever" really heated up. She found her way into nearly every conversation, from saloon small talk to sermon sub point. Prudence became a celebrity, a veritable unseen presence in every public setting. Even her surname came into more determined use as nightshades were pulled down snug to divert her ever-present gaze. The Nightshade craze reached a highpoint one morning as Seth worked hard at setting the type for the next edition. As the shop doorbell rang, Seth turned about to see an attractive young woman entering the room. She had long red hair, sported a green parasol and wore a fashionable dress of tailored gingham. Seth offered, "May I help you please?" The woman stared ahead as if she did not hear him, standing stark still before the door. "Please come in and have a seat," Seth beckoned as he escorted the beauty away from the print table. She fairly floated across the floor, sat in the only cushioned chair in the shop and placed the parasol deftly across her lap. Still not uttering a word, Seth nodded slowly in an attempt to break the silence. She swallowed twice, breathed out a long draft and said, "I have a confession to make." Seth widened his eyes and continued to nod slowly as she fairly burned a hole through him with her gaze. "I am...Oh my! This is so hard for me!" "Please, go on! You are safe here. The honor of the press is at stake!" Seth assured. "I am...Oh! Why did I come?! No...no...I must go through with it. I am...I mean to say...I truly am...Prudence Nightshade!" Seth gasped in disbelief, drawing one hand over his heart and the other covering his gaping mouth. Springing up from his stool he motioned for her to stay put as he dashed across the floor for a writing pad. "Now tell me everything. *Do not* omit a single detail!" Seth implored as he leaned forward in feigned interest. Her silence soon turned into a torrent of disjointed verbiage that came so fast that Seth could hardly keep up. "Well a girl like me has her principles, but who would ever listen, seeing that I am single and only, well...leaving age aside...And why should they in a town of the rich and powerful? Seeing that it's almost Sunday and all... Don't just sit there and stare at me! You're not the only one who knows how write a newspaper you know!" The intensity of her presence practically unnerved Seth. For an instant he nearly believed that she was Prudence Nightshade. Seth was saved by the sounding of the shop bell jangling once again. He and the young woman stood to their feet as a gray-headed matron entered in the print room unannounced. With a determined gait, she strode confidently up to Seth and the younger "Prudence" and announced, "*I* ...am Prudence Nightshade!" Hesitating a moment, Seth replied, "Well, you will have to wait your turn. I am in the midst of the first ever interview with none other than Miss Nightshade herself!" The young woman's face turned as red as her hair. Eyes glued to the floor, she wordlessly marched out the still open door. The elder "Prudence" widened her eyes in ever increasing circles, pointed her nose skyward and with a "Humph!" bustled out into the street. As Seth closed the door behind the two, they put as much distance between themselves as possible, all the while casting unfriendly glances over their shoulders. Seth laughed so hard he could hardly return to the typesetting tray. He shared the whole story with Shamus who quipped, "Well...they could have been her!" Little did Seth know that this would be his last lighthearted contact with Prudence. From here on out, his life as Prudence Nightshade would descend into chaos.

There was no way to soften the impact of what happened. Some things are so irreducibly evil that they allow no room for interpretation. The ugly specter of the dismembered torso was just one of those things. The unbridled brutality of the scene shattered the collective psyche of the city. The heinousness of the crime so wrecked those sensibilities that preserve civility, so dismantled the unseen barriers that distinguish the human from the bestial, that everyone, be they man or woman, felt personally assaulted. The safety and self-assurance of the city vanished like a vapor only to be replaced by a pervasive fog of terror that reached into every heart. The contorted body of the young prostitute, cast to the ground with such savage disregard, cut deep into the soul of the people. Their faces spoke the sad story of profound disappointment, not just in the person who did such a thing, but in the fact that humanity had so insanely failed itself by killing one of its own. A dreary pall hung over everything and to make matters worse Prudence vanished along with the last vestige of innocence that good hearts so desperately sought to hold on to. Weeks went by without as much as a word from Prudence. Many said that the sheer horror of the crime had stunned Prudence into

Seth Garner: Part One

silence. Others claimed that she had quit Pittsburg altogether, abandoned them during their darkest hour, and wasn't worth a second thought in such troubling times. When it seemed that things could get no worse, a second body literally surfaced beneath the Fourth Street Bridge. Prudence could forebear no more.

> *My dear friends:*
>
> *Many of you have inquired concerning my whereabouts during these sad days. I am aware too that some unkind words have been said in regard to my person. I could care less about these things because I care more for you. All that I pray is that you withhold judgment and make place for a word of explanation.*
>
> *How can the mouth speak when the heart is torn in two? How can one put quill to parchment when one's inner world is so cloaked in darkness, a darkness that makes this tepid ink pale in comparison? How can one force this fragile medium of the word to bear the weight of such crushing sorrow? I cannot speak. I cannot write. I cannot find a way to express the tempest that rages in my soul! A storm, I say, a storm that threatens to dash me against the cold, flinty shore of man's inhumanity to man! Do I want vengeance? Never! Lest I sink headlong into that moral abyss in which this killer dwells! Do I*

Prudence Nightshade

crave justice? More than life itself! Would I settle for the cessation of this madness that looms over us all? In an instant! For the preservation of the living is worth more than the eternal torment of the damned. Every fiber of my being cries out for mercy for my fellow sisters. Yes I said "sisters" for no vocation in life, no matter how vile, can expunge that essential humanity that joins us all! And let not one of us entertain some twisted notion of divine retribution, a season of wrath, some terrible plague of murdering judgment being visited upon the outcasts of our town. Banish that thought! Were it not for the veritable grace of God we all would be wracked and bound by those base motions that lurk within.

And now an open appeal to the one who has done the unthinkable. I implore you, no...moreover I beg of you, leave off these crimes at once! I mean what I say. Would that myself be sacrificed on the altar of your hate if it would mean the end of it all! At the very least, leave the fair environs of our place, never to return. At the most, I pray that you cast your soul upon the mercies of the living God and be healed in heart and mind.

Although I have not expressed the half of what burns in my heart, I fear I have said too much.

Seth Garner: Part One

Yet again I write directly to the killer, if it will help in any way, I will sign off in my usual way:
Until we meet face to face,
Prudence Nightshade

Prudence's letter had a profound effect on the readership. Prayer meetings were organized to seek the protection of potential victims and known women of ill repute were welcomed into private homes. Bands of volunteers patrolled the city streets at all hours of the day and night, and there was a general increase in care for the less fortunate. As the weeks stretched by, some entertained the hope that Prudence had even touched the heart of the killer, for the murderous rampage had come to a halt. Slowly one could sense that a degree of normalcy had returned to the city. That sense was short lived.

The crumpled brown paper in the door was nothing new to Seth. He had received dozens of notes addressed to Prudence in the past months. Most were addressed, "Dear Prudence" if the writer was female, but a very few notes from men read, "To Miss Nightshade." For the most part, all were written cordially, reflecting the measure of respect due to one like Prudence. But this particular note was different. It simply read: "Get this to Nightshade." It was written in pencil on coarse paper and by a heavy hand. One could actually *feel* the words in the paper. It simply read: "I have what you're looking for. Go to the well on Market Street. Come tonight. Alone." Seth folded the letter up, tucked into his housecoat, and tiptoed back upstairs to his bed.

Yet sleep eluded him. As he tossed and turned, he rehearsed the few words of the note over and over in his head. "What you're looking for... Come *tonight.*" The letter was unsigned as most of the messages to Prudence were. Yet this one had left Seth feeling uneasy. There was something ominous about its brevity, its demanding tone and short notice. "What you're looking for," it read. Whoever wrote these words no doubt had valuable information. . "Come *tonight!*" it said. The letter presented an opportunity that with each moment he lay in bed was rapidly passing him by. Of course, Prudence could not come in person, nor could he ...unless? A plan hatched in his head of a dangerous kind. If things went perfectly, he might obtain that bit of information that would solve the case. On the other hand, this could be his last day in Pittsburgh...or worse. Springing up from the feather bed, Seth hastily threw on some clothes, bound a kerchief about his face and quietly worked his way down the stairs. Grasping the bell over the door to muffle its telltale ring, he stepped into the night.

He was well aware that time was running out. The night was well spent already and Market Street was several blocks away. At last he made his way to the well. No one was there. Seth's mind raced ahead in all directions. Was he too late? Did the messenger back out at the last minute? Was the whole thing some kind of prank? When he had just about given up, he noticed a corner of paper protruding from beneath the water bucket. Snatching it up, he held it close to his face and didn't like what he read. "I'm watching you..." Seth snapped up his head and peered about through the gloom. Nothing. "I'm watching you...if you are not alone...I'm gone already. But if you know what's good for you and everyone concerned, go to the old foundry warehouse on the waterfront." Stuffing the note in his pocket, Seth hurried along in that direction.

The massive wooden door slid haltingly aside on rust-encrusted rollers. Seth hesitated. It wasn't too late to turn

Seth Garner: Part One

about and go home. He stepped inside, shoving the door closed behind him. Though the first hint of light was appearing in the east, it was pitch black within... he could see nothing. As he shuffled forward, he sensed something tacky beneath his feet and a strange smell filtered into his nostrils. "Don't turn around." The voice had an icy edge to it and yet was strangely familiar. As Seth wracked his brain in vain trying to place it, the voice growled. "Where is *she*?!" "She? Oh, um...you mean Miss Nightshade?" There was complete silence. Seth could sense unseen eyes boring a hole through him in the dark. As Seth shifted his feet in the film, the voice boomed out, "Don't turn around!" Seth froze in place as if made of stone. He snapped his head down toward the floor and squinted his eyes shut in sheer terror. As he stood there trembling, he could hear the breath of his tormentor pulsing through the dark. Not knowing what to do, Seth stammered out, "Uh...uh...she couldn't come. Um...she gave me this note...and ...and...asked me to come in her place...so I..." "Shut up, you filthy little liar!" No sooner had the voice died away than Seth heard a match strike followed by the creak of a coal oil lamp being lit. In that instant between the strike and the wick catching to, Seth could just make out a crimson stream trailing off before him. As the globe of the lamp was lowered and light spread across the room, it was then that he saw her. The young woman was lashed to the wooden bracing at about eye level, her body forming a human "x" across the frame. She had been gutted from stem to stern like an animal, yet her eyes still retained that wisp of humanity, pleading for mercy that never came. Seth's cry was a mixture of anguish and fear, an echo of human suffering throughout the ages, that primal response in the face of pure evil. As he turned about, he was fairly blinded by the light hurtling down from the loft above. As two heavy boots slammed into his chest, every bit of air left his body as he skidded across the mixture of dirt and blood. Lying senseless for a moment, he vaguely heard footsteps about him and the sound of the lamp being hung in the direction of that poor soul who had lost her life in such a savage fashion. No sooner had he scrambled to his feet than a pair of vice-like hands seized about his neck and began to crush the life out of him, cinching down the kerchief from about his face. In that instant it all came together. The voice. The newspaper article about the Fallen Angels Saloon. The stump speeches for sheriff. "So did you think a little newsroom rat was going to ruin me?! It'll take more than some faceless strumpet snitch to end me!" As Seth pushed and clawed and gurgled to suck down a slip of air, he stared wildly into the face of Springhauser. "I've done this town a favor and everyone knows it save the lying, spineless, holier-than-thou types like you, and that old crazy crone you work for, and...and...that pitiful excuse of a woman..." As Springhauser's hate-filled tirade grew ever louder, Seth's arms felt like lead as the muscles in his neck went limp. As if standing outside of himself, he watched as his head lolled spastically to one side...and then...his eyes slowly closed. An unexpected calm washed over his body. A profound sense of surrender enveloped him as he just floated there.

Then of a start, Seth's arms jerked upward, a sudden spasm powered by an untapped reserve of strength. Clawing along the planking, the warmth of the lantern faintly registered in a fading mind. Weak finger tips curled about the cold steel of the handle as Springhauser bore down hard, driving him toward the floor. With one quick snap of his wrist, the glowing lantern came crashing down on his tormentor's head. Hearing him howl, Seth could feel the death grip slip from his throat as he slumped to the floor. Eyes opened wide, he looked as through a fog at a flaming orb crashing first this way and then that. As life-

Seth Garner: Part One

giving blood coursed again through his brain, his vision cleared and he saw Springhauser, now a roaring ball of flame, swatting madly about, setting on fire rotting coils of rope and sailcloth. Smoke and heat began to fill the place when Springhauser suddenly stood stock still; tatters of burning cloth were sloughing off a body writhing in pain. As in a nightmare, the doomed man mechanically spread his arms and stiff-legged across the floor, intent on drawing Seth into the conflagration. Seth's mind fired off commands that his body was slow to obey, "Get moving! Don't just stand there! Get moving!" he shouted to himself as Springhauser staggered closer and closer. At the last second, with the sound of fire raging about, Seth ducked under Springhauser's grappling arms, crab-walked across the floor, and groped wildly through the smoke for a way out. Falling hard against the massive wooden door, he tugged with all of his might but lacked the strength to slide it along and make his escape. The heat seared his back and Seth could smell the smoke from his own body as his clothes quickly rose to kindling temperature. He cried out loud and pounded against the door, being crushed under a sudden weight of despair. A dark thought raced through mind: he had escaped from the strangling grip of Springhauser and slipped through his flaming clutches, but he would be burned alive with him just the same. As he fell to his knees, the end had come. With his last ounce of strength, he marshaled one, last, momentous force of will and screamed, "My God... Jesus... Help me!"

All he could remember was falling and slamming face forward into the dirt. The fact that someone was dragging him along by his shoulders barely registered. He could just hear the shouts of people running about and someone yelling in his ear, "Boy! Boy! Are you alright?!" The roaring inferno behind him had awakened the riverfront community to a blazing inferno.

Prudence Nightshade

Clean, sweet air flowed into his lungs again. Seth could feel life-giving strength spread to his limbs. Suddenly, without thinking, he leaped to his feet, his mind whirling about as he looked into the concerned face of an old man. Aged hands locked onto his shoulders, steadying Seth as he reeled one way and then the next as a drunken sailor. Still in a stupor from the strangling smoke, and seeing all as a threat, Seth flailed away at his helper, broke loose from his arms and tore away like a madman.

Driven along by sheer panic, he raced down the waterfront, colliding with the gathering crowd bound for the fire. After wrenching away from those that tried to stop him, Seth could hear the shouts, "Seize that boy! Seize him!" trail off behind him. Thus the link between him and the fire had already been made even before he had run a hundred yards. Thinking irrationally, but at lightning speed, he could see the headlines already:

Riverfront Warehouse Burns to the Ground!
Remains of Missing Girl Found!
Editor of Pittsburg Herald Flees the Scene!

A cartload of sundries crumbled under his weight as he tumbled over. Turning about, he could see a handful of men in hot pursuit. Righting himself again, he ran backwards a few steps, and then turned to pick up speed, only to plunge headlong into a skein of fishing nets. Caught in a web of corks and cordage, Seth struggled as the men drew closer.

Ripping free and running like a wild animal now, he tripped over bulkheads and dodged pilings without any clear notion of where he was going...except always just further away, just beyond the reach of those bent on his capture. Looking ahead, a double dose of fear shot through his heart. The wharf was coming to an end and only the

81

Seth Garner: Part One

rain-swollen Ohio lie beyond. His mad dash for freedom would soon be over. He was trapped!

Yet he pounded on without letup, even as the "After him's!" and the "We got him now's!" met his ears. As the last set of planking disappeared beneath him, Seth raised his gaze to take in what had floated on the edge of his peripheral vision for some moments. He had seen a linkage of river barges drifting lazily downstream, the majority of which had already cleared the end of the pier; but not all. His mind raced ahead of his feet, firing off questions, "Can I make it? Is the timing right? Would the last one be past when I run out of pier?"

As his pursuers closed in, the last bit of wood disappeared from beneath Seth's feet. With a shout, he launched himself into thin air, wind milling his arms and legs, hurtling forward and downward toward the river.

His feet hit the water first, soon to be followed by a bone-jarring impact to his upper body over a rough-hewn wooden gunwale. He had made it....halfway at least, but it was enough. His legs dangled in the cold Ohio, but from the waist up, he hung over a work-worn wooden deck. By sheer force of will, he had just caught the stern of the last flatboat in a flotilla of six. Hauling himself aboard, he lay prostrate for a few moments, basking in the safety of the solid deck beneath him.

It was then that he felt the distinct imprint of a large boot, right between his shoulder blades.

"Ah cain't tell iffen yer bin cut, shot, strangled or bernt...praps all tree. An' ah dōn keer war yer a'runnin from but ah kin tell yer wars yer run too. Dis heerza werkin barge, an iffen yer ain't cum to werk, ah'll tho yer smoldrin carcass in da river n' snuff ya'out!"

"I've come to work!" Seth felt the pressure ease off his chest as he pushed himself to his feet. He looked into the severe but strong face of a swarthy stevedore, one who had seen many seasons on the river. Tendrils of smoke still curled off of Seth's shirt. Purplish lines criss-crossed his neck where Springhauser had seized him in a grip meant to kill. Blood still leaked from the corner of his mouth. "My name's Seth...Seth Garner." "Folks call me Raif. Git ta da quartermaster an' fetch sum new duds. Mite'az well hab sumpin' ta werk fur!"

In short order, Seth was outfitted with a new set of buckskins. In those first few hours, as he stumbled about the flat trying to take in what life on the river was all about, the rest of the crew cast a wary eye in his direction. These men had worked together for a long time and there was an innate suspicion of newcomers. Seth knew that acceptance into their world would be a long time coming. For now, he stayed close to Raif. The riverman had spent years on the water and if anyone could teach Seth about river work, it would be him. In any case, from the moment Raif's boot had pinned him to the deck to the first bass tones that boomed out of his mouth, Seth had connected with Raif. After all, he could have thrown him over the side, but he didn't. He could have immediately heaved the boat over to shore and turned him in to the screaming mob back in Pittsburgh, that bewildered mob that was falling farther and farther behind even as the swift current of the Ohio swept them along. He didn't do that either. Seth sensed that this rough, unschooled waterman, for whatever reason, was for him. Yes...it would serve him well to stick close to Raif.

Even as all kinds of new orders were being shouted his way, Seth was having difficulty concentrating. His mind was still awhirl with all of the happenings back in Pittsburg, and with thoughts about Shamus and Penelope. After all, they had taken him in when he had no one in the world. His heart ached over what they must be going through because of him. What was he doing in that warehouse? How is it that two people died in the fire, but Seth escaped? If he was innocent in this matter, why did he run? And perhaps most painful of all, Seth knew that they must be asking over and over again: Why has not Seth returned to them; the ones who cared for him as their own son?

As he went about his initial chores on the boat, his brows were knit together in worry and stress lines began to crease across his young face. He was present in body, but absent in spirit. As Raif hollered, "Heave to port!" Seth nearly jumped out of his skin. Tying off to their first stop on the Ohio, Raif strode up to Seth and stared a long, uncomfortable stare directly into his eyes. "What's eat'in ya son?"

"Raif, I'm wanting to go into town before we shove off again." "Wat fur? Dares a heap of werk t'be dun rat cheer on shore." "There's something I've been needing to do since I left Pittsburg. I need to get this off my chest or I'll not be worth anything for work." "Well, be back cheer in two airs or ah'll float widdout cha!" Raif hollered as he jumped from the gunnels to the slippery bank.

Seth followed suit, waved a hasty farewell and fairly ran to the stage coach office. Taking quill in hand, he wrote:

Dear Shamus and Penelope:
I am . . . Prudence Nightshade.

As the flatboats glided silently along, Seth had a lonesome feeling that he would never see his parents again.

Spies Among Us

It didn't take Seth long to feel that he was back on the Pennsylvania Road with Trader Jack. Indeed the flatboats were a lot like floating Conestogas, built and manned for one purpose: trade. Yet, unlike the goods he sold on the trail, this was heavy merchandize: kegs of nails, barrels of gun powder, tubs of lard and the like; even chickens, hogs and a few goats were on board. The plan was to run the Ohio west to its confluence with the Mississippi. Their business was to skip along the riverbank, stopping in at thriving hamlets, most of which had been settled during Seth's short lifetime. All sales were made at dockside, wholesale, and most of the goods on board were swapped for one priority item: whiskey.

85

Seth Garner: Part One

The early spring rains had swollen the Ohio, and the flatboats made swift progress down the river. On the north shore lay the Ohio Territory, his home of not too long ago. This was the closest he had come to his parents, Nathaniel and Elizabeth, in nearly two years. As they glided along, Seth gazed into the dark forests that crowded down to the water line and wondered once again how they took the news of his leaving Heathshire. The dark thoughts of Krupsteiner were with him still. He knew that the old headmaster's letter had berated him in every line. Seth imagined that Rev. Garner would be at first disappointed at his only son's "failure" and that in time his disappointment would give way to anger over a bright future lost. Yet as things would have it, he also knew that in the end, the good pastor would be filled with concern for him. As for his mother, there would be nothing but worry from beginning to end and that grieved him most of all. He was still their "Seth" but he had undergone a world of change since he jumped over the split rail fence at Heathshire and made good his escape. As the flatboats glided silently along, Seth had a lonesome feeling that he would never see his parents again.

Turning away, Seth walked across the damp deck of the scow and looked wistfully across the river, his gaze being fixed on the tree line on the south shore. Here lay the "Kintuck" territory, a wild and beautiful place that beaconed new settlers to leave the security of their homes in the east and venture into the unknown. Even as their flatboats made their way toward the Mississippi, the Scotts and the Irish poured in like a flood. The clear streams of Kentucky reminded them of the Old Country their forefathers had left not that long ago. And just as their forefathers, these new immigrants carried on the age-old tradition of coaxing out the heady brew from grain as hard

Spies Among Us

and dry as gravel, distilling those spirits that in one way or another was driving them along.

As the days slipped past in easy succession, Raif clearly explained the nature of their business. "Diz her'za one way trip!" Raif bellowed. "Were'ah hedden down dis ole river till hit run slap dab into a bigger ole river!" "What's that, Raif?" "Dats da Mighty Mizzazip!" Seth inquired further, not quite getting the "one way" part. Raif continued on. "We're a'barrelin' down ta' Kaskaskia." "To Kaskas...what?!" "Dats war da Ohio and da Big Muddy cum tagetha, 'an dats war we a'floatin. An' dats war weez cain't take deez floats no furder." "Why's that, Raif?" "Well, ya' jist full of'em taday, aint'cha Seth! Well ya see, deez spindly skiffs, well dey cain't handle da Mighty Mizzazip... no siree!" "What will we do with the boats once we get there, Raif?" "I-dee-clair, Seth! Aint'cha got a curious spirit taday! Well, in Kaskaskia weez gonna break deez wrecks up! Sell 'em fur clapboard ta' bilt new towns. Dis here cuntry's a growin' son!" "But with no boats, Raif, how....?" "Weez gatta go nort ta go sout! Make our way, however we kin, ta' St. Louis! Wait till ya see St. Louis, Seth!" "And after St. Louis, Raif? What will happen then? Where will we go from there?" "Well...ah cain't answer dat.... not in da way dat hit should be answered." "Why's that, Raif...don't you know?" "Oh ah knows alright! But dats an answer fur da Mighty Mizzazip! Anyhoo, ahm plum wore out wid all ya' questions." With that, Seth held his peace for some days.

With the coming of summer, the heavy rains of late spring began to taper off and with that the current began to slack as well. At times the force of the river failed them altogether. It was then that the men labored hard at limber push poles, jamming them into the bottom and walking the full length of the rig in order to move them along. Just when Seth felt he could take no more of this frustratingly slow pace, the Ohio widened and the banks on both shores seemed to peel away. As they drifted into an expanse more like a broad lake than the confines of a river, the activity of the men picked up considerably. Someone at the lead boat yelled, "Mark twain!" and then proceeded to cast a weighted line over the side. As he let the chord slip through his fingers as if he were fishing, all eyes were fixed on him. When the line went slack, he looked up, cupped his free hand to the side of his mouth and yelled, "Two fathoms!" With that the men dropped the long push polls on the deck. Soon stout oars were creaking in well-worn locks, the crew heaving back with all their might to draw the craft forward. With all of this, Seth surmised that they had, at long last, reached Kaskaskia. Unannounced, one river had flowed seamlessly into another, so Seth couldn't tell where they had left the Ohio behind. Yet the churning brown water and the wide expanse that lay before them meant that, in the summer of 1811, they had indeed entered the Mississippi River.

The confluence of the Ohio and the Mississippi was of strategic importance to many peoples and nations. Various Indian tribes had inhabited the area from time immemorial. The first Europeans to visit the region were the Jesuit priest, Jacques Marquette, and the French-Canadian explorer, Louis Jolliet. They descended the Mississippi from the north and made a tentative claim for France in 1673. From that time on, Kaskaskia became a fur trading center for French *voyageurs* or *coureurs des bois* ("travelers of the wood"). Yet they lost it all to Great Britain in 1763 when the French were defeated in the French and Indian War. Some fifteen years later on July 4 1778, just two years after the Declaration of Independence, the Americans wrested Kaskaskia from the British. The conquering hero here was none other than George Rogers Clark. He, together with Meriwether Louis, would lead the famed "Corps of Discovery" on the greatest exploration of the American interior to date. But for now, Clark's victory over the British paved the way for American settlers to pour in to the Mississippi valley. They came by the hundreds from as far away as Virginia. The influx of settlers was hastened by the Louisiana Purchase in 1803, that grand transfer of all lands east of the Mississippi from France to the United States. All of this meant that the entire Mississippi River Valley was being settled at a staggering pace. So when Raif's flotilla silently glided past the mouth of the Ohio, Kaskaskia was fast becoming a political and commercial center for the region. In fact, just two years earlier in 1809, Kaskaskia was made the capital of Illinois Territory.

As Seth took stock of their situation, he surmised that Raif had planned their trip perfectly. Indeed, no sooner had they offloaded the last of their wares, than the sledgehammers began to fall on the empty flatboats. Just as Raif had explained earlier, the broad and long planks were themselves sold on the spot and became part of the proceeds for their Ohio River venture. So within hours of arriving in Kaskaskia, Raif and Seth were standing on solid ground with considerable money in their pockets.

For all of this, as Raif explained, Kaskaskia was just a waypoint on their journey. The real heart of business and the future of westward expansion for America lay some 150 miles to the north in St. Louis. Seth assumed that just as Lewis and Clark had done in 1803, they would launch pirogues and paddle upriver to St. Louis. Raif countered that that was in November, when the river was swollen with the rains of fall, and the Corps of Discovery barely made one mile per hour against the current. Even in the slack water of summer, they together could not due much better. Besides, the bends and turns in the river would more than double their trip. No, they would go overland to St. Louis. He had done this before, and in short order both he and Seth had signed on with a wagon train going north. The agreement was that they would provide the backbreaking labor to load and unload the wagons in exchange for food, transport and a few extra coins in their pockets. And so it was that in just over a fortnight, they had arrived at what was quickly becoming one of the most important cites of the new America; the city of St. Louis.

Standing atop the high chalk bluffs on the western shore of the river, Seth could sense the pulse of St. Louis. Scores of men struggled below to get their boats dockside. From there, folks began slogging up and down two long ramps that had been carved directly out of the cliffs yet angling down from opposite directions. These gentle slopes were needed to haul the heavy river freight up from the water level below. Stout and shaggy draft horses hitched to ruggedly built carts greatly aided in the work at hand. St. Louis was a hive of activity.

As Seth looked upstream, he could make out a dark, sinewy ribbon of wood hugging the shoreline as far as the eye could see. As he turned to Raif, his mentor lit in. "Well, dares ya' answer!" Raif shouted as he swept a majestic arc through the air with his arm covering the wide expanse of the river. "Strings a' timber, ah say miles a' logs a' cummin' down from up nort! On da mighty Mizzazip! An' dats war we're a'goin! Gonna ride dem logs all da way down to New Orleans! But we cain't go right yet. Weez got ta' lay over in St. Louie for a spell. We dun run outta water! Dares no goin' down til' hit cum a rain, an' ah mean a goodun' too!"

Indeed, as Seth surveyed the river, there were sandbars aplenty. Although wide, he could tell that for a good part of its breath, especially along the sides, the river was shallow. He could tell too that except for the channel proper, there was little or no current. It was just past mid-summer now, and the river was at low pool. The rush of the spring snowmelt was over, together with the early rains of the season. If there ever was a time when the "Mighty Mississippi" was not as mighty, it was now. Even Seth could tell that the massive log rafts that Raif had just described would not clear the many snags and sand flats sticking above the waterline. So it would be impossible for a crew, regardless of their skill and power, to pole such giant swaths of timber all the way to New Orleans. They would be in St. Louis for a while.

As Raif had promised, St. Louis was a sight to behold. Nearly 50 years prior, the Frenchman, Pierre Laclede, had traveled up from New Orleans to establish a fur trading post at the site. Being centrally located and high above the floodplain of the Mississippi, Laclede declared that this city, named in honor of King Louis IX, was destined to become one of the finest cities in America. No doubt St. Louis was well on its way to claim this title, numbering over 2,000 strong at the time of Seth's arrival.

As Raif and Seth made their way toward the town center, Seth was struck by the names of the streets: La Grande Rue, Rue d'Eglise, Rue des Granges, and so on. Sensing that Seth was about to embark on a barrage of questions again, Raif decided to cut him off at the pass, so to speak. "Now Seth, dis place has swapped hans quickern' da first biscuit offa hot griddle! At the start, hit twas French...so the street names. But den the Spanish took over fur a spell, but dat didn't make a lick of diffrence. Dey give hit back to the French a moment, but all secret like, an' if dey, da French ahm meanin', don't up and sell da whole dern thang to Tommy Jefferson! Now hits airs but da French parts hang on here 'n dare. Do ya follow?" "Yes...but..." "Now ole Lewis and Clark...you heard'uv 'em, aint'cha Seth?" "Of course! I know all about...." "Nuff said," Raif continued. "Well, dey lit outta St. Louie on the great trek west. An' ah tell ya, dey started summpin! Why days folks a'follerin dat path all da way to Oreegun! An ah

Seth Garner: Part One

mean *all da' way* to da big ocean! An' dats what you an' me will be a' doin' now an' agin while we're a'waitin on the river to swell." Seth raised a finger to speak, but Raif continued. "We're a'goin ta hep dose brave souls get dayselves underway, hep dem be outfitted for the big trek out west." "That sounds g...." "Now Seth," Raif drove on, "dis here settlement aint zackly settled." "But President Jefferson..." "Ah knowed he bought hit fair n' square, but the French had a bad habit a' divvying up da' land by word a'mout only, doncha know. Now we don't reckon dose titles fur real, so dares a whole passel a' French folk dats fightin' mad wid' us Amurikans." "So what you mean is..." "What ahm'ma meanin' is dat even though St. Louie is airs, ya gots ta' look lively. Do ya understand what ahm'a sayin' to ya?" "Indeed I do....." "Now da British..." "The British!" Seth interjected thinking that their part was over and done with. "Well...dats a whole nudder story fur a nudder time, ah 'speck. But let me say, Seth, dat you're a wonder t'talk wid...ya hep me frame m'thoughts, an ah so 'preciate dat." Seth just smiled as they walked down La Grande Rue, or as it would come to be known, "Main Street."

Raif soon renewed acquaintances from days gone by and arranged for piece meal work for him and Seth. The take was handsome enough from the flatboat enterprise, but Raif was not the kind to sit around idle. "Now mostens' deez folks aint goin' to take the big jump jist yet." "The 'big jump' Raif?" "Da long haul out ta' Oreegun country. Why jist crossin' da green mountains back east ta' git here is a heep a werk! Iffen dey lit out now, dey would probly freeze over, an dat not halfway dare! Naw....bess ta' take hit in pieces, da smart ones do leastwise. Dare aint nuthin', an ah mean nuthin,' twixt here an da big ocean. A body has ta' tote everthang, an ah do mean everthang, wid'em. A cuppla' hunnert pound a' flure n' lard, a hunnert a' rice n' beans, a half a' hunnert a' shuggah an salt pork, a quarter a' coffee, an' so forth an' so on. An' dats not a'countin' medicine, cookin' gear, long arns, pistols, powder n' shot. Den dares oxen, an' wagons, an den, above all, dey muss 'lect a gov'nah. He's da' trail boss dat knows da way to Oreegun country...leastwise *he says* he does. Dares only been a bucket full a' folks dats achly made da trip. Anyways, dares outfits dat pays a gov'nah a cuppla' hunnert dollar, jist ta' lead da way! After all a' dis, a good bunch stumble on west to St. Joe, and wait till sprang. An den....*an only den*....do dey make da big jump." "Raif, it sounds like an awful lot of preparation just...." "Hit tiz! A pareful lot a' werk! But hits a matter a' life an' death. An weez here to see dat dares more life dan death."

With this orientation to the job at hand, Seth worked hard stockpiling supplies for those with the courage to leave everything behind and make a new start. In spite of all the dangers and uncertainty involved, Seth found the thought of striking out into the unknown exciting. As he laded wagons and handled livery, he gleaned all the information that he could from the travelers. In short order, he found out that practically no one knew much about what lay ahead. They were literally the first of the first, so there was little to go on. For Seth, such intrepid souls defined the meaning of "trailblazer."

The hard work on the Ohio and the heavy lifting here in St. Louis suited him well, both in mind and in body. Seth's physical growth during the past two years had been phenomenal. His height had increased by half a foot and his chest following suit, granting Seth a barrel-like profile from the waist up. His biceps stretched out the normally loose folds of a buckskin shirt, linking smoothly to two heavily muscled arms, only to end in massive hands capable of a viselike grip. All of this was riveted to trunk-sized legs, firmly grounded on solid feet that carried Seth along with an easy but confident gait. At nearly seventeen,

Seth Garner: Part One

he was head and shoulders above most men twice his age. The food needed to see him through the day was prodigious. He always ate what was set before him and also to the right and to the left if not claimed in time by others. Those who hoped for leftovers were oft disappointed.

Seth was indeed impressed with the polyglot nature of the city. As he went about his tasks, he often overheard French and German spoken throughout the town. Not a few betrayed a heavy Scotch or Irish lilt in their voices. Although less in number, Seth even detected another strain of English, one he latter discovered to be a thick London brogue. As it turned out, Seth soon befriended one such speaker of Cockney, one Sedgwick Carlisle.

Sedgwick was a bright-eyed, garrulous young men who in short order drew Seth into a bond of confidence. He was a quick thinker and had a knack of controlling the conversation. Oft times he would pull Seth aside and launch into long musing of how things were and how things ought to be. In all of these talks, Sedgwick was surprisingly keen on all things British. He spoke glowingly of the military successes of the English and was oddly silent about the American victories during the Revolution. To the contrary, he stressed the virtues of loyalty and gratitude and so crafted their conversations that Seth, despite his better judgment, often found himself agreeing with Sedgwick. One such occasion occurred at a local tavern, one frequented by them both, a time which Sedgwick called "tea."

As Sedgwick dunked a crumbling scone into a steaming cup of black tea, he started in. "Now Master Seth, truth be told, you be of British stock, aye?" "My grandfather fought the Redcoats at the Battle of Concord Bridge, I'll have you know!" Seth retorted with a measure of indignation in his voice. "No doubt...no doubt. But he

Spies Among Us

was English....by blood I mean...he did stem from the British Isles....did he not?" "Well...yes...but..." "And your dear mother, Elizabeth as I recall, ..." "Scottish," Seth deadpanned. "Ah...a fair child of the Commonwealth. I dare say that some of your kin fought for the *other* side, as is commonly expressed in these parts." "It's been told." "Told by your parents, I wager. You know... the Americans...." "You mean *we* Americans!" Seth interjected. "A trifle...a mere trifle. The King had an agreement with the Americans, and they broke their word. Now Seth....I know that *you* are a man of your word....am I right?" "I was taught that the colonists were taxed but were not allotted any members in Parliament, as I recall." "As *you* recall. Temporary! A temporary necessity to raise capital. You're a smart man, Seth! You know what it takes to make a go of business, don't you?" "What are you saying, Sedgwick?" "What I am saying, dear friend, is that things could easily tip the other way around here and the next time we enjoy tea together, we could be paying with this." Sedgwick coolly pushed a British pound across the table to Seth. Seth picked up the coin, examined it for a moment and then handed it back. Leaning closer to Seth and lowering his voice to a whisper, Sedgwick continued. "I think it's time that I share a secret with you, my friend. We have a society, Seth, one that is destined for great things." "What are you saying, Sedgwick?" "What I'm saying is that I like you, and I want you to be a part of grand future, one that will outpace this back woodsy misadventure in no time. Moreover, we could use a man of your intelligence and promise. Allow me to speak plainly. I would be honored if you would join in with us." With that Sedgwick pulled out a penknife from his sleeve and scratched a flattened **X** into the top of the table. "What's that?" "The Saint Andrews cross, Seth, our symbol," whispered Sedgwick as he rose to

Seth Garner: Part One

leave. "Because this affair is not over. There are big plans afoot. Think about it."

As Seth walked out of the tavern he felt strangely unhinged. No one had ever talked to him like that, much less a friend. For days, he reflected upon every word that Sedgwick had shared that afternoon. On the face of it, everything that Sedgwick said was a fact. At the same time, it didn't ring completely true. So over and over, one burning question ran through Seth's mind: "Can someone state the facts yet not be true?" Try as he may, he could not tease out a definitive answer here. He talked little for the next few days. He avoided Sedgwick altogether. Even as he and Raif packed goods up the ramps from the river below, for all of the labor and sweat, Seth's worry shown through. None of this escaped Raif's gaze.

"Well...are ya' gonna tell me what's a pullin' ya' down?" "Something pulling me down, Raif?" responded Seth, trying all the world to sound light and cheerful. Raif just lowered his chin and looked up steeply from under bushy eyebrows, the perfect picture of doubt. Seth stared back for a moment to see if his ruse would carry through. Raif didn't blink. At last, Seth let out a long sigh and then came clean. "Remember some time ago, when you were telling me about what all St. Louis has gone through?" Raif slowly nodded. "And you mentioned the British?" Raif again nodded knowingly. "And you said that the British, well, they were another story for another time." Raif straightened up and folded his arms expressing increased interest. "Well ...I think the time has come and I've heard the story...or at least part of the story." Speaking for the first time, Raif opened his eyes wide and said, "Is dat so?" "Well you see...Sedgwick..." "He's a nice lad, Seth." "Well...yes...but, he's shared a secret with me, and it's weighed heavy on my mind ever since." "Dares no secret 'tween friends. An' we be friends, aint we Seth?"

"Indeed...true friends, Raif. Well, Seth says that with regard to the British that 'this affair'...I take 'this affair' to mean our independence, well...it's not over. What do you say to that, Raif?" "Well hit aint!" quipped Raif. "What?! You don't mean..." "Now Seth, hits a matter a' seein'. We sees hit one way an' da Redcoats, well....dey sees hit a'nudder way. Da way dey sees hit is dat us Amurikans, well we be hemmed up right nicely east of the mountains. Now iffen dey could take, let's say, New Orleans, an' ah heered dey tink dey can, an den dey come up here to St. Louie, well dis thang could tip da' udder way. An' iffen dey kin muster up nort, say in Canaday an' cum sout, den we be mashed tween da Mizzazip an da Atlantic." "That's exactly what Sedgwick said!" Seth exclaimed. "An, he be right! Why last summer, they burnt down da capital in Washington, doncha know! An' ah heerd dat weez hard pressed for money, dat is, as a people. So like ah said, dis thang could go da utter way!" Seth raked his hands down both sides of his face, hardly believing what he was hearing. Taking in a deep draft of air, Seth went on. "And Sedgwick said that they have a secret society." "Do dey now?" Raif mused. "And he invited me to their secret meetings and all. I don't know what I should do." "Ah tink dat ya' should go." "What?!" Seth shot back once again. "Ah been raised dat when a body is invited, all tings bein' da same, dey should go...dats all ahm a'sayin'. Now, come on...let's git ta' work."

Days went by and Seth never brought up the subject again. Neither did Raif. The same did not hold true for Sedgwick. As expected, Sedgwick set up another "tea" with Seth. Once the meeting got underway, it didn't take him long to get to the subject at hand. "Listen, Seth. Our numbers are growing. Now's the time to join in. My word is my bond. *The rewards will be enormous.* Tonight. Midnight. Red Fox Inn. Look for the St. Andrews Cross." With that, the meeting was over. Sedgwick pushed a note Seth's way, tipped his hat and was gone.

Seth sat pensively at the table, took a last draft of tea, looked about and then opened the note. "For King and Crown. **X**." For the rest of the afternoon, Seth's mind was racing. Perhaps "this affair" was not as settled as he had thought. Raif was a practical man. If any one had a firm grasp of things, that is, the unvarnished facts at hand, then it was Raif. "Things could tip the other way," Seth muttered as he hurried through the last task of the day.

Seth turned into his bunk without saying a word to anyone, not even to Raif. He lay awake for hours. Sleep fled from his eyes. Again Raif's counsel ran over and over in his head, "If you're invited, then you should go." When the chimes of the town clock struck eleven, Seth sat bolt upright in bed. Hesitating for a moment, he swung his legs to the floor and made his way to the Red Fox Inn.

Stepping into the tavern, he immediately sensed that something was out of sorts...strange. There was nothing of the usual lighthearted banter so typical of the place. The atmosphere was tense, the faces were grave and every eye was on him. There was no barkeep. Only a single lantern hung from a rafter above, the wick trimmed so low that its pale light did little to illumine the room. The orange glowing bowls of pipes smoked in dark corners seemed to float in midair. No one spoke to him as he walked slowly towards the rear of the room. He could then barely make out the pattern of two brooms crossed at the center, next to a darkened doorway. "The St. Andrews Cross," he said to himself as he reached forth his hand to turn the knob. Yet the door opened of its own accord, but only partway. Seth could make out the silhouette of someone peering steadily through the crack. There was not a sound. Then the door swung full open and there stood Sedgwick Carlisle. "Welcome, my friend. Come in." The room was packed.

Spies Among Us

Though smoke-filled and dim, Seth could barely recognize some of the faces present, having seen them in the workaday world of St. Louis. Yet he knew none of them by name, save one, and that was Sedgwick.

Once in, a wave of low murmurs spread throughout the room. "He's alright," assured Sedgwick. "I can vouch for him personally." At Sedgwick's word, Seth could literally feel the tension drain from the room. Soon those present embarked upon deep-toned conversations, the whole of which escaped Seth, except for a few troubling phrases here and there: "the time is coming,"... "the tide will turn." As Seth strained to take more in, the sharp rap of a gavel sent a jolt through his system as he gripped the edge of his chair even harder than before. "Hear! Hear!" shouted the moderator as the idle chatter faded away. "Now you all know why you are here tonight, and if you don't know, then it's not to worry." At that point he drew out a musket, cocked the hammer and laid it upon the podium. A few ominous snickers rippled trough the room. "All rise for the oath!" As if one body, all present stood in unison, placed one hand over their hearts and said: "We do solemnly swear, by all things sacred, to pledge our lives, our fortunes and all that we might hold dear, to defend King and Crown to the last ounce of our strength, to the last drop of our blood, to the very last breath that we might take in this mortal world. So help us God!" "All say 'aye'," boomed the moderator. A rousing "Aye!" fairly shook the rafters as a cold chill ran down Seth's spine. "All be seated," intoned the moderator as he melted into the shadows. Seth was shocked as Sedgwick rose and strode toward the platform. He surely knew that his friend was of a radically different mind, but that he was the leader?! Every muscle in his body stiffened as he could hardly believe what his ears were hearing.

"Fellow members of the Commonwealth, it is good to be on the right side of Destiny and *we are* on the right side!" "Hear! Hear!" shouted one as a smattering of "ayes" joined in. Sedgwick continued. "There is no need to rehearse the number of setbacks we have experienced at the hand of the rebels..." That word *rebels* stuck in Seth's heart like a dagger. How could Sedgwick??? "No...no need at all! For we know that all setbacks, no matter how many in number or how severe in effect, do not equal defeat!" A rousing affirmation erupted in the room as the crowd spontaneously commenced to chant: "God save the King! God save the King!" Sedgwick lifted both hands toward the crowd, palms down and gently tamped down the noise. "Dear Friends, grand plans are in the making, plans forged by greater minds than I, greater in scope I say, but totally of the same spirit! And I can say with confidence that we here, in this very room, occupy a strategic place in these plans!" Someone started a low drumbeat on a tabletop. Others joined in, increasing in tempo and volume until the noise reached a resounding crescendo. Once again Sedgwick quieted the crowd. "As my oath is my bond, I am now at liberty to share with you, and this is in the strictest confidence, that our meeting this night is one among many throughout the land." At this, gasps of surprise were heard throughout the room. "Yes...yes...for quite some time now, secret consultations have been underway, kept secret by necessity, but now made privilege to Loyalists like yourselves, from the mouth of the Mississippi in the south all the way to the great Hudson Bay in the north. The time draws nigh. The full details will be shared a fortnight hence, Greystone's barn at the foot of Rue des Granges, midnight, under the St. Andrews Cross." With that, Sedgwick strode majestically from the podium to the middle of the room. Those present began to chant softly, "To God and King! "To God and King!". They enveloped

Sedgwick in concentric circles until all fell silent. Sedgwick then looked about those gathered with a face as hard as flint. In hushed tones he drew the circle in closer. "Now gentlemen all! I do not have to remind you of the grave import of all that was said in this room tonight. I do not exaggerate! The fate of nations hangs in the balance! At this moment in history, the power of the British empire does not depend upon cannon or riflemen, but upon secrecy!" With a flourish Sedgwick hefted a document high above his head. Again a muttering undertone spread throughout the room. In the dim light, Seth could barely make out a royal seal of some kind affixed to a scroll, complete with ornate blue ribbons trailing beneath. "It's time for us to take the most solemn oath of all. The blood oath!" With that he motioned for Seth to come forward. As he took faltering steps toward the leader, the crowd melted away before him. Drawing near, Sedgwick bid Seth take the document, unfurl it and hold it out before him so that it could read. Commanding the attention of all, Sedgwick somberly sounded out: "Before the presence of all and in the name of Almighty God, I being of freewill and sound mind, and with a clear conscience, am hereby bound by utmost secrecy for the furtherance of England, the promotion of the Commonwealth, the defeat of her enemies and full support of her allies. To this I commit my pledge and upon pain of death, I herewith signify *in my own blood*!" At once Sedgwick pulled out a knife from his sleeve and slowly drew it across his thumb. As the blood trickled down, he thrust his thumb high in the air, turning about so that all could see. As he came back around to face Seth, he jammed his thumb into the parchment. Still holding the knife, and with a wild look in his eyes, he glowered at those standing about. The soft light of the lamp made for a most frightful sight as each man, one after another stepped forward, laid hold of the knife, sliced open

Seth Garner: Part One

his thumb, and pressed it firmly into the document still held forth in Seth's trembling hands. At last, Sedgwick motioned for Seth to hand the pledge to the one next to him. Before Seth could do anything, Sedgwick snatched up the knife, laid hold of Seth's right hand, and struck smartly across his thumb. As Seth winched under the pain, Sedgwick pressed his thumb at the very bottom of the bloodstained paper, glaring full-faced into Seth's eyes with the most hideous, hate-filled stare. As Sedgwick rolled up the scroll, he shouted, "Until a fortnight!" as the men filtered away into the darkness.

As dawn broke, Seth felt as if he had been beaten all over. As he wrapped his thumb in a makeshift bandage, his head ached, he felt sick to his stomach and his thoughts sped through his brain at a dizzying pace. As he prepared to meet with Raif, he mused that a hard day's work would serve him well. He was tired of thinking. Yet within moments of meeting with his old friend, Raif asked, "Cut ya' thumb?" For a moment Seth thought of making up some story about an accident, but he had never been untrue to Raif and he was not about to start now. "I kept the invite." Raif's puzzled look begged an explanation. "I took the blood oath...at least I think I did." When Raif completely left off the work at hand and wrinkled both eyebrows into a quizzical knot, Seth unloaded all that had been on his mind. "I went to the meeting with Sedgwick and..." "Oh did ya' now? Ya' kin tell me about hit whilst we load up dis here wagon." "No, Raif. I took the blood oath, like I said." "Naw, what ya' tolt me is dat ya' *tink* ya' took da' blood oaf." "Well, when the time came, Sedgwick snatched up my hand, sliced across my thumb and mashed it down on the pledge paper with the rest of them." "So den ya' didn't, cuz Sedgwick took hit fur ya' 'an dat don't count." Seth cocked his head to one side in a pondering moment then commenced to tell Raif everything that

Spies Among Us

transpired at that fateful meeting. Raif let out a long, low whistle. "Like ah said, Seth, dis thang aint all settled jist yet. A fortnight, huh? Dat would be sumairs 'round two weeks from now. A cross on a barn?" "Well not to worry, Raif. I don't plan on going!." "Got ta' go now. Dey knows ya' face an' ya' knows dairs. Fact is...dey knows dat ya' knows what dey knows an ya know it." By that point Seth wasn't exactly sure what he knew. "What ahm a' sayin' is, in fur a penny, in fur a pound. Iffen ya' don't show fur dat meetin' ah'd say ya'd be deed befo' da' day's done." Seth's face blanched as his mouth went dry. "Not a bad thang, dough. Bess ta' keep all bases covered, like ah said, dis thang *could* tip da' utter way. But furgit hit, Seth. Like da' Good Book say, we don't know what a' cummin tamorrah, leeswise in fourteen day. Now, tho dat sack a' fluer in da' wagon."

In the end, Seth was right about one thing. The hard work preoccupied his mind and helped him forget his problems for a time. In any case, he kept his distance from Sedgwick, and apart from a knowing glance now and again, Sedgwick kept his distance from Seth. But all the work in the world could not forestall the dreaded date. The fortnight was now upon them. The grand meeting was at hand.

Seth had grown to trust the counsel of his rough-hewn friend, and so as that day drew to a close, he was especially attentive to what Raif had to say. "Now Seth, ah'd lay low at da meetin. No need ta' say a thang." Seth ratcheted his head in agreement. "Ah speck in a meetin' like dis, bess ta' go unarmed. Yu'll be searched, an' iffen dey find a weapon, dell plug ya' right dare." Again, Seth nodded. "Not talkin' don't mean ya' not listenin'. Ah'd tuck away everthang dey say. Ya' neva know when hit'll cum in handy. Now, ya' got any questions fur me?" This time Seth shook his head in the negative and prepared to take a path not of his choosing. He felt trapped by the whole situation. If he

Seth Garner: Part One

went, he was nothing less than a traitor in his own eyes. On the other hand, from all what Raif had said, he was afraid not to go. And this was the most puzzling part of all. On the face of it, Raif was right on all the facts. But as was the case with Sedgwick, something didn't quite square. "Are ya' skeerd?" Raif's question snatched Seth back to the problems at hand. "Maybe...a bit." "Well ya' oughta be. Deez folks are a danger! Now bess be on ya' way." As Seth turned to go, Raif untied the red bandana from about his neck and interjected, "Seth...do yassef a favor. Hits ma' lucky kerchief. Hit'll do ya' some good." Turning back again, he took the cloth from Raif, smiled a weak smile and continued on his way. Seth paced the floor as he waited pensively for the witching hour of twelve midnight. At half past eleven, he tied Raif's kerchief about his neck and stepped out into an ink-black night. The place was not hard to find. There was only one barn out at the Grand Prairie Common Field, land that had been allotted for the general welfare of St. Louis. So when he came upon the crossed staves in the middle of the road, he was double-sure that he was in the right place. As he approached the barn, there was absolutely no visible light whatsoever coming from the structure. All windows had been blanketed over. As he walked up to the door, Raif's take on the situation proved true again. Two men stepped forward and searched Seth for weapons. Satisfied, they walked Seth around to the back of the barn and whisked him through a small door at the rear. Once inside, Seth could hardly believe his eyes. A half a dozen men, clad in scarlet red British uniforms stood at attention at the front of the room, muskets at the ready, bayonets fixed. The place was packed. Every available space was taken. The crowd even extended deep under the overhead loft at the back of the barn. Seth had no choice but to sit on the front row, even as the sergeant at arms took note of each person present.

Spies Among Us

In short order, Sedgwick strode to the front and mounted a makeshift podium. "Welcome one and all to this auspicious occasion. We are all privileged to be part of history-making events that will, in due season, rewrite the map of North America. And now, it is time for me to step aside and make room for new leadership, leadership destined to direct us to our finest hour." These last words were totally unexpected, inciting a rolling murmur that worked its way through the crowd. What happened next caused Seth's jaw to drop clean open. From out of the shadows stepped a British officer, in full uniform, complete with a shimmering saber strapped to his side. You could have heard a pin drop as the officer majestically strode to the platform. "Gentlemen! I am Colonel Lionel Fitzpatrick of the Blackwatch of his majesty's Royal Guard. I have been given charge of all British operations on the central Mississippi. All praise to Mr. Carlisle for the fine work he has done here in St. Louis. Let me assure you that his service has come to the attention of the Crown and he will be rewarded handsomely. Now to the matter at hand! As you have already been made aware, what's happened here is one part of a coordinated effort that spans the continent. Even as I speak, plans are well underway to wrest New Orleans from the Americans in the south. Once this objective is secured, England will have control of the mouth of the Mississippi. We will then move northward to St. Louis. Compatriots in Canada will march south to Detroit and then move on to Chicago. The noose is tightening on the necks of the rebels and the trapdoor will soon fall! In what will prove to be England's finest hour, we will then march eastward, driving this craven rabble to the sea. Once there, our warships will mow them down like a sharp scythe cuts spring grass."

At that moment a resounding crash broke forth from the loft above as a heavy-framed door was kicked clean through. "Drop ya' arns!" Seth snapped his head upward as Raif's booming voice filled the air. In an instant, the room descended into chaos. Chairs tipped over and men tumbled forward, grappling past one another in an attempt to clear the loft overhead. The security intended to keep folk out now became a trap that kept folk in. And then the unthinkable happened. A British rifleman shouldered his weapon and touched off a shot that zipped just inches past Raif's forehead. Even before the report could clear the air, the colonel pulled forth his musket and dead-centered Raif's chest. Without thinking, Seth sprang to his feet. Coming down hard with his right hand, the colonel's pistol discharged harmlessly into the floor even as Seth's left fist followed around and delivered a crushing blow to the officer's jaw. Complete pandemonium broke out as Raif's musket sent a white-hot ball of lead through the throat of the first shooter. The remaining British soldiers then prepared to fire, dropping to one knee in military discipline, all rifles trained upon Seth's brave friend above. Seth lunged low to the floor to clear the line of fire planning to disrupt a few of the soldiers before they could shoot. Just then a dozen riflemen stepped forward on the loft, flanking Raif on both sides. As the big riverman pulled two muskets from his belt, he shouted, "Mind the red kerchief!" Simultaneous, ear-splitting blasts rang out from above and below as the lead flew and gun smoke filled the air. The British soldiers were shot to shreds as the Loyalists made for ever available exit, diving headlong through blanket-clad windows, completely heedless of how they might land on the outside. As the shooting continued, bodies crumpled to the floor even as terrifying shrieks and cries of pain pierced the air. Turning about, Seth was horrified to see a body tip forward and tumble from the loft, crashing pitifully to the floor, the man clearly dead before he hit the ground. Sheer panic seized Seth heart as he watched Raif level both muskets at his head and drop both hammers at once. In that instant, time ceased to exist for Seth. He was sure that the dual puffs of smoke from his old friend's weapons would be the last things he would see in this world. Slapping his hands over

his ears, Seth instinctively bowed low as the blasts reverberated throughout the cavernous expanse of the barn. Surprised to still be in the land of the living, Seth wheeled about only to see the colonel on his feet again, the tip of his sword now only inches from his face. As two gaping wounds leaked out the colonel's life's blood, a broad grin spread across Raif's face. It was then that Seth caught movement out of the corner of his eye as Sedgwick tried to make good his escape. Three strong strides and a leap later, Seth had Sedgwick knocked to the floor. Twisting Sedgwick's left arm behind his back, Seth jammed it upward nearly to the back of his neck. Somehow Sedgwick clambered to his feet only to have Seth step forward, plant his boot in front of Sedgwick's left shin and

Seth Garner: Part One

give him a mighty shove forward. As Sedgwick's face plowed into the filthy barn floor, he growled, "Betrayed by a colonist....again!"

With Sedgwick secured, Seth yelled a warning to Raif, "The escaped Loyalists! Don't go out there! We're trapped!" Raif paid no heed as he pointed out orders to his men and briskly stepped outside. Seth stole away to a doorpost and peeped around the edge, fearing the worst. Instead, he discovered that Raif had previously established a perimeter defense around the barn. All of the Loyalists were already subdued and laying on the ground like cordwood.

By the time Seth caught up with Raif, he had pieced together the main parts of the plan. "Why didn't you tell me that the Sedgwick goings on was rotten from the start?!" "Well, Seth...ya' were ma' way in. Iffen ah leveled wit ya', den ya' mighta' tipped ya' hand to da Redcoats. An' where'd we be den? Ah'll tell ya' where we'd be! We'd all be a'talkin' English b'now!" "Raif, we are talking English." "Ahm a'meanin' *London* English, an' ya' knowd full well what ahm a'meaning!" Raif's face flushed red, the perfect picture of frustration and exasperation altogether. Seth laughed heartily as his friend calmed a bit and continued on. "An' so ah kept ya' secret secret so dat way, we' all know. Ya' see?" "I understand." "An' my red kerchief, did hit not bring ya' luck? Luck so dat ya' not shot full a' holes! "I see that too, now.' "Ya' don't see da' half, Seth ma' boy! Da' fortnight part ya' tolt me gave me 'nuff time ta' spread da' word. Dare been raiden' parties, jist like we dun here, aginst da' Redcoat meetins' up an' down da Mizzazip! Ah'd say ya' plum messed up da British plans from New Orleens ta' Canaday! Ah'd say too dat you a' right proud patriot, an' dat widdout eben tryin!" "No Raif...it is clear enough that you are the only hero around here." "Could be...could be. But Seth, ya got a' mean left hook!" "But I didn't mean...that was the first time.." Again flustered, Raif interjected, "Sometime ya' jist gotta mean to, son! An' jist in time, for ma' part! Or ah'll a' had a nudder hole in ma' heed!" A heavy slap on the back spoke clear enough...the Redcoat affair was over. It was time to move on.

Throughout the fading weeks of summer, Seth and Raif busied themselves with outfitting the last few families in preparation for their journeys out west. It was heavy but happy work for Seth, for his mind raced ahead of the wagons, picturing the wild environs that they would slowly but surely pass through. He had no idea that he was about to begin an even wilder journey of his own. For somewhere down the rampart, a rifle accidentally discharged. What happened next would cast the die for a good portion of the rest of his life.

At the shot, a team of horses bolted, breaking away from their handlers, lunging ahead straight up the rampart road. As long as the beasts strained against the steep incline, their speed was kept in check. But as soon as they topped the rise, the horses gave full vent to their fear; the clattering of truck falling from the wagon drove them wilder still. Seth stood riveted to the ground, frozen in place by too much happening too fast for a mind accustomed to thinking things through one step at a time. Raif, a man of impulse and action hollered, "Gang way! Gang way!" sounding out a warning to those in harm's way. As folk peeled away from the melee, the wagon roared past Seth and brought him back to his senses. Meaning well, he tore after the wagon waving his arms and yelling, "Whoa!" at the top of his lungs. His efforts only tended to speed the horses on further still. In an instant though, he was brought up short by a sight that struck sheer terror to the core. Far up ahead, instead of fleeing as all others did, a young girl, casting aside all natural instinct for self-preservation, stepped directly into the path of certain death. As the horses bore down on her, she held her hands out, palms up, as if offering the mad beasts something good to eat. Her face was perfectly calm and there was not a trace of fear in her stark blue eyes. When it looked like she would be surely crushed to death, the team began to sink back on their haunches, stiffening their front legs as their hooves cut deep furrows in the mud. At the last instant, they reared up wildly into the air, she snatching one of the reins as they came back down to earth. As Seth dashed up from the rear, the beasts struggled and jerked their massive heads, their wide eyes nearly all white for fear, nostrils dilated and quivering, laboring hard to draw in air to overburdened lungs. Through it all, the girl held firm to what she had, nearly being lifted off the ground as the huge draft horses began to backpedal in a desperate bid to be shed of the unseen torment that had so suddenly fallen upon them. When it seemed that she could take no more and all threatened to break loose once again, Seth drew up just in time to grab hold of the remaining harness. Lending full weight to well-muscled arms, he dragged their heads low to the ground, finally bringing the horses under control. Above the din of whinnies and snorts, Seth could hear her quiet but strong voice speaking gently to the team as their terror ebbed away. As calm followed mayhem, he stood there speechless, staring wide-eyed at a beauty matched only by courage as the girl softly stroked one muzzle then the next. When the owners of the rig drew nigh, she smiled at Seth and simply said, "Thank you, mister." He still struggling for words, she leaned to one side and shouted, "Johnny! Over here!" A black-headed boy of about fourteen, perhaps a year her senior, trotted up, took one cool look at Seth and said, "Let's go, Abigail!"

    It all had happened so fast that Seth just stood there waving lamely as the couple ran back to their families. Only a heavy hand on his shoulder snapped him out of the trance he'd fallen into. Raif stood there with one eyebrow raised as Seth asked dreamily, "Who is she?" "Ah don't reckon ah know in particular, but she's wit da' Stewart clan. Don't waste ya time, Seth. She's not worth it." "I beg to differ, Raif. I'd say she's worth about everything." "Well maybe in five year or so. But what ahm a'meanin' is dat dey taint gona last dat long. Why mostens deez folk don't know what dey gittin' into. In short order, dell be froze, or a'hungered, or scalpt or sumpin' mortal. An dats what ah means when ah say she taint worth it. Tings bein' as dey are, dey not gonna make hit." With unusual defiance, that is, as far as things related to Raif, Seth held his ground. "I'll wager that if anyone is going to make it….she will."

While Seth fixed his eyes on the two youngsters, Johnny left go of her hand as loving parents rushed forward and embraced an extraordinary daughter, one who, just moments before, they nearly lost forever. Being totally absorbed by the scene, Seth jerked as a deafening clap of thunder jolted him back into the present once again. Pulling up his collar, he peered about for a moment, spotted Raif, and slogged on in his direction. It had started to rain.

Abigail

Seth Garner: Part One

Indeed their floating village was a part of the network of trade that plied the silt-laden waters of the Mississippi.

The Big Float South

The recent rains in St. Louis were just the leading edge of larger storms further north producing deluges that had raged on for weeks. This massive influx of new water signaled the start of the big float south. As the river continued to rise, the islands grew smaller and the snags and sandbars had all but disappeared. The big river was coming into its own once again. And just as Raif had promised, strings of timber soon arrived from upstream, each requiring a healthy number of skilled men to take them further along.

A much larger crew was needed to shepherd so much lumber down the Mississippi; larger, that is, than the men that piloted the swift flatboats down the Ohio. So when Seth leaped aboard for the next phase of his life, he recognized some of the men, but not all. Once again he was faced with becoming part of a loose-knit society of men. The group was temporarily held together by the job at

113

Seth Garner: Part One

hand, but its membership was subject to change any time they put into shore. At these times, some would find a better opportunity, settle up with the paymaster, and never be seen again. On the other hand, a new face would appear now and again, some homeless soul that would just as soon drift down a muddy river as to shuffle along a dusty road. As for Seth, he was with Raif for the long haul, wherever that might lead.

After a couple of days of miscues, cursings and dropping gear over the side, Seth found his place among the crew. There was no official chain of command on board. One's craft was one's calling, and if it was real, then it was recognized and respected. One man could handle ropes, another knew the river currents and sand bars, and another could render a meal for a dozen that otherwise couldn't feed a few. In time their small floating world developed an economy of its own. No time nor parts were wasted. A squirrel shot off the forward bow, would be field dressed and skinned amidships, then its liver used for catfish bait by the time it reached the stern.

It didn't take long for the men to know that Seth's craft was "book larnin'." After sunset, a campfire was build right atop the raft logs. The green logs and the constant moisture seeping up from the river forestalled any hazard. A lantern was lit at the prow, pipes were kindled, and yarns were spun for hours. Alas someone would shout, "Young Seth, read us sumpin'!" He would then take out a copy of Dickens, or a work on ancient history, and at times even the Bible, and read to the men as they drifted along. The last selection was known by most, even if practiced by few. Regardless of what he chose, nothing was despised. Keen interest all round. "Now... tell again Seth, who cum first, da' Romins, da' Partians, or was it the Gypshins?" Seth would always patiently explain again, knowing that the details were not important. What was important was that

114

The Big Float South

these roughs had come to understand, in a general sense anyway, their place in history. Gradually the men gained an orientation to the grand pageant of human affairs. They came to appreciate their connection with the wider river of time. One of their favorite recitations came from Seth's knowledge of the Lewis and Clark expedition. The famed "Corps of Discovery," commissioned by none other than President Thomas Jefferson some eight years earlier, had kept a meticulous logbook, and the men never tired of its story. As Seth recounted their description of the Rocky Mountains, and the arduous journey to the Pacific, one shouted out, "And hit ain't a'stoppin there! Noooo sireee, hit won't! Weez part of hit now! Weez part a' historee too!" Hearty "Yea's" sounded out around the fire. Even as they were moving down river, they sensed that America was on the move, and that they were marching along with it. Often at reading times there was more smoke from tobacco than from the fire. "Here now, take a draft or two!" called a neighbor as he thrust a fine porcelain-stemmed pipe before Seth's nose. For a moment he was inclined to simply pass it on. The religious sensitivities of his home life were deeply engrained on his conscience. But then he thought better of it. The offer was not to entrap or corrupt, but was a sincere offer of goodwill and fellowship. So Seth sucked down a bit of the stuff, coughed out a couple of puffs of smoke, and then passed the pipe back to its owner.

As the group broke up and turned in for the night, Raif pulled Seth aside and fairly stared a hole through him. "What is it, Raif? Is there trouble?" The powerful riverman looked one way and then the other. Satisfied that no one was watching, he whispered, "Will ya' tetch me ma' ciphers, boy?" "Say, what Raif?" "Ah cain't read, needer. Not a' lick!" Seth was humbled by the request and a bit taken a back. "Indeed I will teach you to add and subtract and to read as well, but under one condition. You must teach me to load and shoot a long iron." "Ya' mean ya' don't know?!" he fairly shouted back with eyebrows knit in disbelief. As Seth looked at his elder in silence, both men realized the same truth. All knowledge is powerful, even if of a different kind.

The lessons in marksmanship and reading were to be done in private for both Seth and Raif felt a bit self-conscious at not knowing the basics of life, that is, the basics as pertaining to their respective spheres in life. The chance to learn came soon enough when the raft put in to take on supplies. As they slipped away from the crew, Seth lost no time in teaching Raif the building blocks of all knowledge: the "A, B, C's." "Now repeat after me. 'A' as in 'Apple'." "At's rat, a 'Apple'." "No, Raif! You need to say the whole thing. Now, try again. *'A' is for 'Apple'*." "Okay, den. 'A'...dat goes fur 'Apple'." "Now then. 'B' as in 'Ball'." "Hang far, Seth! Gist how long is dis gonna' take?" "Forever, if you don't get with it! There are twenty-six letters in the alphabet, but once you learn them, all the words in the world are at you're command. Now... 'C' is for 'Cat'." "Don't like 'em mich, but anyways, 'C' is for 'Cat'." "Good... 'D' is for 'Dog'." "Ah heerd ya', ...'D'." Seth snatched off his hat and threw it on the ground. "You've got to say *'the Dog'*, Raif. I'm teaching words here too!" "All rat! 'Da' Dawg'! Hey if dis spot ain't purfic fur shootin'." It was Raif's turn to teach.

Raif held forth the Kentucky Long Rifle at arms' length and stared into Seth's face for a long while. Finally, Raif commenced his lesson. "Na' Seth...dis cheers a raffle. Hits a killin' thang! Hit'll kill ya' or hit'll kill sumpin' else. Ahm'a here ta' teech ya' ta' kill sumpin' else!" "I understand, Raif." "Ya' got's to be keerful, Seth, an' ah don't mine a'sayin' dat twiced. Na' hear, to." Raif held up a round ball as if it were a diamond shining in the sun. When Seth took notice of the shot, Raif nodded in acknowledgement and

The Big Float South

then hefted the powder horn. "Na' Seth, dis cheer's da' thang! Ya' gots ta' do it dissa ways an' no utter. Do ya' understand me?" "Yes, Raif...go on." "Now, say after me...'Powder...Patch...Ball...Primer'."
"Powder...Patch...Ball...Primer'."
"Ya' dun good. Na' watch keerful like." Raif's eyes bulged with intensity fairly forcing Seth to lock on to his every move. "Powder!" Raif tapped the nipple of the horn just enough for the gray-black grains to pour down the barrel. "Patch!" The frontiersman quickly moistened a small square patch of cloth with spit and placed it over the barrel. "Ball!" his eyes opening even wider than before. Then Raif rocked back a bit for emphasis and with a flourish pulled out the ram rod like a sword. Turning it end for end, he placed the butt of the rod over the ball and patch and rammed it home. "Primer!" he yelled. Cocking the gun sideways a bit and arching one eyebrow until Seth drew closer for a look, Raif spilled out a bit of powder into the pan. Standing straight and tall again, Raif continued. "Ya' see dat piney cone a' way up yonder!" No sooner had Seth turned to gaze in that direction than an ear-splitting roar belched forth from the rifle and the pine cone was shattered to pieces. "Now dat piney cone's deed, an' weez okay. Ya' know why?" His head still ringing from the blast, Seth dully said, "Why?" "Cuz we wuz keerful ta' faller da' sequence, dat's why! Hit's a thang dat kin onlys be done onced and be done rat!" "Why's that, Raif?" "Cuz iffen ya' fergit, an' load hit twiced, hit'll splode an' kill ya', or render ya' rat homely fur da' duration! Like ah said ba'for, hits'a killin' thang, one way or da' utter. Na' hits your turn." Seth grabbed the powder horn and raised it toward the barrel. "Whoa, boy! What's da' sequence?" "Raif, I know the loading order, there's no need..." "Na' Seth, ya' made me say 'Da' Dawg' so ya' need ta' say da' sequence!" Groaning in exasperation, Seth recited, "Powder . . . Patch . . . Ball . . .

117

Seth Garner: Part One

Primer" as he went through the process of loading the rifle. "Na' shoulder da' raffle and aim at dat knot on da' big pine. Mash da' set trigga, da' one behinds the farin' trigga, an' when ya' ready, pull the business trigga. Now dats prit near 40 yard, so..." Again the gun exploded with a riotous blast sending a cloud of white smoke in the direction of the tree. When it cleared, Raif lit in again. "Now ya' missed da' whole dern tree. None ta' worry...hit'll cum in time." Ignoring Raif, Seth marched resolutely to the tree and placed his finger over the bullet hole. He had aimed at a much smaller knot than the one Raif intended and he hit it dead center. As Raif drew up, his jaw dropped in amazement. "Na' do dat agin an' ah'll fix ya' supper!" he said as he guided Seth back to their starting point. "Powder...Ball....Patch...Primer" Seth recited dutifully as he loaded the firearm a second time. After the shot, Raif joined in, "Now ya' pult off cuz ya's skeered of the gun kick, which is only natral at da' start. Hits happened ta' me...." "Are you sure, Raif? I held steady. I can't see how I could have..." "We'll let's take a look see, but don't lose hart iffen ya' plum missed it all." As they examined the tree it was plain to see that the first bullet hole had doubled in size. In fact Seth's second shot overlapped the first by just a bit. "Well... ah lived ta' see hit!" shouted Raif. "Dat ends da' shootin' lesson. Ah cain't teach ya' nuttin'. You're a' natral. You wuz born ta' shoot. Ah can tell ya' bout huntin' an' trackin' an' specially bout da' 'hostiles', but dats all ah can do! Ya' shoot bettern ah'll ever shoot! Der ain't one in a tausand souls dat can do dat. Hitza gift dat can't be made no bettern den hit's rat now! You can shoot, shore'nuff but ah still cain't read a lick!"

And so it was, as they walked back to the raft Seth sounded out, "'E' is for 'Elephant'," and "'F' is for 'Frog'," and so on. Raif would, without warning, blurt out, "What's da' sequence?!" and Seth would have to recite the loading sequence once again. In the days to come, Raif learned to read and write his own name and was right proud of it. In turn, he became Seth's mentor in practical living on the frontier. "Book larnins' pareful stuff Seth, shore nuff', but yu'll plum die a' readin' iffen ya' ain't got grub!" Raif counseled. "An' in da' long haul ya' gots to kill hit or trade fur it!" he continued. "Mostens it cain't be kilt lessens ya' got da' truck ta' kill hit wit, as ya' know, ya needs a raffle. Do ya' foller what ahm a' sayin'?" "Yes, Raif." "So wat ahm a' sayin?" "You're saying that one way or another it all goes back to trading." "Zackly!" Raif shouted while thrusting his arms in the air. "But I already know everything about trading from my time in Pittsburg and our time on the Ohio." "Well hit aint da' same ever wars!" Raif howled, with eyes glaring and veins bulging in his neck. "Dare ain't no need out here fur needle an" tread, and kaleeko! Mostens don't eben have foldin' money out cheer! Ya' needs ta' know what ta' trade fur, and how much and so forth and so on," he explained. As Seth listened wide-eyed to every word Raif was saying, a sudden smack aback the head sent his long blond hair flying. "Wastin' ya' air, Raif! Ya' can't larn city boys nuthin' bout nuthin. Dey tinks dey knows hit all. Dey cain't be hepped!" As Seth brushed the hair out of his eyes he saw the lanky frame of Tuck Franklin amble past. Taking Seth's hand and leading him off a piece, Raif comforted, "Don't wor' 'bout 'em. He's got a burr in his belly, or a whole poke a' burrs shuved sum'airs. An' ahm not mad atcha, needer. Ya' jus gotta lissen betimes. Now nixt time dare cumma' tradin' post, ya' keep an eye on ole Raif," he said while squinting his eyes in a shrewd kind of way. And he *was* shrewd. Seth was amazed at how well Raif and the other men conducted business even though most simply scrawled an "X" for their name.

Seth Garner: Part One

The trading posts were little more that ramshackle huts built at strategic fords in the river. They carried flour and lard, and a bit of sugar if you were lucky. Gun powder and shot were often the first items sought after, followed closely by whiskey. Although Seth had never fully swallowed the "devil's brew" as his father called it, he was impressed with its effect on those who took more than a sample or two. Whiskey loosened the tongues of men who normally might grunt a few times in an entire day. And those who never expressed a single human emotion, not even those common to bodily pain, would pour forth sob stories of long lost loves, pitifully whining of broken hearts and forgotten promises while pea-sized tears coursed down tobacco-stained stubble. Then when sobered, a man would deny it all with such conviction that Seth came to believe that he had truly forgotten how foolish he had acted mere hours before. The drink truly possessed a power of its own, a power of which Seth would soon learn firsthand.

When Seth read to the crew, he felt accepted... to a degree. In the main, though, he sensed that there still was a barrier between him and the men. Yes, he was the youngest one of the bunch, and he had studied longer than all of their school years combined. But there was something more, something unseen that shut him out of the inner circle. His sense of alienation was never more palatable than at the nightly tale-telling sessions around the fire.

The earnestness with which the stories were told and the bonding effect that they had upon the group practically took on a religious quality. Indeed there were high priests of the craft and none could best Silas Hollinger for doling out a good story. He could spin an epic yarn from little more than a lint ball and always drew a crowd about the evening fire. None could cement the invisible ties that joined the men together better than Silas. As he began one night, Seth stepped closer, secretly wishing that he too would be fully drawn into the group, to be bound up with that spiritual cordage of true friendship. It was then that Silas launched in to his tale.

"Well ahm a' tellin' ya' dat tommy-hawk twas on hits way afore ah had da' hammer back on ma' long arn!" bawled a bleary eyed Silas as a bottle was passed around. That's how Silas always began his stories. He simply started midstream without any introduction and then he waited. It was his way of gaining the floor so to speak in this informal gathering of souls, and it worked very well. Seth stepped closer to the circle as he heard another call out, "Ya' say what, Silas?! Hit twas a' cummin' atcha! Do talk a spell!" For that invitation Silas gave a quick nod and passed the bottle on. "Oh, yeah... ah seen hits blade a glintin' in da' moonlit as hit twuzz a' turnin' rat tward ma' nose!" "Oh law!" shouted a raftsman while another whined pitifully, "Hits a cryin' shame ya' got ya"sef kilt! Ah heered dat you wuz a pretty good feller!" A number of the men laughed and pointed at the jokester even as Seth blurted out, "What on earth did you do?!"

At that moment all talking ceased and eyes slowly turned to peer at Seth in the night. As he withered under the steely glare of the raftsmen, there could be no doubt that he was in breech of frontier etiquette some how. No words were spoken; each face was as blank as in a game of high stakes poker. Nevertheless the message was clear: you are an outsider. They had accepted him as a fellow raftsman, but he was not yet one *of them*.

"Aw go on, Silas!" moaned one of the group as buckskin clad shoulders turned in unison toward the fire. "Dat injun had ya' good!" another shouted. "Nat gist one, Mistah... twas two a' dem sabbages gist a' tearin' rat behin' dat tommy-hawk! Dey wuz affer ma' top knot sa' bad dat

Seth Garner: Part One

dey wuz a' gainin' on dat war club as hit twuz 'bout to cleave me in twain!" "Den dare'd be twice as much trouble from ya' as dare is now!" chided a friend. Again laughter and backslapping went around the circle. Yet apart from the joking interruptions, Seth was amazed at how disinterested his fellows were in the actual story. They simply took it in, bits at a time, not demanding more than Silas was want to give. Not so with Seth. He was practically dying with suspense. "Oh lands, man! Two against one! How on earth did you ever..." "Why don'cha ya' jus sit ya'sef down an' let da' man finnish hiz tale?!" bellowed one as the bottle tipped skyward again. There was a shuffling here and there and a small opening appeared in the ring. It was an unspoken invitation for Seth to join the group. He accepted and settled down across from Silas. "So dey twas two of 'em, ya' say!" chimed in another in an attempt to get things moving again. "What ah cud see of 'um, leese wize," Silas continued. "Ah hauled back on ma' sef to buy a pinch a room 'tween me an' da' trouble," he continued as he bent as far back as he could without tipping over. Silas' eyes bulged out as if he was staring at a whirling blade speeding towards him. All the while Silas' finger pointed out in thin air, but you just knew that tomahawk was the last thing Silas was going to see this side of eternity. Seth leaned back a little too, totally caught up in the tale. His comrades smiled placidly as they stared blankly into the blaze. Straightening back up, with Seth following suit, Silas unleashed a gut-wrenching belch and downed another swig of spirits. He continued. "Cuz ah wuzz a' needen' a mite more space at da' time, dōncha know," he explained as he nodded knowingly about the circle. Seth too ratcheted his head while the rest seemed unmoved by the scene of abject terror that Silas painted, one word stroke after another. "An' den ah gist mashed da' trigga' as ah flopped back on ma'...ma'...well...ah wuzz a' sittin' plum on

The Big Float South

Mutter Ert when hit twus all over." The story man lowered the bottle between his knees and just stared philosophically into the fire along with the rest. Not a word was spoken for a long while. Here and there a head nodded with deep understanding, being completely satisfied that the tale was told. Seth looked about unnerved. Not a one evidenced the need to know that burned in Seth. He could bear no more. "When it was all over?! What do you mean, 'When it was over?! You've got at least two men bent on your mortal destruction and a razor sharp blade about to cleave you in two, and you say, 'When it was over,'?! You must have shot, or run, or ...or...?" Silas remained unmoved. A group of the men started at Seth with consternation; a few shrugged their shoulders and one twirled his finger about his temple signaling that Seth had finally snapped. Then, as if on cue, they all turned back to the fire. After a few long moments, Silas took a, long, slow draft from the half empty pipe bowl. Puffing forth a few lazy smoke rings, Silas took hold of the bottle, and held it up before the fire to judge its fill. Looking now directly at Seth, he joined in again. "Well...dats da' bess part. I don't rattly know what happened nixt, not zackly anyways. Ah kin only tell ya' what ah bleev." Again he sank into a somber, contemplative mood as the flames licked higher toward the night sky. A few barely audible "So true...so true." and "Daz' zall a body kin do," sputtered in places about the ring as a nameless soul poked the fire with a burning stick. Again all present seemed quite satisfied with the tale as told. Seth's pleading glances garnered no sympathy from those present whatsoever. He searched the faces desperately seeking one like his own; but found none. Not able to refrain any longer, he stood to his feet and fairly shouted out, "What you believe?! "Well......" drawled Silas as he took another long draft on the last glowing ember of his pipe. "Iffen hit heps ya' some." Seth

Seth Garner: Part One

dragged both palms down the sides of his face, stretching it long and groaned, "Yes...please...that would help right nicely. Go on!" "Well azzah said, ah mashed down on da' trigga, as ah wazz a' sayin', an' ah half thought, 'Wat a time fur a misfar!'" "My God, man! You had a misfire!" shouted Seth. "Naw...naw...ah jus half thought dat, dazz' all. Naw, Ole Reliable did hits part an' drive me back a foot or two. An' dat's gist when ah think hit happened. Dat tommy-hawk gist a' stopt in mid are, hit gist a' quivrin' an' a' singin' as hit dropped ta' da' grown. Az da' smoke cleared a might more, ah seed a wundrus thang, a thang dat made a way fur me to be here gist now. Dem two redskins heaved forward on dey faces, jus a' skiddin' rat up ta' ma boot bottoms." Silas tipped back his feet and wiggled the soles of his boots for emphasis. "When a cum ta' masef, ah raised up and prized dem bōf ovah. Dey wuz bōf deddern yistaday's biskits, bof offem shot rat 'tween da' eyes gist az pretty az ya' pleez!" Before the "ya' pleez" faded from earshot the crowd erupted in laughter, it all punctuated with robust backslapping and rib poking. Seth looked about gap-jawed, completely wowed at the turn of the tale. Without speaking, he slowly folded back to the deck and crossed his legs, as the rest howled and laughed themselves silly. "Da' bullet muzza hit da' tommy-hawk dead centern an' bust in twain. Den a'corse da' parts went on ta' kill da' injuns. An' dat iz why ahm a' here ta' tell dis story!" "Hear! Hear!" they shouted. "Dern iffen dat tale don't get bettern ever time ah heerd hit," hooted another. "Hit don't make me weery, needer, though ah must a' heerd hit fifty time, an' ah cans tell hit bettern Silas!" crowed another as the rest joined in the fun.

As the bottle was thrust toward his chest, Seth instinctively reached out and took it. He sat there slack-jawed, stunned by the sudden knowledge that all present had heard this story many times before, save for him. It

The Big Float South

dawned on him too that he had been lured in, strung along for sport. The whole thing was an unrehearsed, homespun joke on him, and he marveled at how smoothly it was pulled off. He had underestimated them. Just because they hadn't gone to school like he had, didn't mean that they weren't cleaver. They had set a trap for him and they caught him good.

As he was slapped on the back and punched in the shoulder, first on the right side and then on the left, he sat there speechless for the first time since the story began. His mind raced trying to tease out what parts of the tale were true, knowing that how these men lived and occasionally died, nearly all of it was surely true. He was so dumfounded by it all that he was not even aware of having taken the bottle. Half smiling and looking about at the mirth-filled faces and crooked fingers that pointed at him across the fire, he quaffed down a good measure of the drink.

It didn't stay down for long. Seth suddenly wretched forward, sensing the increased heat on his face and elsewhere. The searing streak of white-lightning retraced the path from whence it came and spewed out into the night. As the heady blast approached the fire, it caught to, and erupted in a great ball of orange flame. A cacophony of "Hey thar's!" and "Oohs!" sounded off as one shouted, "Nuthin' tops a good story morin' a far-breethin' dragun!" The laughs and cackles rolled on as Seth joined in as well. Indeed the joke was on him, but now, at last, he sensed that he was one *of them*. The bond was made. From time to time one would say, "Now don't get dat boy mad. He'll breathe far! Ah seed 'em do hit!" Such antics only strengthened the friendship that he now had with a hardy, and for the most part, good-natured crew of frontiersmen. And he learned too that it was not the story told that was important. It was the time spent together that mattered

125

most. Though none would ever admit it, nor acknowledge the need for such, it was a sacred time, one with its peculiar rituals, sacraments and procedures. There was no written liturgy of course, but it was plain to see if one was willing to enter into their simple but honest world. Seth had entered in and... he was learning. He turned in for the night and slept the contented sleep of acceptance. Regrettably, his restful slumber did not last long.

It was one of those cases where events outpaced the mind. With a stinging pain in the center of his back, Seth awoke with a start. At the same time, he had the strange sensation of being weightless and welcomed the short-lived comfort that he was dreaming. But quicker than can be told, he realized that in fact he was in midair; and just as quick, he was slammed hard onto the deck again. He landed on the top of his shoulders, continued to roll backwards and came to rest on his hands and knees, facing forward towards the bow of the raft. It was then that sheer terror coursed through his body. Through the moonlight, he could make out a frothy mountain of water looming up ahead of the raft. The rest of the crew staggered before the phantom wave like specters groping for a place to hide. But there was no place to run when the big wave hit. Men flew into the air as the sinewy length of wood bull-whipped from stem to stern. Seth braced for the impact as he too found himself catapulted skyward once again. This time, he hit the deck face down and felt every bit of air leave his lungs just before blacking out. Coming to moments later, an ear-splitting roar peeled on and on as huge swaths of earth cleaved off the banks and fell into the river. These launched tidal waves from opposite shores that rocked the raft like a cradle, making it impossible to stand on one's feet. The severely wracked raft pitched and yawed in the midst of the tumult, as shouts of "Earthquake!" could be heard above the din. From out of the darkness the panicked cries of man and beast could be heard as everyone hung on for dear life. Indeed, at two in the morning on Dec. 16th, 1811, a massive earthquake had ravaged the Mississippi Valley.

In the wake of the first big jolt, Seth and the rest of the men clung to the logs, longing for the light of day. He had never felt more helpless than now, for there was absolutely nothing he or anyone else could do to better their situation. Through it all, aftershocks rattled their craft and their nerves as the hours wore on. At last, a welcomed sun cleared a cold horizon and shed light on the devastation. The normally sleek string of timber was now in disarray, zigzagging in a mangled mess aft wards as far as the eye could see. Cabins on shore were reduced to splinters and even the river had changed its course here and there. Moreover, lakes drained dry in minutes as the land was thrust upward and new ones were formed as acres subsided and allowed wild floods to pour in.

Nevertheless, all of this ruin was only a harbinger of things to come. Just past 7:00 in the morning, a second quake hit with mind-numbing power. They were all knocked to the deck once again and watched in disbelief as the mighty Mississippi appeared to reverse its course and flow upstream. Sand boils erupted throughout the land, sending geysers of silt and mud high into the air. The men shrieked in fear as massive trees walked across the ground, outpacing the raft as the earth moved along, swaying wildly before they too came crashing down. Seth could see the panic-filled eyes of strong men as the blood blanched from their faces, looking to him for some kind of answer in the midst of the tumult. "It's alright!" he shouted. "It will pass! We're safe on the river!" Seth yelled as the horror bore on. Yet he too could not resist the one thought that weighed heavy on each heart: when would this all end?

127

Seth Garner: Part One

Mercifully, the dreadful shaking did come to an end. Nevertheless, constant aftershocks harried the men and rippled the surface of the river, sending droplets of water jumping into the air like rain in reverse. A low rumble would sound off from time to time, but no big jolts were forthcoming. Through it all the men were tense and fairly paralyzed with fear, not knowing what to do. Leaping onto a barrel head, Raif took the lead. "Don't jis stand dare gap-jawed an' a'starin! You men git ta' werk! Wrangle in dose stray logs an' mend dis mess tagetha! We got ta' git down dis river!" His heavy-handed commands worked like a tonic as the crew laid trembling hands to hard labor. Walking about with all confidence, he secretly pulled Seth aside and whispered, "Dist thang is over, aint hit Seth? Ah mean, da quakes, dey done wit, aint dey?" "I don't know, Raif. No one knows. All we can do is hope for the best."

For three full weeks, all was calm and the crew entered a period of normalcy. The rafts of timber were truly in a shambles though, and the men worked from dawn till dusk just to straighten things out. Block and tackle creaked and groaned as the massive logs were drawn up again. Moreover, all of the storage sheds and shelters had to be rebuilt. Worse yet, they were marooned on an island of logs. They made no progress downstream for nearly a month.

And so it was that as the New Year dawned, the days were filled with backbreaking work and harrowing tales of the quake. Folks would ride down to the shore and shout out the bad news to the men on the raft. For a start, the damage spread much further than any one had imagined. The quakes could be felt as far away as Canada and New York. Church bells in Boston rang of their own accord due to the violent shaking of the earth. The first steamboat on the Mississippi, the New Orleans, was nearly swamped by the rogue waves that coursed across the river in every

The Big Float South

direction. There was nary a chimney left standing for hundreds of miles around. Untold numbers had lost their lives and livestock was either scattered or killed throughout the land. No one, not even the Indians, could recall a catastrophe of such magnitude. To a man, all gladly bid farewell to the tragic end of 1811. It was just then that the unthinkable happened.

At about a quarter past nine in the morning on Jan 23rd, a third quake bludgeoned the earth. An immediate wail of pain arose from the crew; a spontaneous chorus of fear that that betrayed a sea of worry, a world of fear lying just below the surface of every man. Once again, men lunged and lurched across the pitching timbers. One panicked soul, like a frontier Jonah cried out, "It was me! It was me! I done it!" and then made a fright-filled dash to plunge over the side. He would have succeeded too if it were not for a friend who tackled him in midair and dragged him to the deck. Seth glared stoically downstream as a temporary waterfall formed across the whole breath of the river, and then just as fast, disappeared beneath a boiling cauldron of foam. In a moment, all of the work they had done during the past month was undone. Worse still, picking out the few landmarks that remained, the crew could tell that they were several hundred yards further *upstream* than they were just moments before the quake. No one could tell whether the land had moved or the water, or perhaps both had shifted in some unnatural way. What they could tell was that they were going backwards rather than forwards on their tortured journey south.

The men were fit to be tied. They yelled and screamed and scuffles broke out here and there as they took out their frustration on each other. Small knots of discontent formed as some shouted, "I'm done!" or "I want off this wreck!" In short order, a full scale mutiny swept through the crew. Raif broke up one skirmish, pulled through

129

Seth Garner: Part One

another mass of rebels and clambered up a large snag to get high above the melee. "Ya' through! Is dat what ah hears?! You wants ta go ashore? Is dat what ya wants? An' fur what, ah asks?! Ta' get ya heed stove in by a tumblin' rock? Is dat what ya wants?! Ah heered a whole church fell in on folk while dey wuz a' prayin. Is dat what ya wants?! Den go on, ya empty heeded goats! Go ashore an get pinned to da groun by a splintery brainch like a passel of folk ah heered of. Do wants ta be a'runnin from fear and fall into folly?! Have da ground open hits merciless maw and swaller ya up?! Why dares hunnerts a' bodies dat'll never tell us where dey buried!" A voice hollered out, "Uh... Raif? A body caint tell us where hits buried!" "A'specially deese!" Raif continued without pause. "Ah heered dat a nimble footed pony caint pick hits way through the bumblin' mess a roads dat waits for ya ashore! An when ya finally gets ta where ya wants to go, what'll ya find? A tangled wreck worsen what we gots here, dats what ah heered! Oh yeah, St. Louis is all broke up as is all da rest of the towns for two hunnert mile. Go on, if dat's what ya wants! *Or* ... ya kin stay here, like young Seth said, da safest place around, just a floatin' in the midst of the Mizzazip! Why iffen a nudder big shake cums, ah wager folk will be a divin' into da river trying ta gits ta us. An' ah gotta mine ta charge 'em a dollar ta climb aboard, too! But go da utter way, if ya wants too. Ahm not a stoppin' ya!"

With that, one could literally feel the tension ebb away from the men. Raif's speech had made them realize that there were no better options than what they had at hand. Everyone's world had been turned upside down. As they began to shuffle away in silence and not in a little shame, no one needed to tell them what to do. Once again they laid weary hands to thankless work, just trying to get their floating world back together again. Raif climbed down from his perch, folded his arms and looked menacingly at

The Big Float South

the men as the walked by. It took a strong man to rule strong men in times like these. As Seth drew up to Raif, he quipped, "You'd make a good preacher, Raif." "Dat twernt preachin! Dat twas jist da Gawd honest trut!" he grumbled in response. Seth smiled as he pondered Raif's point.

The men had made their choice, but they were frazzled. Even the fourth and final quake of February 7th could not shake their resolve. This time, there was no panic or cries of fear. There was no running about, either. When the rumbling started, everyone just held onto whatever they could and braced for the worst. This temblor was as bad as all the rest and it cruelly tore down all that they had build up. But this time the putting together was practically a matter of routine and the men went about the work without complaining. Yet they were sorely dispirited, through and through. The nightly campfire became more a time of solace than joyous fellowship. Nearly all of the nonsense stories of the past had ceased and the whiskey flowed less liberally. Additionally, they would have Seth read from the Bible at nearly every setting. And so it was that Seth found himself reading from Psalm 91:

> "HE THAT DWELLETH IN THE SECRET PLACE OF THE MOST HIGH SHALL ABIDE UNDER THE SHADOW OF THE ALMIGHTY. I WILL SAY OF THE LORD, *HE IS* MY REFUGE AND MY FORTRESS: MY GOD; IN HIM WILL I TRUST. SURELY HE SHALL DELIVER THEE FROM THE SNARE OF THE FOWLER, *AND* FROM THE NOISOME PESTILENCE. HE SHALL COVER THEE WITH HIS FEATHERS, AND UNDER HIS WINGS SHALT THOU TRUST: HIS TRUTH *SHALL BE THY* SHIELD AND BUCKLER. THOU SHALT NOT BE AFRAID FOR THE TERROR BY NIGHT; *NOR* FOR THE ARROW *THAT* FLIETH BY DAY; *NOR* FOR THE PESTILENCE *THAT* WALKETH IN DARKNESS; *NOR* FOR THE DESTRUCTION *THAT*

Seth Garner: Part One

> WASTETH AT NOONDAY. A THOUSAND SHALL FALL AT THY SIDE, AND TEN THOUSAND AT THY RIGHT HAND; *BUT* IT SHALL NOT COME NIGH THEE."

Once finished, a solemn silence fell over all present. It was then that someone asked the fateful question that all feared to ask out loud. Looking up to heaven, from out of the darkness, a quavering voice said, "Young Seth, is it something that we done?" There it was. The awful, heart-rending question of whether all that they had suffered was some kind of divine punishment for their sins. Seth paused for a moment, let out a long sigh, and then offered his thoughts concerning all that had happened to them. "No...it's not something that we've done, not in particular. Nothing worse than the numberless souls that live in this troubled world, anyway. It's more like what has been done, since the beginning that is, with that awful misstep of the first man Adam. Since then, the world's gone wild. You both know and have experienced that! This whole place, without exception, is full of danger, disease, and sooner or later, for every living thing on earth, is full of death too. Not only this, but we fight and war and abuse our neighbor. We all know it's true, if not a sorrowful thing to admit. And for some reason only known to the good Lord, we've been thrown into the midst of a sorrowful and hurting world. No...it's not something we have done; but yes...in some sense...it's something we all have done. And so whatever the case may be, I reckon it's a good time to pray..." "Well I fur one taint a goin' ta pray!" hollered out Tuck Franklin. "My maw and paw were a' prayin folk! An' what did it get dem?! Dey be scalped and gutted by da hostiles! Dat's what! No sireee! No prayin' fur me!" "You pipe down, Tuck Franklin!" shouted another. "Let da man be!" hollered another. "Ya' all pipe down!" yelled Raif. "Young Seth was asked a hard thang, one ah dare say we all been a' thinkin'

The Big Float South

on one way or a'nudder. An he give a fair answer, in ma opinion. Now ya' all go on an do whatcha want. As fur me, ahm not shamed ta say, ah am goin' ta have a little talk wit ma Maker, iffen ya don't mine!" As the men broke up for the night, a few men gave Seth a handshake and lightly patted him on the back. Not so with Tuck Franklin. He glowered at Seth through the gloom and then stomped off toward his lean to on the raft.

Once again, a great deal of time was lost in getting the raft river worthy again. Indeed, it took nearly two months to get the operation underway. By that time the spring rains had begun to push them along at a good pace and some sense of normalcy returned to the crew. On the first day of May, he and Raif figured that they had passed the midpoint on their journey to New Orleans. On this day too, Seth turned 17 years of age.

As the raft snaked its way southward, it was literally being sold out from under the river men. New settlements were springing up throughout the Mississippi Valley. Solid hardwood lumber from the north was needed to feed the steady growth of villages and older towns along the river. This was especially true in the wake of the destructive earthquakes that pummeled the southeast at the start of the year. Entire sections of the raft were sold off to meet the demands of new construction and repairs. Seth was impressed anew that their floating village was a vital part in a network of trade that plied the silt laden waters of the Mississippi. And high up on the bluffs, always above flood stage, stood the centers of the entrepreneurial spirit that powered the new nation; the frontier trading posts. Whenever possible the men would leave their floating island of wood and make landfall at the trading posts so that they could catch up on the latest news and to trade a little. And so it was, a shout went out from the bow that a

133

Seth Garner: Part One

post had been spotted ahead and that the men should make ready to go ashore.

"Now ya' gist clap an' eye on ole Raif, an' yull be a rich man!" Raif exulted as he prepared for the excursion. "Don't say nuttin dis furs time, an' hit'll serve ya' good!" he continued. Seth was eager to get on with the trip. He had enough of the raft ride for a while and he looked forward to something new. "You just take the lead and I'll follow," assured Seth.

A gruff voice from behind asked, "Mine iffen ah tag along?" Tuck Franklin was a master at inviting himself to things, especially when money was involved. He was a swindler, a shyster, a slight of hand artist who took advantage of the naiveté or goodwill of others. He had a way of getting people to part with their valuables, then lighting out to parts unknown. The present rouse was to gain the trust of the uninformed along the way, lift a few coins from each, and promise to return with finery from New Orleans. He was such a master of deceit that those hoodwinked suspected nothing until Tuck was way on down the river, never to pass that way again.

Seth shot a worried look toward Raif as he replied, "Ya' don't need a ticket to go ashore. Dees stores'll 'cept anybody, iffen day got truck to trade." Several more joined in the party as they wound their way up the muddy bank side. Before the group topped out, the trail led to a cave opening. A crude sign on a shingle read, "McIntire's Post-- Welcome." As the men stooped to enter in, pine pitch torches lit the interior. A cask of whiskey stood near the rear of the cave, together with a small keg of powder. Apart from some tangled coils of rope and a makeshift table, there was little else about.

"Cum on in! Cum on in!" shouted a weather-worn soul as he held out a flagon of drink. A vicious scar slashed across his cheek, and not a few teeth had finished their time of service. As others from behind the old crone shuffled a few feet forward, one of their own party reached out to take the mug. As Seth's eyes panned slowly from one dimly lit corner to the other, he sensed something was wrong, but couldn't place it. A confused look toward Raif was not comforting. His eyes were knit in anger as he peered into the gloom and filth. Turning back toward the aged leader, Seth barely caught sight of a gnarled hand as it shot below his chin and seized him by the throat. Through panicked eyes he looked into the wrinkled face of the old rogue laughing wildly even as he crushed the breath out of him. As torch lights began to fade, a flashing blade came down hard and sliced through the spindly forearm that held Seth fast. As Seth slumped to his knees, the graying stump of a hand still held tight to his throat. Prying the limb off in horror, he heard several muskets shots go off, in such quick succession, so close that they sounded as one cannon shot. Bodies were falling everywhere. As the acrid smoke of burnt powder filled his eyes and nose, Seth let out a pitiful cry. Seconds later the roughened soles of his bare feet slapped hard on the mud path outside. He had made no conscious decision to run, but he found himself knocking branches and briars out of the way as he frantically tore down the trail. Coming to his senses he felt shamed at his cowardice and turned back toward the cave. Lurching forward and staring at the front of his blood-soaked shirt he met his own men on their way down.

As the men sternly filed past he looked searchingly into Raif's eyes. "Wha...What happened?" "River pirates!" was Raif's curt reply as he brusquely marched past Seth without another word. As the party filed past him, Seth stood stupefied on the trail above them. He shouted down, "Don't you think we ought to do something? We can't just leave them there!" The group continued toward the raft as if Seth hadn't said a word. As they pulled away Seth made a few steps toward the cave. As he approached the opening, a huge explosion rocked him to the ground even as a wall of fire rolled over him mere inches from his nose. Instinctively turning face down, Seth clamped both hands over the back of his head for protection, winching under the heat, hoping and praying that it would not increase the more. As the heat abated, Seth sat up, wiping bits of gravel and dirt from his mouth, staring gap-jawed as a roaring flame poured out of the mouth of the cave. What had once been the entrance to the "trading post" a few moments before was now a raging inferno. Pulling himself together, Seth surmised that after the bullet-riddled bodies were left on the cold stone floor, someone had set the powder keg to explode. It troubled him not a little that that "someone" might have been Raif.

From far above, Seth could see the men approaching the raft. The foreman called out, "Heard a ruckus up there! Anybody hurt?" "Not on our part!" was the reply. "Then it looks like you got the better half of the trading!" he yelled back in jest. Seth could hear the rest of the men laugh as his friends piled aboard. Men had been killed. *He* had come close to dying, and for them it was just another day on the river. In an instant he had come to realize just how strange and dangerous their world was. Like it or not, now it was his world too. He must learn how to live in it soon, or he wouldn't have to bother. "Young Seth! Ya' cummin' or do ya' still have some tradin' ta' do?!" Again laughter rolled up the river bank as Seth plodded downward in silence. As soon as he realized that he needed to change, it dawned on him that he had already changed and that he would never be the same person again. He wasn't near as young as he had been just moments before. Seeing, better yet, experiencing the thin margin between life and death had added years to him and that in an instant. As Raif held out a helping hand to haul him aboard, Seth certainly was not the same person that he was when he awoke that morning. He still had a lot of growing up to do, but the conflict with the river pirates had done its part in making him a man.

Tuck kneeled near the edge of the raft cleaning blood off the long, sharp blade of his knife. "Thank you Tuck for saving my life." "Savin ya'!" he snarled. "Is dat wat ya' tink ah did?" Seth stepped back a bit as a firm grip on his elbow turned him about. Raif led Seth to a stump by the fire and handed him a plate of beans. "Bess leeb him alone a spell. Now eat up!" Grateful to still be in the land of the living, Seth wolfed down the beans with gusto. Looking up from the plate he saw Raif staring back at him with one eyebrow raised sharply toward the brim of his hat. "What?" Seth muttered as he shoveled in another ladle of beans. "Ya' were a mite slow back yonder, son." "Well...I..." "Heer wat ahm a' sayin," Raif continued as if Seth hadn't spoken a word. "Slow in dees parts means death! Do ya' know wat ahm a' tellin ya'?" "Yes, I believe..." "Well dōncha ferget it nun too soon!" he warned as he stood up and walked off into the darkness. Seth realized this was about as close to an expression of care that he was going to get on this raft, so he took it to heart. But the lesson had already been learned high up on the riverbank. An unguarded trust could get a man killed in a hurry out here. Indeed, unbeknownst to Raif, the survivor's instinct had already taken root in Seth. It was just a germ of caution, and it had a lot of growing to do, but that element of reserve that would save his life and perhaps the lives of others had already started to grow in his heart.

The next day continued just as if nothing unusual had happened the day before. The tedium of chores rolled on, thankfully punctuated by a practical joke here and there to break up the monotony. As evening fell, Tuck Franklin brandished a deck of cards above his head, and like a town crier, sang out, "Cards! Cards! Anybody heer fur a game

Seth Garner: Part One

a'cards?!" All walked away wagging their heads save Tuck and one other. As they pulled up to a rough hewn table, Tuck called out to Seth, "Ya' play cards, boy? Ya' eva play da' game?" "Well...no...you see..." "Sit down cheer. We'll teech ya'. Give ya' sum larnin'. Book larnin' costs money and card larnin' can cost money too! Do ya' have any money, son? "Five dollars in coins..." "Dat'll work! Jus' nuff fur da' first lesson!" Tuck assured as he pointed to an empty chair at the table. Settling in, Seth was pleased to see Raif suddenly walk up and take a seat too. "Think'll gist play a round er two ma'sef!" he said as he smiled at Tuck. "Sure! Sure! Da' more dey iz...well...da' more dey iz!" Tuck said a bit awkwardly shrugging his shoulders. Tuck dealt out the cards with lightning speed, and even before anyone could see what fate had wrought he snapped, "Whatta we startin' wit...lemme see...say...five dollars?" "Dat's a titch steep fur da' furs hand, don'tcha say?" said Raif. "We're a'headin' ta' New Orleens man! Ah'd say weez all wantin' sum pocket money?" countered Tuck. Seth emptied his pockets onto the table, soon to be followed by Tuck and his friend. Raif cast a somber look in Seth's direction and followed suit. Now twenty gold coins rested in the center of the ramshackle table. Seth had never seen that much money out in the open. "All rat Raif, what'le ya' take?" "I'll jus kep ma' hand," Raif replied. After Tuck and the other traded in for a few new cards, Tuck barked, "Okay, son, how many cards do ya' want?" "Well...I don't exactly..." "Gist chuck three cards," Tuck interrupted while reaching out to snatch a cluster of cards from Seth. Unsure of what to do, Seth reached out and took three more from the deck. Tuck was the first to reveal his hand, and at that Raif and the other man folded. "Well hits gist me agin' you, Seth. Watta ya' got?" "Well that's what I'm trying to tell you. You see... I've never really played cards before," Seth explained. "Don't matta now, gist tells me watcha got?" "Well...I've

The Big Float South

got three 'A's' and two 'K's'. Is that good?" Tuck was crestfallen. Every inch of exposed skin turned blood red. Raif let out a howl of laughter while slapping his knee. "Is dat good?!" hollered Raif. "Hit means dat ya's won all da' dern money, dat's wat hit means!" he cried while pushing the pile of coins toward Seth. Tucks eyes narrowed to a malicious squint. Taking a deep breath and scrunching up his face with his free hand as if trying to wipe off grime without water, he sighed, "Well dat's fare. Watta ya' say we play agin? Startin at...let's say...ten dollars?" "That's too rich for me," muttered Tuck's sidekick. "Ah gist think'll sit dissun out," drolled Raif as he pushed back from the table a bit. He sidled up a little closer to Tuck, watching his every move. Seth looked at the pile of coins and then back at Tuck. Tuck's smile looked as if it was pasted on. His lips were smiling but the rest of his face was not. Seth was somber. He knew something was up, but didn't know what. "Watta ya' say, Seth, are ya' in?" Seth hesitated. He really didn't have a reason not to play; he was winning. If he backed out, it might look like he didn't have the nerve. This was a chance, albeit a small one, to prove that he wasn't just a kid anymore. So as a small crowd was gathering about, Seth replied, "Well... that was easy enough...deal me some cards." As Seth divided his winnings in half and slid ten dollars to the center of the table, he shot a quick glance toward Raif. His face was inscrutable. Again Tuck held firm to the cards as he flicked them across the table. "Dat makes five each!" Tuck said as he slung his arm sharply down toward the floor. As he did, a card slipped out of his sleeve and skated across the surface of his palm. Tuck tried to wrap his greasy fingers around it, but only managed to clip the edge of the card so as to bend it a little before it sprang loose. The card flipped up in the air a bit, rose above the surface of the table, and swirled on to rest at Seth's feet. Reaching down, Seth slowly picked up the ace of spades,

Seth Garner: Part One

held it up for all to see as a stream of tobacco juice dripped from the corner of Tuck's mouth. "Well....what do we have here? Another 'A' card. I believe this belongs to you, Tuck!" Tuck's jaw set and his face flushed crimson with rage as he peered into Seth's eyes. "An' ..ah...bleev...dis...b'longs ta' you!" snarled Tuck as he reached for the long knife strapped to his side.

As Seth peeped over the top of his cards, he spied the steely tip of Tuck's knife speeding toward his chest. The mind can do strange things in cases like this. Time itself yields to its power and simply melts away. Somewhere between the unseen spaces that separate seconds and inches, Seth's thoughts coursed through another realm and that at lightning speed. The border between rational thought and feelings collapsed. "How could the same weapon that saved my life yesterday end it today? What did I say....What did I do to deserve this? No!. . . Not this way!. . . I'm too young to die. Dear God...if you can hear me....."

From the corner of Seth's vision a figure thrust through, snapping him back to the here and now. The table crashed over even as Raif shot into Tuck's side like an arrow piercing a deer mid stride. The force of the impact jarred the knife loose from Tuck's hand, and Seth heard it clattering across the wooden deck. The two men barreled across rough hewn logs, swinging and kicking and biting as they tumbled along. Tuck pummeled Raif's face with a fury that was inhuman. Blood and tufts of hair flew everywhere as the men clawed and punched in a wild scramble to end it all. As a crowd gathered about the two combatants, Seth looked about to see if any one would halt the fight. He met the same dull faces that he had once met around the evening campfire, but this time there was no story telling, no inside joke to explain the reticence of the men. Seth picked up the knife and stretched forth his hand to get it to

The Big Float South

Raif. A fist came down hard on his forearm and the knife once again clattered to the deck. He looked into the angered face of a burly deckhand, and stepped back. Suddenly Tuck left off striking and stretched with all his might to reach for the blade. His craven fingertips were barely stroking the handle, trying to rake it a few inches closer so that he might grasp it full and run Raif through. With a momentous effort Raif arced a booted foot and managed to kick the knife further away. Raif was getting the worst of it, though he was far from giving in as the men cheered him on with their words, but lent not a finger in the fight. Suddenly standing up Raif landed a savage round house punch that sent blood and teeth flying as Tuck crashed to the ground. Turning his back and peering at the men through bloody eyes, Raif's message was clear: Tuck's been beaten in a fair fight. The issue has been settled. He owes no one anything. He's paid the price of being a fool.

As the crowd began to break up, Tuck rolled to his knees groping along until he bumped into a pile of stove wood. Wrapping both hands around a length of hickory, he suddenly lunged back toward Raif as he walked away. The makeshift club came down so hard on Raif's skull that it knocked him clean to the deck. Lying on his stomach and moaning, barely conscious, Tuck moved in to finish the job. But at the last instant, Raif wheeled over and faced his attacker as Tuck swung the bloodied stick again, following it all the way down to where Raif lay. Turning his head aside, the hickory thudded harmlessly on the raft only to be followed by a sickening splitting sound. From the firelight Seth could see the point of Tuck's knife slice clean through the buckskin on Tuck's back and stick some three inches beyond his body. Tuck let out a gasp as he rocked back on his knees and then staggered up to his feet. His eyes opened wide with a mixture of surprise, disbelief and terror as he stepped backward toward the edge of the raft, all the while holding the hilt of his own knife protruding from his chest. "Raif! Ya' dun kilt me!" Raif, standing now, stepped forward, gripped the handle and planted his boot in the center of Tuck's gut, sending him over the side. Seth ran forward as Tuck thrashed about in the current. "I believe he's still...," "Nat fur long!" Raif growled as the men departed and Tuck's still flailing body was slowly swept down river. "But yesterday..." "Dat wuz yesterdays!" Raif snapped as he marched back toward the fire still holding the weapon in his hand. Midway Raif wheeled around and shoved the knife towards Seth's stomach. Seth jumped back and spread his arms open as if he was about to hug someone. Raif peered seriously into Seth's startled eyes, then flipped the blade in the air, caught it by its tip, and said, "As da' man said, dis b'longs ta' you!" Raif extended the knife toward Seth as he took it in his hand. "An' Seth...ya' still a mite slow...ah worry fur ya'... honestly ah do!" Raif continued his march on to the fire as he prepared to wash up and recover from the brawl.

That night Seth made his bedroll some distance apart from the rest, all the while thinking hard on what had happened. In the span of a day he had nearly been killed... twice. Moreover, he had seen more than half a dozen men die a violent death. Something in him had died too. The schoolboy at Krupsteiner's had passed away, blown to bits in a cave high above the Mississippi and just now mortally swirling away in its muddy currents. Seth audibly groaned at the notion of how he must appear to his fellow travelers. They were men of action who judged others on the basis of action. He had not acted well today. At this moment, they could know nothing of the seismic change that had taken place within his mind and heart. But they soon would.

As the night wore on, his thoughts wandered about the universe of his own life, contemplating his transport from the ordered world of Boston to the rough hewn life on the

The Big Float South

river. He then began to do something that only humans can do; he talked to himself. As so often is the case, the soliloquy was illogical, self-pitying and disjointed. "'A mite too slow!' What does that mean? 'I'm worried fur ya'!' Well don't bother old friend! I'm as fast as *they* are, even faster, when need be. And my eyes, why I see things before they even know there are things to be seen! I'm just not suspicious to the point of being sick in the head, *like they are*. They're not a wit more alert than I am. Touchy is not the same thing as being observant. They're edgy and edgy is not the same as being on guard. It makes you wonder. But then again, they did survive the last couple of days, while fast near a dozen others didn't. 'A mite too slow.' Well, it won't happen again! Not planning on it, anyways. Not if I can help it and so there it is."

And thus he rambled until his mind was tired of its own thoughts. As heavy eyelids closed out the splendor of the Milky Way only to unveil it once again, he didn't know whether he was thinking or praying. All he knew was that he had run away, and that's for sure. He had run away from his home.... from his parents. Now he was slowly drifting away from everyone he had ever known and from everything he had been taught to believe. He was no longer sure of exactly where he was in the broad scheme of things, if he was ever that sure. He was less sure of where he was going. All he knew at that moment was that deep down inside, he felt a profound sense of loss.

Seth Garner: Part One

The Treachery

It is no mere happenstance that one is always described as "riding" a raft. For in the arrangement between man and raft, it is the former that gives up a good measure of control. The raft goes where the water flows. Indeed there is always a bit of steering and coaxing here and there, but in the end one fact remains: the river of timber they called "home" rode on the back of an even greater river of water. The Indians called it the "Mitchasippi" or the "Father of Steams." The frontiersmen dubbed it "The Big Muddy" or the "Mighty Mizzazip." Those having a broader grasp of the world referred to it as the "American Nile." No matter what one called it, the river remained the same. Its strength was untamable, its depth unfathomable and its course unalterable. The only real say the raftsmen had in the whole affair was to sell off the enormous logs that creaked and groaned beneath their feet. This they did as they flowed past the towns and hamlets that sprouted along the river bank, all the while planning to offload about half the timber before journey's end. That's when they would cash in what was left of the raft at New Orleans.

Yet there were miles and miles to go before then, and the raftsmen glided toward an uncertain future. It was told that at flood tide, a swift canoe could make the run from St. Louis to New Orleans in ten days, while the norm for the trip was closer to two months. With their slow craft, and the months of delay caused by the earthquakes, they were already into the fall of 1812. Raif ventured that they would be in New Orleans sometime around Christmas. One thing was for sure; regardless of human plans or commerce, the whole thing was relentlessly rolling toward the south and Seth and his friends were simply along for the ride.

Seth Garner: Part One

The violent episode with Tuck had altered Seth in ways that he could neither understand nor change. Since that time, he didn't talk as much and joked even less. On the other hand, he worked harder and helped others more whenever he got the chance. If an occasional, "Thank ye'" came his way, Seth just continued on and made no reply. As always, he listened to the long tales around the fire at night and would smile at the jesting and silliness as the brown jug was passed around. But he seldom laughed out loud anymore. He wasn't angry or bitter. It was just that he was coming to know what it took to live on the frontier. It had become plain to him that regardless of how he felt on the inside, he would have to grow up on the outside if he were to survive for long in this rough and tumble world. For all of this, his friendship with Raif became more important than ever. Raif knew about everything there was to know on the river and beyond. More than ever, Seth was determined to glean all the knowledge that Raif had to offer.

"Na' Seth, as ya' well know by na', da' river is like a big artry, a' runnin' da' full lent of da' land...from nort ta' sout," Raif proffered. "Tiz all green an growin' along da' sides real nice like, but a ways out from da' banks...well ...tiz all different." "How so, Raif?". Seth asked the question because he knew that Raif wanted him to ask. In any case, even though he had come to know a lot about the wilds, he was never quite sure of what Raif was going to say.

"Well tiz different cuz of da' folks dats live dare. We cum past Tennersee an' Kintuck...da' 'Dark n' Bloody Ground'." "Dark and Bloody?" "Oh, yeah hit' tiz...Seth...real dark an' bloody...an' dat long b'fo weez cum along. Da' Injuns bin a' fightin an' a' scrappin' here since...since...well nobody's quite sure how long...but a long, long time." "Is that so, Raif?." "Sho'nuff. Tennersee an Kintuck iz da' bess huntin' territory east side of da' Big Muddy. One trab says

The Treachery

hits dares an den a nudder trab says hits dares....den dares wore...den weeze cum along an' thangs get worsen den befo. Aw hit'za awful mess!" An' da' worse part is da' captives." "The captives?!" "Oh, hit'za thang, Seth! Dis trab loses warriors in battle, so dey needs more folk, so dey takes captives ta' replace 'em, directly dat is, an' den dat trab is short a' beins, and so dey take captives, an' so forth an' so on, till a turrable a' tumblin' mess gets a' goin', an well...dare jist ain't no end to hit." "I can see that, Raif. I surely can." "Na' kin ya' see dis? 'Bout da captives. White folks, iffen dey took young, dey wants to stay Injun. Why when dey been 'rescued,' as weez prone to think, an' as soon as dey let alone, dey runs off to da' woods an' back to da' trab!" "That is a peculiar thing, Raif, I must admit." "Peculiar hit tiz but true hit tiz! Pray dat ya' don't eva see hit, fur hitz hard ta' get over. Na wares ya' long nafe?"

As Seth marched off to retrieve his knife, he knew that Raif's rambling talk about the "Dark and Bloody Ground" was only partly educational. It was Raif's way of helping him get back on even keel after the events of the last couple of days. As Seth sorted through his gear, he also sorted through his thoughts. He came to accept that life on the raft could be hard and unforgiving, but also that it was a place of good times and real friendship. He came to know that all in all, life on the frontier was about overcoming and moving on, and in all cases, sifting out the joy when it came along.

"Ya' caint go a' carryin' a pound or so a' razor sharp steel lac hit'za wooden spoon! Da point of ya' weapon is always ta be away from ya'." Seth pondered the double meaning of Raif's counsel as he handed the long knife to him. Grasping the knife, Raif headed off to his small lean-to and pulled out a piece of saddle leather. Shaking the rawhide in Seth's face, Raif bellowed on. "As Tuck went a' swirllen down da' river, ah had a lowly thought. 'Dare goes da' scabbert!' ah thought. Ain't dat a shame? A living being flowed down da' river an' ah thought, 'Dare goes da' scabbert!' Awful but true. Anyways, a nafe an a scabbert goes hand 'n hand. One ain't much use without da' utter, leesewise, not fur long! Ya' need a scabbert an' ah aims ta' teech ya' ta' make one."

Over the next few days Raif tapped out a pattern on the leather with a sharpened horseshoe nail. Borrowing a real awl from a workmate, they cut and sewed the heavy hide into a first rate sheath. The scabbard had a heavy loop at the top for Seth's belt and two long leather laces at the bottom to tie about his thigh. In time Seth slowly but steadily impressed the letters of his name into the leather after it had been moistened with warm water. He then filed a star-shaped pattern on the blunt end of a thick iron nail. With it he hammered an attractive pattern around the edge of the scabbard just inside the stitching. Raif was very impressed with the finished work and from that time on the long knife and scabbard rarely left Seth's side. He settled into the easy going life of the raft, becoming more of an equal deckhand with each passing day. He was already looking forward to arriving in New Orleans when it happened.

"Help us please! For the love of God, save us!" The frantic cries shattered the lazy routine of the raft. All heads swiveled toward the eastern bank, the Kentucky side, as the men quickly pieced together what was happening. The woman, with a babe in arms, screamed out once again the most pitiful plea for help. As some of the men seized weapons and primed them for action, Raif was making long strides toward the rear of the raft. As he picked up speed and loped past Seth, he shouted out one word: "Captives!"

Reaching the stern of the raft, Raif untied one of the canoes and was soon on his way, making long powerful strokes toward the far bank, even as orders were given to heave the hulking raft ashore. Seth watched pensively as Raif drew closer to the mother and child. It vaguely registered in his mind that Raif's long iron rested against the lean-to. He then turned his focus on the woman and child as Raif paddled steadily on to their rescue. At about a hundred yards out, Seth's keen eyesight saw some movement on shore and he quickly looked about at the rest of the crew. They showed no interest as they labored to get the raft to dock. When the woman's head turned back toward Seth, he thought that he could see a slight smile spread across her face. When Raif stopped paddling, Seth took off running, snatched up his rifle, and collected Raif's as well on the way to the back of the raft. By that time the woman was holding forth the baby, and looking intently upward into the woods. Strong bronze-colored arms swept up the baby while another set pulled her up the bank and out of sight. At that moment a half-dozen rifle muzzles emerged from the forest and belched forth flaming death toward Seth's only friend in the world.

The shock of the rifle fire set the crew into confusion. Some were straining on the push poles frantically trying to get the hulk of a raft to obey their will. Others were clattering about with ramrods, staggering along the pitching deck, preparing for battle while a handful shouted orders that went unheeded. None of this registered with Seth as he lunged forward to reach the remaining canoe. If it was the last thing he did on earth, he was determined to help his friend.

After heaving the rifles into the boat, Seth slipped the long knife from its sheath and sliced through the fibers of the mooring rope. In that sliver of time between the report of the rifles and the drawing of the long knife, he instinctively cocked his head back to keep track of Raif and his attackers. Even as his strong hands stretched forward and wrapped around unsteady gunnels, Seth saw bits of wood and water explode near the bow of Raif's canoe. "Out of range!" Seth shouted in his head as he slunk down and jammed the paddle into the brown water of the river.

Indeed in their haste to make good on the ambush, the Indians had fired too soon. The long arch of the speeding bullets ripped through the bow of the canoe and tore gaping holes in its floor, dangerously close to Raif's outstretched legs. As water flooded in, the momentum of Raif's canoe carried him closer to shore, even as Seth laid into the paddle with powerful but steady strokes. When Raif rolled out of the sinking boat, three Indians hit the water and thrashed wildly toward him. To Seth's surprise, Raif, though unarmed, made no effort to distance himself from the Indians. Instead, he repeatedly went under and thrust off the bottom again and again. As the Indians closed the gap, one pulled ahead of the others drawing ever closer to the bobbing Raif. As the lead Indian slowed and reached for his tomahawk, Seth laid his paddle in the floor of the canoe. He quickly shouldered his rifle.

The small waves on the river had little effect upon the heavy raft yet played havoc with the canoe. At one moment, the front bead of Seth's rifle was high above the head of his target, the next it was square in the center of Raif's forehead and then a moment later, it was leveled at the water. And so it went for a couple of cycles before the Indian raised the hatchet high to put an end to Raif. At that point the world was lost to Seth. All things were shut out save the shining brass bead at the end of his barrel and the deadly threat bearing down on his friend. As the sight smoothly swept below the black hairline of the Indian, Seth squeezed the trigger.

What was once a living face broke into pieces and was alive no more. No sooner had the smoking gun landed in the floor of the canoe, than Seth laid hold of the second and

The Treachery

nestled the butt plate to his shoulder. In the midst of it all Raif kept lunging wildly toward Seth even as Seth's canoe glided steadily toward the melee. Each time the big riverman surfaced he babbled and choked some incomprehensibles Seth's way. Seth paid no mind. Having drawn closer, the shot angle facing Seth was much steeper than before. After taking aim, the gun barrel rested square in the center of Raif's chest as he pushed off the bottom once again. As the remaining Indians closed in, Seth eased his finger off the trigger, raised his head off the stock, and coolly assessed the situation. Settling back in, Seth put pressure on the trigger once again. When Raif went under, Seth held off a moment and then squeezed off the shot. The timing was perfect. As the second Indian slowly sank, Raif popped up right in front. As the third treaded water for a stroke or two, Seth took up the paddle again to cover the last few feet to Raif.

"Ah'm shamed ta' say!" hollered Raif as he slipped under the surface. "Dat...hee!...hee!...ah kin read an' write!" coming up again and spitting mouthfuls of water. "But..ah cain't swim a lick!" In spite of the deadly seriousness of the time, a slight smile spread across Seth's face even as the last attacker beat the water into a terrible froth, driven mad with anger at the loss of two braves, madder still that a well-planned trap had in turn trapped them.

As the canoe reached Raif, he clambered to take hold of the bow of the canoe even as he felt a strong hand grab him from behind. Raising a knife of his own, the Indian planned to end the riverside drama once and for all. "Down!" Seth yelled as Raif pulled the bow of the boat low struggling to haul himself to safety. The increased pitch raised Seth above the flashing blade of the attacker even as Raif dutifully squinted his eyes shut and plunged his head toward the bottom of the canoe. Seth gripped the hilt of his long knife with both hands and swung with all his might, screaming at the top of his lungs, transferring every bit of strength to the singing blade as it cut through the air. The blade met his opponent's wrist with a loud "crack" and continued on to catch the Indian just under the jawbone. Without so much as uttering a sound, the Indian's grip loosened as he slipped under the muddy waters. Quickly sheathing his knife, Seth grabbed the top of Raif's waterlogged britches and hauled him aboard. Tumbling in, Raif set the small craft to see-sawing as the current swept them downstream toward the main raft. Taking up the paddle, Seth drew a couple of strokes backward to swing the bow down stream and gain control of the boat. No sooner had Raif uncoiled himself in the front of the canoe than he lit into talking again. "Ha! Ha! All dis time on da' river an' ah don't know how ta' swim! Not a lick! Well dares no hide'in hit now!" Intent on getting back to the crew, Seth paddled on in silence. As they approached, they could see the men on the raft aligned in battle array. Every available rifle was leveled at the near shore of the river, expecting an ambush that never came. After a few awkward moments, Raif continued. "Naw...dares no hide'in hit now...nooo sireee! Hee!...Hee!." As the adrenaline ebbed away Raif continued in a more serious tone. "Ya' done good, Seth...dat ya' did. Ahm pareful sorry 'bout all dis. Ah shouda knowd hit mighta been a trap. Ah heerd a' such but never seed hit." Seth spoke for the first time since the ordeal had ended. "Well we both got an education here! We both are heading back to the raft and that's the important thing. But there is one thing you can do for me Raif." The big man twisted around and arched an eyebrow in Seth's direction. "You really should learn to swim, living on the water the way you do."

  Their laughter could be heard a long way off as the crew laid into the long poles again to get the raft under way. As Seth cast what was left of the mooring line to a deckhand, someone shouted, "Hear! Hear! for young Seth!" As they climbed aboard the men set up a cheer for Seth. He was more than accepted now. He was more than an equal. Seth was a hero and that in the eyes of every man present.

The raft continued its lumbering yet relentless journey south through Arkansas and then through the previously French territory of Louisiana. What the river lost in speed it gained in power. One could sense the ominous deepening of the channel and the broadening of its banks. As a finely honed athlete, the rivulets and currents became like the rippling of steely muscles and sinews, flexing in power between the broad shoulders of brushy banks and levees, unstoppable in its surge to the Gulf of Mexico. Even then the briny green of the wide ocean yielded to the mountains of silt carried down from the continent above. Massive brown plumes pushed out for leagues into the Gulf driving back Neptune's realm with ease. For all of this, the river was a land-mover and a land-maker, building up square miles of delta at its mouth. It was a deceiver taking away *terra firma* and replacing it with a confusing patch of swirling eddies, and then suddenly, piling up sandbanks where there were none just moments before. In the end, the people along its edge abode in the shadow of its benevolent mercy, drawing freely from the river's bounty, yet only a spring's storm away from sudden destruction. You could work on the river, live by the river, even swim in the river, but you could never fight against the river. Within its banks, it was the master of all, and nothing on earth, especially frail humanity, could alter that fact.

In the lazy weeks to come, Seth sensed that they were running ahead of winter. The fall foliage of the lower Ozarks gave way to the rich and humid land of the lower Mississippi. Although never experienced before, Seth anticipated the coming of a warm Christmas. In the meantime, he went through his chores on the raft as an

Seth Garner: Part One

expert now, not thinking about what he was doing, but simply doing it well by rote. Gone were the days of awkward strides and lurches across uneven logs, dropping tackle over the side and such. He had forgotten those early days and so had the crew. His thoughts were more caught up with where he was on the inside than with what was happening on the outside.

The fight to save Raif's life was an unfolding lesson for Seth. He learned that he was powerful in his body and his power was matched by his speed. He could act and act quickly when needed. He learned too that in some way he had been granted incredible eyesight. In a flash he could bring power and speed to bear down on what he saw with deadly effect. For all of this he experienced something that he had not felt since he fled Heathshire in Boston. He felt confident.

But the fight taught not just by giving answers but by raising questions as well. He was troubled not a little that he had killed three men. Indeed, if he had gathered anything from his frontier-preaching father, those he had killed were real men, just as he, regardless of their race or creed. He was troubled too that he could not wrap his mind around the forces that led to the conflict in the first place. How could a white woman conspire against her own people to commit such treachery? How could she appeal to the tender mercies of human care to bring about ruin? What was the purpose of the ambush? Surely the slaughter of his friend Raif would do nothing to stem the tide of white settlers pouring into the Mississippi Valley. What concerned him most was that he was forced to kill in order to save his friend. He was truly sorry for that, but he did not regret it. Indeed, from his time on the raft, he had come to know that there is a real difference between sorrow and regret. Somehow he knew too that this difference would play a large part in his life from here on out. There would be times for sorrow; sorrow for what had to be done. But at the same time, there would be no cause for regret.

Seth Garner: Part One

Battle in the Bayou

At last, the word came that the city of New Orleans was but a few days downstream. From that time on, the tenor of the crew changed dramatically. The men spoke little and no one gathered about smoldering embers of the fire to tell stories late into the night. Instead there was a shuffling and a gathering and a binding up. This was the frontiersmen's way of saying goodbye without actually saying it. All knew that the big float south was coming to an end, and with that, so would their time together.

As the crew disembarked on the outskirts of the grand city, they drew their pay and went their separate ways. Some headed back north, others pressed further west, while a few loitered about the city waiting for the next phase of their lives to unfold. Seth and Raif were among this last group. They didn't have long to wait. The city was preparing for war.

New Orleans was a jewel in the crown of the young nation. The city numbered among the five largest in America, but its strategic importance outweighed its numbers. Whoever controlled New Orleans held sway over the heart of the continent. All river traffic bent on shipping goods to the Gulf of Mexico and all international trade flowing in from the gulf must come through New Orleans. To capture New Orleans was to seize America by the throat. To that end, the British had assembled an expeditionary force of nearly 20,000 men to take New Orleans. Of this number, over a thousand were black soldiers from Jamaica, Barbados and the Bahamas, the British staging ground for the attack. Under the command of General Edward Pakenham, fifty British warships had already anchored off the mouth of the Mississippi. Armed to the gunwales, they awaited his order to strike. Some British forces had already sailed into Lake Borgne. They

Seth Garner: Part One

secretly made their way up Bayou Bienvenue just east of New Orleans. The enemy was within eight miles of the city and was poised to attack.

Raif lost no time making his way to the conscription office, beckoning Seth to tag along. All the while Seth protested that he knew nothing of soldiering. "Jist stay close an' let me do da' talkin'," Raif assured. "Dare a'needin' fightin' men, an' you da' bess raffle shot ah seed. Dey'll sign ya up, yu'll see." The recruiter had no qualms about signing Raif on, but cast a doubtful eye at young Seth. "Oh! Dis'un...heeza scout, an' a dern goodun ta' boot! An' he can shoot da' fuzz off a peach at'a hunnert yard!" With that recommendation, Seth became a soldier.

In short order Seth gathered that he was not the only one who had not tasted of battle. The American national treasury was nearly empty and had precious little funds to conduct war. So with no standing army at the ready, New Orleans' hope lay in a rag-tag lot of volunteers. The "army" consisted of buckskin-clad folks like Raif and Seth. They were called "Kaintocks" by the locals. Of the same spirit but of a totally different quarter were the pirates of Barataria. These French brigands mostly sailed outside the law, but they had one thing in common with the Americans; a burning hatred of the British. Their commander was the flamboyant Jean Laffite. In return for fighting with the Americans, he had negotiated amnesty for past transgressions, both for himself and for his men. Emancipated slaves, or free persons of color, joined in the fight as well. These comprised the First and Second Battalions of Free Men of Color, and numbered about six-hundred men. Their commanding officers were drawn from their own ranks and they were the first fighting force of its kind in America. Even Choctaw Indian warriors cast their lot with the Americans at this dire point in her history. The Choctaws hated the pro-British Creeks, and

Battle in the Bayou

this was enough to draw them over to the American side. Yet perhaps the most strategically important force was the inhabitants of the bayou country, the Cajuns, those immigrants of French descent who counted the Louisiana swamp as their home. They were the eyes and ears of the entire undertaking and in a real sense the fate of the city was in their hands.

This unlikely assembly of patriots and partisans, outnumbered by almost five to one, all came together for one audacious purpose: to stand down the best equipped and most highly trained army in the world. All of them, Seth included, were the only thing standing between the hard fought gains of the American Revolution and Britain's bid to hold on to vast tracts of the American interior.

Within a few hours. Seth joined a band of other scouts, most of which were not American at all, but French. They were indeed the pirates who were under the command of Jean Laffite, the deadly privateer and sworn enemy of the British. For some time Laffite plied the waters of Barataria Bay of southeast Louisiana, wreaking havoc on anything that might fall prey to his canon. So Laffite and his men were just the kind of help that the Americans needed. They were native to this strange and dark land and knew it intimately. So for his part, Seth was more than glad to be in their company. The briefing of the scouts was to the point and their mission was clear. Travel south along the river undetected and meet the enemy. Take stock of their numbers, provisions, and if possible, their intended movements. Return under cover of darkness and report. That was all. By midnight Seth found himself pressing deep into the delta, far out ahead of his own troops, on reconnaissance.

He and his French partner slipped silently down river in cypress pirogues, these craft being little more than narrow wooden shells with only a couple of inches of

Seth Garner: Part One

freeboard above the water. But his pirate friend handled the boat as if it was part of his own body. On the other hand, Seth was at a complete loss as they glided through the night. His only point of orientation was the occasional "No! No!" and "Oui! Oui!" of the French paddler behind him. By contrast, the Frenchman laid into the paddle with confidence for he knew exactly where he was going. He was going home. This French privateer had been born and raised in the murky swamps of the delta country. After some hours, the clattering of materiel could be heard up ahead. Seth looked behind but his mate paddled on. When the unmistakable scent of campfires was met, the pirate gave a few quick strokes to one side and they were ashore.

Seth belly-crawled to within a stone's throw of the British lines. Guttural commands hissed throughout the camp. Above the din that always accompanies preparation for battle, Seth could clearly hear strange voices, but could make no sense of them. Neither could any of his fellow scouts. Jean Lafitte's men explained the dilemma in broken English. "Monsieur Seth, zee soldiers, zee no parley Englais. Zee soldiers are vom zee islands of zee Caribbean; Jamaica...Barbados...Bahamas. Zee parley Carib. Dat tongue is vom Africa! An doze dat zee Engais dey speak, zey vom Schottland!" Indeed, Cajun informants had said as much in recent days. These French immigrants from Acadia had escaped from Canada in search of religious freedom. They chose the French-speaking portion of Louisiana as their new home. Sending down deep roots in the black soil of the delta, they knew every inch of the bayou country. Nothing passed through these dark swamps without their knowledge. They had already told notables in New Orleans that "foreigners" were among the British invaders. This came as no surprise to those familiar with the British war machine. They knew that George Washington had fought Hessian mercenaries at Trenton during the Revolutionary War. These Prussia soldiers were fighting for a fee, serving their British paymasters' vain attempt to hold onto a crumbling empire. So once again, the English crown had employed professional soldiers to kill Americans.

As Seth lay facedown in the marsh, he struggled to appraise the strength of the enemy, and if possible to know something of their strategy. Campfires sent out luminous orbs through the thick fog. Men and materiel appeared as ghostly figures, nondescript through the gauzy haze. That combined with the strange tongue dashed any hope of getting accurate information. As the mumbling and shadows continued, Seth's heart sank. He knew his commanders would want details, not impressions. This much was sure: the British invasion force was an awesome machine going through the motions of war. They were professional soldiers bent on completing another foreign campaign. Seth could tell that the British were supremely confident of the outcome. They would crush the Americans, take control of New Orleans and then return to their homes oversees.

The situation of the American defenders at Chalmette plantation could not have been more different. They were not fighting for a fee, but for a future. They had no certainty of the outcome. Fueled by a mixture of fear and indignation, these young patriots were determined to fight to their last ounce of strength. The grating sound of whet stones against steel bayonets sent a chilling message throughout the American camp. Grant no quarter to the enemy. Their lives or yours, and your family's beside.

They were glad to have Andrew Jackson as their supreme commander. "Old Hickory" had proved himself a merciless foe in battle. In truth he was tougher than hickory, born to fight...and to win. His fighting spirit was not confined to the battlefield, either. Jackson would engage in at least thirteen duels in his lifetime, the most celebrated of which was with Charles Dickenson. It was this duel that would define the cold, steely nerve of Jackson under fire.

Dickenson had impugned Jackson's honor, accusing him of infidelity and bigamy. For a gentleman of the South, such an insult could not go unanswered. Jackson penned a fiery note to Dickenson demanding satisfaction on the field of honor.

Dickenson was a quick and accurate shot. Jackson was neither. Ever the realist, Jackson's strategy was as fierce as his character: let Dickenson fire first, take the slug, recover, hold steady, then gun him down.

On the day of the duel, Jackson draped a large dark blue coat over his slender frame. Survival was measured in inches in this deadly game, and perhaps the slack coat would be enough for Jackson. As Dickenson raised his pistol to shoot, Jackson stood stock still awaiting the impact of bullet. Witnesses saw a small fleck of dust erupt from Jackson's coat on his left side. He clasped his hand over his heart and bent forward slightly. A crimson stain quickly spread across Jackson's chest. His left boot began to fill with blood. "My God! Have I missed him?!" Dickenson exclaimed as he stepped back in horror. "Back to the mark, sir!" shouted Jackson's second, a kind of referee present to make sure that the rules of engagement were followed to the letter. To his credit, Dickenson stepped forward, folded his arms and faced Jackson. In the meantime, Jackson straightened up, raised his weapon, took careful aim and fired. Dickenson crumpled to the ground never to rise again. Jackson refused help as he feebly limped to his carriage. Once inside, he collapsed to the floor. When medical help arrived, it was quickly determined that the wound was inoperable. The bullet was lodged just inches below Jackson's heart. Massive blood loss so weakened his body that he lay motionless in bed for a month. Yet Jackson refused to die. He literally willed himself back to health and within weeks was commanding troops on the field of battle. Indeed, that thumb-sized chunk of lead nestled just below the general's heart as he planned to beat the British in New Orleans.

Seth pushed up from the rich dark soil of the delta and made his way back to the pirogue. Upon arrival, he motioned for his French friend to shove off. "No...no...Monsieur Seth. Zee Englais vill meet zee Debil right 'ear and dat Debil vill be French! Vive la France! Vive la Americans! Vive Jean Lafitte!" In vain, Seth tried to hush his French compatriot. Considering the number of British soldiers at hand, Seth figured that one more "Vive!" would get them all killed. So he leapt into the pirogue alone, rocking wildly right and left, slapping the water hard on each side to stay upright. He could hear his French partners laughing as he zigzagged through the marsh threading his way back to New Orleans.

Seth had paid no attention on the outward journey of the mission. There was no need. The pirates of Jean Lafitte were the best guides that one could hope for. But it had not occurred to him that he would travel back alone. Thus he became completely disoriented on the return trip to New Orleans. With luck, however, he finally slipped into to the main channel of the river. Once there, his plan was to simply paddle against the current until he intercepted the American lines. Even so he strayed up one false cut after another, only to run aground time and time again. Overhanging limbs raked across his face as he looked up into a moonless night sky. With each stroke, Seth sensed the confidence that he had gained on the raft ebbing away. Alas the faint gray light of dawn revealed some of the spires of the city. He was exhausted both physically and mentally. He was totally unprepared for what was to come.

Seth Garner: Part One

No sooner had Seth stepped out of the pirogue, than he was spirited away for debriefing. The weight of his report bore down hard on Seth. The British had already captured five American gunboats on Lake Borgne. A more serious skirmish occurred on the Villeré plantation on December 23rd. In this fight, the British had sustained nearly 300 wounded and almost 50 killed. The American suffered a little over 200 wounded and some 25 killed. Although the fighting ended in a stalemate, but the cost was high on both sides. All of this meant that the big fight to come was going to be a bloody one.

He was taken into a small tent and surprised to see just about every officer seated inside. Now these were *real* soldiers. Bedecked in immaculate uniforms, their very presence emanated strength and surety, as they smoked small cigars and talked in low tones. One medaled warrior barked, "Scout Garner, report!" Seth slowly rose to his feet; his hulking body making the cramped quarters feel even more crowded. He cut a striking figure. Tall, broad shouldered, heavily muscled. But his blond hair was mud-spattered and a thorny briar had made a red welt across his cheek. His eyes were opened wide as he slowly panned from one side of the tent to the other, overawed by the military bearing of the officers. He swallowed twice trying to repress the growing fear welling up in his throat. He sensed that this meeting was not going to turn out well. "Well son...do you have something to report?" Seth could sense the tension in the officer's voice as if he were trying to control his anger or refrain from shouting. "Well sir... there are a lot of them, and they are well armed." After a few awkward seconds and sidewise glances, an explosion of laughter erupted from the officers. One soldier jeered, "And the army pays scouts for this?" "All quiet!" the order came. Each officer tried to put on the best poker face he could manage while the blood-red flush of Seth's face slowly ebbed away. A few muffled giggles leaked out here and there just the same. Gaining his composure, the officer asked kindly, "Son, do you have anything else that might help us win this battle?" "Yes . . . I believe I do," came Seth's firm reply. He stood in silence slowly nodding his head in the affirmative. The officer pulled off a kid glove and raked his hand across his face as if to sweep away his nose and mouth. Taking a deep breath he leaned forward to within inches of Seth. With trembling voice he commenced again. "Well then son...take your time and share with us what you know." "They are fixing to march northward....generally...in our direction...as far as I can tell." Another roar of laughter fairly shook the tent to tatters. Mortified, Seth feebly protested, "The fog...and the language...and the Caribs. . . " "Dismissed!" groaned the officer in disgust even as Seth tried to redeem himself. A nameless soldier took Seth firmly by the arm and pushed him through the tent flap into the early morning air. So ended Seth's first official mission for his country.

 He skulked from the tent and eventually found Raif. As he hunkered down behind a massive cotton bale, for there was no finer means of defense in this boggy country, Raif could sense that Seth was smarting from his first "intelligence report." After hearing the embarrassing details of the meeting, he tried to comfort his friend. "Ya' toll 'em rat. Eva' body knows dat plans iz da' furs ta' go in wore. Why ya' coulda tol'em da' drawers size of eva British solja an' da' number of each piece of enmy artillry an' hit woodah made no difference. Dares gonna' be fightin' an' plenny of hit. Plain and simple. Dat's da' only thang dat ya' can count on when da' time comes. If by da' grace of da' Almighty we kilt more a' dem, den we win. On da' utter hand...."

 January 8th dawned swathed in a gray shroud of thick fog. Suddenly, through the gloom, a bright flash on the horizon caused every head to snap to the source. An instant later a cannon ball slammed into a rain soaked cotton bale with a thud. The shock telegraphed for a hundred yards in both directions up and down the rampart. In what seemed to be a ridiculous span of time, a booming blast followed, rattling their eardrums. The ratcheting of rifle hammers commenced as if on cue. Suddenly a white stallion raced lengthwise behind the American defenses, its rider calling out, "Hold your fire! Hold ...your... fire!" It was "Old Hickory" himself. The enemy cannon were not really in range yet. The ball that hit their ramparts had actually skipped across the ground like a flat stone on the surface of a pond. It was a "test fire" so to speak, just to see if the Americans were green enough to burn powder to no effect, and to reveal their weaknesses besides. They had passed the test. Not so much as a musket answered from the American side. It would take more than battlefield tricks to defeat this group.

Moments later the fife and drum corps announced that things were about to begin in earnest. It seemed a perverse thing that the prelude to slaughter was a jolly tune. In the gray light of dawn, Seth could barely see the Union Jack wafting in a slight breeze. Then a series of flashes on the horizon silhouetted the advancing army. This time, well within range, the cannon balls smacked the cotton bales like a rifle shot. The concussion knocked the wind out of every American soldier leaning against them at the point of impact. But still, the bales held. Seth detected a murmuring whisper on its way down the picket to his right. "Don't shoot til' ya' see da whites of dey eyes! Pass it on," was the message. Whether this had come from Old Hickory or not, the meaning was plain. Don't waste powder. Make every shot a kill. Adrenalin was pouring into every living pulse along the line. The time had come.

Battle in the Bayou

Seth saw "whites," yet still, no one fired. His keen eyesight had pierced the gloom well ahead of his fellow soldiers. When he could see "blacks" within "the whites," he could forbear no more and squeezed off a shot. An instant later a roar of musket fire erupted from the American side. It didn't matter. Seth had factored out all else except the poor, nameless soul on the killing end of his rifle. He saw the redcoat tip back on his heels like a wooden doll. This was the fourth man that he had sent on to his reward. He felt no emotion at all. For a second it bothered him that he was not bothered, yet he handed the spent weapon to a "loader" at the rear, and without taking his eye off the enemy, he took hold of a newly charged rifle. He had already settled upon his next target, and neatly dropped him in his tracks.

When the smoke had cleared after the first volley, ominous gaps appeared throughout the British lines. Mechanically, in old European style, the spaces were dutifully filled by soldiers from the rear. Seth thought, "Tradition can be deadly." He shouted to Raif, "You think they would've learned since Concord!" There the Redcoats had applied Old World tactics to a New World army. Repeatedly they had marched shoulder to shoulder in match set fashion into a hail of gunfire that came from all directions, right, left, fore and aft, even from overhead. Colonists were firing from behind rocks and trees, and down from every window leading away from Concord Bridge. As the British fled in disarray the "rebels" filtered ahead and wreaked havoc on the fleeing mayhem. The Americans had learned these tactics from the Indians. They had paid a heavy price for their education, but they had learned all the same. The British had not.

As the American cannons creaked back for the reload, the chilling command rang out, "Gunneries load! Grape shot!" War is orchestrated cruelty driven along by a

Seth Garner: Part One

ravenous hunger that's never satisfied. Lead shot, cast in grape-like form, blasted by the thousands from the gaping maws of a score of cannon, is nothing short of a harbinger from hell. But as an anti-personnel weapon, grapeshot is a friend of the battlefield. As the cannon belched forth their lethal load, the British lines fell like spring grass before newly sharpened scythes. Bodies and parts of bodies lifted into the air like marionettes on a string. Moreover, General Pakenham fell from his horse, shot through and through, mortally wounded, only moments from death.

Enemy resistance crumbled. Incredibly, as if on command, the entire British assault force turned on its heels and made for the mouth of the river. Jackson's forces fired another volley at the backs of the fleeing Redcoats. At that moment another sound met the ears of those crouched behind the cotton bales. It was the clatter and thumping of weapons, drums and of anything else that might impede a panicked retreat, hitting the ground as the drive to survive swept over the fleeing mass. The rout had begun, and once started, there was no stopping it. Again, the American commanders bawled out, "Fix bayonets! Charge!" Countless bodies scrambled over the bails and fell upon the hapless invaders like hounds on a hare. Seth's pulse quickened as he clawed and scrambled his way up and over the rampart. In moments, he was caught up in the unbridled fury of the victor over the vanquished. In short order, the game was clear. The wounded were pierced through without regard. White-hot lead tore through the backs of British soldiers, infantry and officers alike.

It was one thing to fire on a company of men at over a hundred yards. It is quite another to look a dying man straight in the eye at arm's length. At a distance the British were "the enemy." Up close they looked unsettlingly familiar. The face of the enemy was a human face. As the Americans pressed forward, what Seth saw was like a dark scene from hell. He had the strong illusion that he was striding along in a nightmare. The shifting fog strengthened the notion that all was unreal. As each boot pounded blood-splattered soil, he expected to awake to normalcy, yet unimagined carnage unfolded before him. It was hard to believe that so much damage was inflicted in just a few minutes. Partially dismembered bodies still housed doomed souls, their dwindling presence in this world only made known by ever weakening moans, trailing off into silence. The humid mists from the river softened the heart-stopping terror of the field, and Seth was vaguely grateful for that. But even this unexpected mercy from nature was stripped away in an instant. Somewhere from behind a powder magazine exploded, forcing brilliant light through the gloom ahead. In a split second, in a flash, the horrid aftermath of battle was burned into Seth's mind. At the speed of light the apocalypse bypassed conscious thought, registering on a subliminal level, yet in unnerving detail. Mental etchings of figures were imprinted in a moment; ghastly figures unfit for mortal eyes, completely devoid of human decency, stripped of all dignity. "God no!" he cried out involuntarily, hearing his own voice as if it called from another. Now his lungs pumped like great bellows, wildly out of control, driven not by fatigue, but by sheer terror. As he staggered forward, a fragment of the flash vision he had just received floated into consciousness. He had seen, off to his left, a quavering arm of a British soldier, barely lifted, fingers outstretched, beckoned for help. Without thinking Seth veered off in that direction. In less than thirty yards, the man loomed into view. He sat upright, his back propped against the belly of a warhorse, one already stiffening under the grip of death. The man looked to be in his thirties, and as far as Seth could tell, wore the trappings of an officer. A single piece of grapeshot had driven through the soldier's midsection, ripping through his stomach and snapping his spine. Disemboweled and paralyzed from the waist down, the young officer was twice dead already, even though he appeared quite comfortable in his awkward repose. Even as Seth was folding into a knelling position beside him, he heard the fallen warrior croak forth, "Water!" Continuing the motion to his knees, Seth groped after the small flask fastened to his belt. As he untied the canteen, he caught a glimpse of movement in his peripheral vision. Slowly turning to lift the canteen to the fallen soldier's lips, Seth starred straight into the bore of a British pistol, hammer cocked, a sickly gray finger steadily applying what strength it had left to pull the trigger.

In less time than it takes for a trap to spring, events crashed together crowding out all things normal. Seth's arm, the one that bore the canteen, continued its arc, yet jerked left as if hit by an electric jolt. Even so his head veered to the right, his free arm dropping to his thigh. A deafening roar erupted just left of his temple, as he felt, yet did not hear his own lips form, "No, you fool!" Blazing light blinded his vision, but not before he took in the crazed grin from the one he sought to help. Blistering heat seared the side of his face as he caught the sickening scent of his own hair burning. The toes of his boots dug deep into the damp soil as he heaved his weight against the hilt of his knife, now deeply buried in the chest of the officer. Somehow, by impulse more than plan, he had unsheathed the long-knife from his thigh, wrapped his massive hands about its haft, all the while steering its deadly point home. As his momentum carried him forward, Seth's face came to rest just beside the one of his pitied victim. Above the ringing in his ears, Seth heard him breathe his last in a thick cockney brogue, "Good form, laddie. Jolly good form."

With that Seth uttered a sound more like a beast than a man, drawing forth the blade as he sprinted backwards, falling to the ground, propped up on both elbows, reeling in mind and body. "Why?" he thought. "The senseless, cursed, stupidity of the thing!" Oddly, Seth felt no malice toward the man that had betrayed his kindness and nearly took his life.

Rising to his feet, Seth took up his rifle and sheathed the long-knife again. To his surprise his thoughts turned to his own father, connecting with words spoken about a kitchen table, in a home filled with acceptance and love. Prayers for the less fortunate had been prayed there. Forgiveness for those who deserved none was implored there. "Father, remember nothing of this wretched day! Hold none of the sins committed here against us or against them! Have mercy on this poor one and grant him peace. And lastly, have mercy on me!"

A massive explosion rocked Seth to the core, knocking him to the ground. His eyes dimmed for a moment, then cleared. A siren was ringing in his ears and he could vaguely sense the chaos of war rushing past him. His mind was clouded. His hands and fingers tingled with numbness; he couldn't stand. For an instant his pulse quickened at the thought of being paralyzed. Just as quickly though, he could hear clearly again and when he felt the damp ground beneath him, he pushed up and lurched forward. Without thinking, he began to run, picked up speed and hurried toward an unknown destination.

The Americans were held up only by the materiel that littered the battlefield. They pursued the British without mercy, cheering each other on with shouts and hair-raising war cries. Once again Seth found himself caught up in the onslaught. Within moments his mood had swung from the cool competence of a rifleman nestled behind barricades, to the benumbed state of near death, to the intoxicating joy that he was still alive and rushing on to glory. So, on he ran in the melee, following the tip of his bayonet as it pierced the rags of fog that still lingered here and there. Soon a red coat loomed up before him. As the man twisted about in full stride, Seth could see the terror of the defeated spread across his face. Without thinking, Seth ran him through, smoothly turned to his right, withdrew the bayonet and raced on.

In short order the Americans were within the British encampment. Officers were being captured and still yet a shot was fired here and there. Seth struggled to keep in check a savage exhilaration born along by the absolute command of victory. It was his first taste of this rare state of lawlessness called "war." The only rules in play were those of his own making. He consciously laid hold of them as he raged on amidst the carnage that turned to pillage. Bursting into a field officer's tent, he was immediately met by an odd sight. It was as if the parlor of an aristocratic dandy had been transported to the black soil of the bayou. Pure wax tapers still burned in fine silver candle holders. A white linen cloth graced a fold-down mahogany table. In the corner was a mattressed bed bedecked with pure white flax and lace, canopied with the most delicate mosquito netting. On the table was an opened bottle of brandy with a half-filled snifter at its side. Close by was a wired pedestal cradling a bottle of French champagne. His time on the river convinced him that he was not a drinking man; however he didn't begrudge those who took a dram or two. Not so his father. Nathaniel Adam roundly condemned the stuff by the drop or the barrel. More like his mother, Seth felt more pity than loathing for those held captive by "the devil's drink" as she called it. Yet for the sake of the good reverend, Seth hefted the butt of his rifle and smashed the bottle of brandy to pieces. In like manner, he shattered the champagne, crumpling its wire vase into a twisted heap. Stepping back he spied an oddment amidst all the finery. A little brown jug was nestled in the corner of the tent. He recalled how some of the barge men jested about getting their corn from a bottle and thought, "The British despise all things American, but not *all* things, especially from the hills of Kentucky!" But as the humble crockery jug also burst into shards, a strange tinkling sound mingled in with the crash. Seth was stunned to see a golden cascade of coins flow out onto the floor of the tent. As he reached down and picked up a handful of newly minted American gold pieces, a long human shadow cast upon the canvas before him. Wheeling around with bayonet at the ready, he was relieved to see his old friend Raif. "Da' sperls a' wore son! Da' sperls a' wore! Keep hit close to ya. Hit'll cum in handy!" Raif slipped backwards through the tent flaps, grinning from ear to ear and casually waving a farewell high above his three-cornered leather hat.

The bugler sounded a series of blasts that signaled to break off the attack. The British were running for their lives. They had been roundly defeated and enough blood had been spilled to drive home the message: don't trifle with the Americans. The newly formed nation was young, inexperienced and at times at odds with itself, yet still it was a forced to be reckoned with.

Within hours of returning to camp decommissioning was under way. Shouts of victory were mixed in with the moans of the wounded. The British had lost over 2,000 men while the Americans lost only 70. The Battle of New Orleans marked a resounding victory for the Americans.

The clatter of returning arms and equipment filled the air even while kegs of gun powder and canon were loaded onto wagons. The military efficiency that had prepared for war was now thrown into reverse. The whole of the operation together with each of its parts was being shut down, packed away and accounted for. This was the end of war. Somehow in the midst of all the hustle and bustle, it

Seth Garner: Part One

became known that the paymaster was ready to settle up with each soldier. As if on queue a ragged line soon formed and Seth shouldered his way in. At the end of a long and harrowing day, Seth received his soldier's pay. As he milled around in the fading light of dusk, Seth was surprised to see the familiar profile of Raif. Waiving him over, Raif led him to a smoldering fire slowly warming a welcomed pot of coffee.

Crouching low near the fire, Raif poured Seth a cup. Seth too folded on his heels, smothered the zinc cup in his huge hands, and looked across the fire at his old friend. Oddly quiet, especially for Raif, the weathered riverman looked off wistfully as Seth sipped his coffee in silence. The battle had taken its toll on all. Indeed, Seth was practically drained of all strength. But Raif looked worse than tired; he looked used up. Taking a long draft of the steaming brew, Raif finally spoke. "Well, Seth...ah'd say we done alright. Jist drinkin' dis here coffee tiz proof a' dat!" Seth nodded in agreement. "We dun our part fur Ole Glory...agin!" he added, ending with a nervous laugh. Once more, a prolonged and award stillness filled the air. Stirring the embers with a broken stick, Raif got to the point at hand. "Seth...ah giss ya' know b'now dat we dun hit da' end of da' line, so ta' speak." "Well, we floated south. I know that much. We can't float north," mused Seth as he took another swallow of coffee. "But we could go west," he added with a glint of adventure in his eyes. His words were not so much a suggestion as an invitation. "Dat we could....indeed...we could do jist dat," Raif affirmed. "But Seth," he offered with a sigh, "an' ah want'cha ta' heer me good...ahm a'feered ahm too long in da' toof fur dat trip. Na... maybe more'n twenty year ago... when ah wuz za young blood like yessef, ah'd beat'cha to da' Pecos, ah wager ah would!" "You'll have no wager from me, Raif. I'm too fond of my money! You'd be way ahead of me, no doubt." Raif smiled, opened his eyes wide and raised his cup in salute to Seth. "Where will we go from here, Raif?" "*We*?" he parried, knitting bushy eyebrows together in real concern. "I'm sticking with you, Raif. Where you go I go." "Naw, Seth. Ah caint let'cha do dat. Like ah' says, ahm too long in da' toof. Fact iz, Seth....ah'd jist slow ya' down, not at first, but directly, ah'd slow ya' down." Seth stood to his feet even as Raif motioned him to be seated again. Settling back down, Raif continued. "Na' Seth, you're a' wonder. An' ah do mean dat! Ah knowd hit da' time ya' smolderin' carcass landed on ma' flatboat a way up on da' Ohio. Dat's why ah pressed da point of work right off. In a moment, ah could tell dat ah wanted ya ta stay." Again, Raif took a couple of sips in silence. "What ahm a'meanin' ta' say iz dat, Seth, ya'z bound to da' future, whereaz fur me..." Raif's voice broke off as he stared blankly across the fire. "Whereaz fur me..." his lip betraying the slightest quiver, "what ah' mean iz dares more behind me dan dares ahead a' me." "Yes, that's true. But what's behind you, Raif, is better than what's ahead of me!" "Naw...naw...Seth. Ah thank ye, anyways." "What will you do, Raif? Where will you go?" "Oh, ah bleeve dares one more float in me, maybe two! Ah don't know...but ah do know diss, dat fur facts beyond me, da' good Lord took keer a' me ta' now, an' dares nuttin' afoot ta' make a change...nuttin' dat ah knowd of...leeswise." With that Raif slowly rose to his feet, again looking mournfully into the coals. Seth followed suit as the silence dragged on. Again, Raif spoke first. "Ya' know. . . a body's a wonderful thang, Seth, but in da' end, dat one thang ya' truly have in dis life, well hit kind 'a turns on ya. Yeah,..hit surely do." Seth nodded knowingly but said nothing as the fire crackled softly on. Even as Raif's eyes moistened, work-worn hands wiped a tear away. "My, dat's a smoky fire!" he said as a nervous laugh trailed away. "It is Raif, a fire ought not smoke that way." Raif

Seth Garner: Part One

looked up as a nervous smile spread across his face. "Ya' know Seth. . . ah' never had a famly to speak of. A'course, ah never had a fine son like yessef, needer." As moments past on in silence, Raif pinched his eyes between thumb and forefinger and said, "Yeah...rat smokey, dat far is!" Stepping back and looking off to the side, Raif continued, "Nah. . . Seth...ah never did." Not really knowing what to say, Seth held out his hand. Raif ignored the handshake, spread his arms wide and wrapped Seth in a big bear hug. Turning about, he shrugged his shoulders a bit and walked off into the night. As he slowly disappeared, he called out over his shoulder, "Ya take keer now, Seth! Remember da' sequence! Ya be quick now, when ya' have too!" and other such counsel. As darkness closed about the only friend that Seth had in the world, he whispered, "And 'D' is for 'dog' Raif, remember that, 'D' is for 'dog'."

With Raif gone, Seth was truly left to his own thoughts. It seemed strange to him that just a couple of hours before he was empowered to wreak wanton slaughter on his fellow man. Now with coins in hand, he was expected to conduct himself as a perfect gentleman, to honor the laws of the land and to seek the benefit of his neighbor. Yet the decommissioning had little effect on Seth. His heart was still driven with the passions of a war, and he wondered if it was so with his fellow soldiers. He pondered too, how long it would take, if ever, until he felt differently. There was one thing, though, that he was sure of: the schoolboy from Boston was long gone. There could be no turning back now. As he pushed through the crowds, he made peace with this fact: he would never be the same again.

Parting the shimmering portal, he entered a strange world.

Two Madams and a Princess

Traveling east from Chalmette, Seth followed the long line of soldiers making their way to the river ferry. As they slowly floated over to the east bank, the sounds of celebration met their ears. Word of the British defeat spread quickly and the entire city was in a joyous mood. The ferry docked at the mouth of a manmade canal that led deep into the heart of New Orleans. It was here that wagons laden with cotton, tobacco and food crops were offloaded directly onto barges. From there the cargo was hoisted onto ships that carried American made goods throughout the world. The converse was true as well. The finery of Europe and all the spices of the West Indies flowed into New Orleans and eventually made their way

177

Seth Garner: Part One

up river as far north as St. Louis and then east to Pittsburg and beyond. So New Orleans was the place where large sums of money changed hands, both legal and illegal, oiling the wheels of commerce. The casinos and bars that lined the Reux de Bourbon stood ready to take their share of the profits. After the Battle of New Orleans such enterprises smoothly diverted the thrill of battle into those dalliances that corrupt the soul and empty the pocket book. As Seth stepped off the ferry, the exotic and alluring offerings of New Orleans were literally at his footsteps.

Hawkers and street merchants shouted at Seth as he walked down the boardwalk. Lively music spilled into the streets and Seth saw sights that should not have been seen. The flickering lamplight, singing, laughter and confusion of smells fairly overwhelmed his senses as he continued on into the city. As he bumped and staggered on through the carnival atmosphere, he was suddenly seized by a ravenous hunger. He had been running on pure adrenalin for the past two days, and as his system returned to even keel he craved food as never before. As a weathered Cajun lugging a pallet of gator hides drew near, Seth called out, "Sir, could you tell me where a man can get a hot meal around here?" "Wi, Monsieur! When ya' smell zee' fleur de bois, ya' knō ya' dare!" he replied, leaning harder into the load, not lessening his gait. "Fluer de bois?" Seth shouted after him. "Zee flowers made of zee wood, Monsieur!" he called over his shoulder as he turned down a darkened lane. Puzzled yet more hungry than ever, Seth pressed on in his quest for food. Rich aromas flowed from every tavern and casino along the way, and Seth was tempted to turn in at a number of them. And then, like an invisible hand, a spice-laden scent stopped him in his tracks and fairly dragged him toward one smoke-filled kitchen. A finely carved flower was pinioned to the doorpost. Below it was inscribed, "Fleur de Lis." "When you smell the wooden flower," Seth mused, "this must be the place!" As he stepped through the open door, the clatter of tableware and undecipherable chatter filled the air. Soldiers, pirates and black marketeers devoured foodstuffs as thick and murky as the bayou itself. "Well ya' goin' ta' set yasef down, o' stan' gawkin' tru da' nite!?" Seth turned to see a mountain of a black man looming over steaming cauldrons, wielding a stirring paddle in his right hand and a butcher's knife in his left. "No sir... I mean yes sir... I am going to sit down... I'm hungry," said Seth. "No suh" and "Yes suh." If dat dōn bern da' buttah! Ahz a freed man a' culah, but ah dun nevah heerd dat befo!" he bellowed out, finishing off with a laugh that raddled stoneware plates and mugs strewn about. The rabble followed suit cackling and wheezing out gaffs punctuated with swearwords and pipe smoke.

Slavery in the Deep South was a tragic and strange affair, a system of injustice sanctioned by the law. The jovial cook that greeted Seth was part of the unjust system that in time would threaten the liberty that had birthed the nation. A freedman or woman of color was a former slave that had been liberated by their master. As such they could own property and run a business, some becoming quite wealthy. New Orleans was a haven for freed persons of color, and had no laws segregating the races on this score. Yet by law freedmen and women could not marry in the city. They would have to travel a little ways up river to Natchez, Mississippi to start a family. Such were the vagaries of the law.

The swarthy cook strode up to the table, his thick brow furrowed as if waiting for something. "I'd like to have a look at my choices, if you will," proffered Seth. The cook rolled his eyes about weary sockets as the regulars dipped their heads behind playing cards and tankards of ail to hide their chagrin. "Weez got tu tings, an jus tu tings.

Seth Garner: Part One

Crawfish Etouffée and red beans n' rice wit Andouille sausage! So wat's goin' down da hatch ta nite fuh yuz?" he barked. "Well, I'll take both, if you please," Seth responded with relish. "Yu'll regret it!" called one from a dimly lit corner. "Dats iffen he lives ta' da'morra!" cat called another. But they were wrong on both scores. Seth did live to see another day and he certainly didn't regret the double order. The taste of the dishes was as rich as the culture of the bayou. Spanish, French and Caribbean flavors mingled together in a culinary dance that enlivened the pallet. As Seth scraped out every drop with an ox horn spoon, the cook said, "Tu bits fuh each, an no bru fuh a chīl like yoo!" Seth blushed at the last remark, but he knew that it came from a good-hearted soul.

Indeed, by count he was a very young man, just a bit over seventeen. His size and beard stubble hid most of that though, but it didn't matter. In a country that had declared its independence just over twice his lifetime ago, years were not the measure of greatness. It was the unseen qualities that made the difference, not the looks of a thing or the counting. Values, an innate sense of what was right and fair, an unquenchable fire for freedom that would rather consume itself and all else that stood in its way rather than submit to tyranny, that was the measure of a thing in this new born nation. A spirit that would gladly spend the rest of its days in violent struggle for freedom than to exist for a moment in the sham "peace" of the conquered, that was the measure of this land, not time. In ways that he could not explain nor trace, all of this had found a home in his heart. All of this was Seth Garner.

Having finished up, the silver dollar snapped from between his forefinger and thumb onto the table. It was money well spent. His time in the Fleur de Lis not only satisfied his hunger, but also met another important need in his life. The social interaction he had experienced there was like a healing tonic to his spirit. Even now he could feel the strain of war draining away. Pushing back from the table, Seth strode forth into the night air.

As he continued down the boardwalk, Seth took stock of his present situation. His time as a riverman was past and that was for sure. He had just survived a brief stint as a soldier and was glad of it. But once the campaign had come to an end, his comrades in arms had all gone their separate ways. The fact was that he was on his own again. He had to make a new start for himself, to figure out where to go on from here. Although against his nature, Seth had to start thinking of himself. He had to take care of himself and chart some kind of path to follow from here on out. At that moment, a swaying shingle caught his eye. It read:

Hot Bath & Shave
$.50

Turning in, he was once again reminded of the cultural blend of the city. With a wide grin, the barber greeted him in broken English, "Bienvenidos, Señior to bonito Nuevo Orleans!" Seth knew no Spanish but the meaning was plain enough; a warm welcome was his in this shop. "I'll take a hot shave, if you can manage it." Handing him a mirror, the barber drawled out, "Lo siento mucho, I mean to say, I so sorry, Señior, bu' I no can werk with dis, mi amigo." Seth had not looked into a mirror for some months. He was shocked by what he saw. The entire left side of his face was black from the powder burn he had received the day before. His blonde hair on that side was singed back to half the length of the rest. "My name, Señior Miguel Sanchez. Por favor, please Señior, maybe a bat' furz, no?" Without response, Seth handed the mirror back to his gracious host, and made his way to the rear of the shop.

Seth Garner: Part One

He stepped through a door into a steam-filled room. A giant copper tub brimming with hot water stood in the middle of the floor. Just then a massive woman pounded in and barked, "Mine nam isht Berta, bud dat' dōn matta vor dū. Rake off da' hides ye call clothes an trō dem in da korna!" Seth could barely understand her German accent, but he knew what she wanted him to do. He wasn't about to comply. "Vat dū vāten fur? Isch seed a tausand men a' munt, an isch dōn memba a vun a' dem!" Sheepishly Seth ventured, "Please turn around, and if it's not too much trouble, close your eyes." Somewhere beneath a mountain of cloth, enough to set sail on a good-sized frigate, overburdened feet steered Bertha about, amid huffing and fuming. Bacon grease, dirt, gun powder and sweat had impregnated Seth's buckskins. When they finally did hit the corner, it sounded more like kindling wood than clothes. Slipping into the tub was like a bit of heaven. More stress melted away from pith and palm. Bertha dumped in another bucket of scalding water, nearly undoing Seth's work of modesty of moments before. Slowly slinking back down again, Seth closed his eyes and drank in the warmth. "Dū vant dis tū! It verks vit da' vater!" Seth opened his eyes to see a one-pound cake of lye soap sailing in his direction, halfway to him already. If it were not for his catlike reflexes, the soap would have done more damage to him than any of the British soldiers in battle. Catching the bar in mid-flight, just inches from his nose, Seth muttered, "When will I be shed of this woman!" Bertha wheeled about and glared, "Dū say vat?" "The water is wet and warmin'!" he improvised. "Da vāy it tiz mos' dāz!" she thundered as she pounded out of the room, "Da vāy it usually tiz!."

Seth breathed a sigh of relief as he slid back down into the hot tub. The lye did not just wash away the dirt; it ate it away, together with a good part of the first layer of skin. With that Seth felt that the past was losing its grip on him too.

The Spanish barber stepped into the room. "Señior Seth, por favor, lemme say, buen amigo, yū cloths no so gōōt,

Two Madams and a Princess

comprende? Permissō, yō tengō, I wan' t'say, I haf a fren', he make cloths muy bonito, he make cloths por tū, sí o' no?" "Sí, yes, of course!" Seth yelled from his watery lounge. Seth was awakened by a pompous sounding, "Ahem!" As his head lay atop the tub's rim, the warm bath had lulled him to sleep. "Master Seth! Sir Edmund Whitbred, skilled artisan in cloth, maker of fine apparel, courtesan of kings, at your service!" Without turning about, Seth replied, "I am in need of a decent outfit, presentable, public wise, if you know what I mean." "Indeed, I do sir. It is my business to know. And what aspect of attire may I procure for the esquire, might I ask?" "From the drawers out, and the boots up! Every stitch." "I see, sir, but...." The tailor hesitated. "Is there a problem?" Seth asked looking back over a lathered shoulder. "Just here we touch on a delicate matter, one not easily put. You may well have beaten my countrymen, or should I say at the moment, my *former* countrymen, but that doesn't exactly establish credit with my establishment, especially on the part of drifters, rebels and the like." Bertha lumbered into the room like a mad grizzly, her face as flushed as a fever, brandishing a board for stirring laundry in a cauldron. "I bin listnen' at the varsh kettle, an' let me tell yū a ting o' tū, Herr English dandi! Mine blūt isht German, but mine heartz is Amerikan! Dōn yū talk a' no kretit 'round heer!" "Alright...alright... We're all friends in this room," Seth said in a calm voice. Dipping his hand into the neck of one of his riding boots he had placed next to the tub, he pulled out a fist of gleaming $20.00 dollar gold pieces, and stated, "I don't need credit; I pay in cash." Indeed, just as Raif had said, the spoils of war had come in handy, and sooner than Seth had expected. "I say, Sir! That changes everything!" interjected Whitbred. "My experienced eye has sized you up, in a general way at least. I'll send word to the local merchantile to deliver some serviceable wear, flannel and flax should do. That should hold you for a couple of days until we can get you some proper clothing. A room at the Magnolia will be acceptable?" Before Seth could respond,

183

Seth Garner: Part One

Whitbred continued, "Consider it done. And the *things* you tossed in the corner, we'll have them burned…" "No! No! They have their place. I'll tend to that," Seth concluded.

With that Whitbred turned on his heels and crisply left the room. As promised, a full set of fine, but rugged clothes arrived within fifteen minutes. Whitbred was a snob, but at least, an efficient one. Donning the new duds, Seth finally made it back to the barber's chair. "Muchas gracias tu no make trouble wit' Señior Whitbred. He a poco loco, but bueno hermano, I tink," crooned the barber. He proceeded to swath off great lengths of hair, bringing the form into balance in light of the singed side. He then went on to give Seth the most luxurious hot shave that he had ever experienced. Turning the chair toward a broad mirror, he crowed, "Mira! I so sorry, I forget sometimes. Look a' tū, amigo! Tū look like a new man!" As Seth peered at his own reflection, he had to agree. His hair was in order, his skin was the picture of health, and his clothes hung on him just right. "And I feel like one too!" He made his way on to the *Magnolia*.

As Whitbred had promised, exactly two days after he had washed and scraped away the toil of battle, a knock came at his door. As he opened it, there stood the tailor's apprentice, bearing all the pomp of his master. "Whitbred's!" he snapped as he waltzed into the room without invitation. He cradled two large bundles bound in brown paper. Nestled on top of these was a beaver felt top hat. Carefully placing all on the bed, he wheeled about and quipped, "Alistair Lewis, at your service. Please disrobe!" Even as Seth was shedding his new work clothes, the shop man was unpacking the fine ware. The crisp white shirt had ruffles at the neck and cuffs, and the pants had a neat crease the full length. The black jacket fit perfectly, and the dress leather boots slipped over his slacks, reaching nearly to the knee. After brushing off the finery here and there,

Two Madams and a Princess

and receiving a handsome tip from Seth, he chirped, "Good day, sir!" and was gone.

Seth gazed at himself in the mirror for a few moments, amazed at the transformation. The bath and barber had done wonders, but this was nothing short of a miracle! He hardly recognized himself. He looked older and more informed. He strode across the floor as a person of refinement and substance. He tried to choke back a laugh and failed. Gaining his composure again, he put on the most self-important face he could manage and stepped into the street.

No sooner had he turned toward the river, was he met with an apparition of pure resplendence, like a finely outfitted clipper, drawing ever closer to him in matchless grace. Her eyes were like limpid pools of sapphire. Her porcelain clear skin was framed by jet black hair cascading down over her left shoulder, coming to rest weightlessly upon white lace trimmed in scarlet. As she glided past him, the most heavenly fragrance wafted about, turning his head as cleanly as a weather vane. A delicate film of a handkerchief slipped from her slender fingers and floated airily to the boardwalk. Instinctively, Seth strode forward, retrieved the piece and stammered, "Ma'am. I think this belongs to you." She pivoted deftly, and in one smooth motion, she grasped the hand bearing the kerchief and pulled it toward her, looping her free arm over Seth's shoulder and about his neck. Caressing his hair in her fingers she whispered in a voice so lithe that Seth lost all bearing. "Mon cheri American, s'il vous plaît, come with me tonight. Bon merci, brave Monsieur, for saving our fair city from the Englais!"

The whole thing had caught him off guard. In his strict upbringing he was never allowed to be alone with a girl in the full light of day, much less "come with me tonight" and so forth. He stammered, "Well, I think....perhaps I should....being a bit shy and all, no...no...you see..." She released her clasp about his neck and spun out to arms length all the while firmly holding onto his right hand. Feigning displeasure she snapped, "Wot iz zee problem? You no like Mademoiselle Rochambeau, no? "Of course!" he said without thinking. "Your delicious...I mean delightful...no, it's just that ...that is the problem... if you get what I mean." Letting go of his hand now, she laughed an easy laugh that spoke of strength and good will. "I understand, mon cheri American," and gracefully turned her back to him while teasingly gazing back over her shoulder. "Please help me with this," she purred as her hands reached behind her neck to take hold of a gold chain. Seth saw that she held a delicate catch and beckoned him to unlatch it from about her neck. As his fingers worked through her hair and touched her smooth skin, Seth felt that he would swoon at any moment. Nothing could have been further from the carnage and cruelty he had witnessed just days before. He stood firm in the face of battle, but his knees were close to buckling in this fair struggle. Clumsily, he managed to open the catch just as she closed her hand about the chain. As she pulled a treasure from the top of a perfectly formed bodice, she dropped the gift into Seth's open hand. "To true love, mon brave American! To true love! Merci beaucoup, mon cheri. Give this to the woman who steals your heart, while your eyes are wide open! Give this to the one who takes your life so that you can really start to live, mon cheri!" With that she drifted away down the boardwalk, gentlemen greeting her on all sides, tipping their hats, and making way for a true Acadian beauty.

Seth stood stock still. Persons walked past him as if he were made of stone. When he finally came to himself, he opened his hand and spied a gold ring adorned with a flat ruby inset. In the midst of the ruby was a pearl white star, its lines crisp and clear against the red background. He had never seen anything like it before, and was struck by its simple beauty. He slipped the jewel inside his watch pocket, fastening the tiny button for safekeeping. "Are you alright, sir?!" Seth stared blankly at a wide-eyed stranger. "Should I call someone?" he continued. "No...no thank you. I'm alright....I think," mumbled Seth as he shuffled awkwardly further down the boardwalk, brushing past folks, putting some distance between himself and the unknown inquirer. Fully present again, he readjusted his top hat, strode on through the night, just bumbling along, not really knowing where he was going. In fact he didn't know where he was going in an extended kind of way, either. The mouth of the Mississippi River was literally the end of the world for him; there was no way forward. Still pondering his future, he spotted a rough-hewn shingle suspended just above head height. The sign had been sawn diagonally through a large cypress log; maze-like worm holes formed odd patterns throughout. Ornate calligraphy added to its spell-binding effect. It read:

Madame Clairveaux

Mistress of Fortune and Fate

Palm Reader

Again, nothing of the sort could have been more at odds with his upbringing. Anything that even hinted of the occult or the curious arts was an abomination in his home. Yet Seth was worlds away from his childhood. He was changed, though not completely. In any case he had time

Seth Garner: Part One

on his hands and money in his pocket, and nowhere else to go. "Why not?" he thought.

Madame Clairveaux's had no door, only brightly colored beads that hung from lintel to threshold. Parting the shimmering portal, he entered into a strange world. Pungent incense stung his nostrils and made his eyes water. A jawless skull rested next to a black candle anchored in a cairn of soft wax. A linkage of dry bones of some sort hung from the wall to the left; straggly strands of hair tumbled down here and there. As he panned to his right he was startled to see a young black girl sitting motionless on the floor, clad in a flour sack, legs and arms crossed swami-style. She had a red bandana tightly wrapped about her head. In the center of it was a crudely painted eye with two bright yellow bars slashed underneath.

Seth spoke haltingly, "I...I...expected someone.... a bit older...I mean..." "O! Ah's not Madame Clayboo! Naw suh! Ah's "Pincess Mafūsoo" fum Afika. Ma' fens calls me "Honeysuckle" meez be'in so sweet n'all. B' rat now ah is da' Pincess, dōn cha nō! Ah nōse a ting o' tū, but Madame Clayboo, she nō eva'ting! She nō who yū be n' who yū will be. Why she nō where yū ben 'n dat choo cummin' too!. Let met tell huh dat choo dun here? Fifty cent!"

Seth let slip a couple of coins on the table. With that "Princess Mafusoo," that is, Honeysuckle, jumped up and raked the money into a drawstring sack tied to her wrist. "Hey... wait a minute!" Seth protested. "That was supposed to be for my fortune!" "Naw suh! Ah din' say dat! Did ja' heerd me say dat? Fifty cent jus ma' part. Madame Clayboo cawses a dollah, fa' startin'. She be out jus na'. Yū wait here!" Seth still protested, "Well, I don't think..." "Please! Please, mistah! Lemme' keep it. Ah's dearly luv lick-o-rich, an ah...". "Alright.... That's alright," assured Seth. "Tank ya'! Tank ya' suh! Madame Clayboo give ya' a *gooood* forchune.

Two Madams and a Princess

Yu'll see. A real good 'un," said Honeysuckle, as she whisked to rear of the room, soon enveloped behind another sheet of colorful beads.

Madame Clairveaux emerged like a phantom. Clad from top to bottom in clear white satin, she was a sight to behold. Tall, graceful...the perfect union of mind and body. The elegantly wrapped turban highlighted the beauty of her olive-colored complexion. The Madame was a *Creole*, literally a "child of the parish," being born of an English father and a Caribbean mother. She was also a "freewoman of color," and more than clever enough to exploit human insecurity to her advantage, both socially and financially. But most of all, she was a voodoo queen; the real thing.

Seth had already surmised that Honeysuckle was her personal slave. As such the "Princess" was another example of the corrupting affects of human bondage. Those once enslaved employed their freedom in capturing others, making profit from their souls and labor. The oppressed had truly become the oppressor in this case. So Princess Mafūsoo represented a tragedy twice over, and it pained Seth to see it. The Princess was quick of mind and very articulate, being as learned as she could possibly be under the circumstances. Yet Seth knew that the social reality at hand had made her into something far less than what she could have been in another place and time.

The Madame glided effortlessly to the table, more akin to floating than to walking. Instinctively Seth laid his hand upon the table, palm up. "Put your hand back in your pocket!" she commanded without lifting her eyes. "I thought... you're a *palm* reader, aren't you?" Seth parried. "Do *you* tell fortunes? The gods of the future require an offering...of a monetary kind." As Seth drew forth a dollar, she drew forth a crystal orb. The Madame began to chant in ever increasing volume, "Crystal before hands! Hands before cards! Cards before...!" She then let out a long slow

Seth Garner: Part One

breath, closed her eyes tightly as if she saw a terror, and then calmed down again. Placing the crystal ball on the table, she gradually opened her eyes and peered straight through Seth. He felt a chill sweep over his body. Slowly gliding her hands over the top of the crystal, as if trying to clear away a mist, she whispered, "Cloudy... so cloudy....No....not clear enough to make out anything just yet." Seth reached down and unhitched a small leather change purse fastened to his left side. Whitbred had taken the liberty to have this made up for him at the saddelry shop. It evidenced fine workmanship and even had his name embossed in gold lettering across the front. At the sound of the tinkling coinage, the Madame crooned, "Clearer now....yes...much clearer! Your life is coming into view at last!" Before Seth could slide the change purse from off the table, her sultry olive-shaped eyes took in the details. "A man of letters in the past, yet gone wild, but now, at last, made civil again.... for a time, I see. Looking up at Seth again, she said firmly, "You are not the man you appear to be on the outside, *Mr. Seth Garner!*" These last words struck Seth like a thunderbolt. "Why I never!" he gasped. "How did you know my name?" he asked in utter amazement. "It is a gift my child... a rare gift" she purred even as she took note of his accent. Looking back at the globe, she continued. "You have traveled from afar...I see it now... from the north country, no?" "Yes!..Yes! Miss Clairveaux, I'm from up north." "Yet your journey is not yet over. And so you come to Madame Clairveaux, no?" "Yes! Yes, exactly! That's why I am here. To learn of my future!" he said anxiously leaning ever closer toward the medium. She placed the ball to one side, and letting out a deep philosophical sigh said, "That is all, my son. That is all that the crystal will reveal for now." "That's all?! But that's not enough! I need to know more. Is there any other way?" "Well....," she hesitated. "As you said, I am a *palm* reader."

Two Madams and a Princess

Seth impulsively slapped his hand on the table, knuckles down, making an unpleasant rap on the hardwood. "Ahem.... The gods of the palm are not the same as the gods of the crystal. Another offering is needed," she whispered. As Seth placed another coin on the table, Madame Clairveaux's languid lids rose like a stage curtain, again peering straight through him. Noticing the reddened flesh of the powder burn on his face, her eyes quickly fluttered back to the open palm before her. Placing her finger on a crevasse between his thumb and forefinger, she said, "You have had a close brush with death in the recent past," she ventured. "Indeed, I have!" he blurted out. Tracing her finger along another crease in his strong hand, she plied on, "But your life line is long. Destiny has spared you for greater things." "You don't mean it! So I have a good future!" Seth continued excitedly. "I said that your lifeline is long, not that it is good...but then again...not totally bad," she offered in an air of aged wisdom. "Enough! Enough! A hand can only say so much!" she said with authority. "Oh, no!" Seth groaned fully into it now. "Please, isn't there any more?" Noticing that Seth placed the coins on the table with his left hand, the Madame whined, "Well.....you have *two* hands, don't you man?" "You mean both hands don't say the same thing if they belong to the same person?" Seth asked in puzzled amazement. "Not if one unusual condition is met," she explained. "And what's that?! What's that?!" Seth fairly shouted to the Madame. "Peace, my child, peace. Fortune telling is a gentle art. The one condition that I spoke of, is if the man is left handed." "Well, bless me, Miss Clairveaux. If I'm not left handed. I got more fortune coming to me yet!" he shouted as he rapped his other hand on the table palm up. "Ahem...," the Madame said, clearing her throat, "Another dollar, please."

There is a difference between being intelligent and cunning. There is a difference between being trusting and

191

Seth Garner: Part One

gullible. Seth was neither cunning nor gullible. He simply could not bring himself to believe...no.... it never crossed his mind that anyone would deliberately plot to deceive and to steal. In this sense his inherent belief in the goodness of people was strength, not weakness. Madame Clairveaux knew all too well how to leverage this strength against Seth.

She explained to Seth that he would have to help her if the left hand was to reveal more secrets. She commanded him to stare intently at the hand of his natural birth and that he would see things that he had never noticed before. As he focused on every fissure and callous, Madame Clairveaux sprinkled a copper-laced powder into the candle flame. A crackling, bright green flash erupted, sending Seth to his feet, he remaining earthbound only by the firm grasp of the voodoo queen. "Easy son....it's the power...it's just the power," she comforted. As Seth folded into the chair once again, she continued. "A long love line I see. There will be passion in your life, stronger than the grave." "That's what the Bible says. There is a love that is stronger than death it says!" "I am duly impressed with your knowledge of spiritual things, dear friend. Allow me to continue." "Interesting. Your wealth line. Clear yet broken. Nothing more here," she said with finality.

At that point, Seth felt something as light as a mouse tugging on the change purse at his side. Looking down he took in the wide-eyed face of Honeysuckle, crouched behind his chair, her long slender fingers already lifting out a few coins. Seth hollered, "Hey! What are you up to now?!" "Ah's dun had!" squeaked the Princess, and made for the beaded door like a shadow. A shank of licorice ropes bobbed over her left shoulder, as the red bandana slipped from her head. The confection was hardly distinguishable from her glistening braids as she fled into the night.

Two Madams and a Princess

"Why you little wretch!" the Madame shouted. "When I catch you I am going to throttle you within an inch of your life!" she yelled with murderous fervor. All of the poise and dignity of the queen was lost in a moment. Her turban slipped at an odd angle on her head, her eyes bulged in their sockets and her nostrils flared in anger. "Now...now...Miss Clairveaus, don't get angry at her. She acted out of need no doubt, and not out of meanness. If you count me a friend, promise that you will not harm the Princess," Seth pleaded. "I promise. But this session is over. The spirits are disturbed!" she barked as she straightened her turban and sought to regain a portion of her regal air. "I understand, but begging your pardon, what I have heard thus far is just traces and hints. Don't get me wrong. I am grateful and all, but is there another way I can see deeper and clearer into my future?" Seth asked.

The Madame's expression fell into a grave and sullen pose. At length she offered, "There is a way, but I do not advise it to anyone. They must choose on their own accord." "Then I choose it," Seth responded. "Don't speak quickly, child!" she snapped. "This is not a game!" she charged with a hint of fear in her voice. Seth swallowed hard once, then again, weakly saying, "I...I...do choose it...come what may."

Madame Clairveaux retrieved a small black velvet bag from under the table. As she opened it she looked straight into Seth's eyes. She seemed changed in an intangible kind of way. Lifeless....cold....dark....morbidly serious. She drew out a small deck of cards and spread them in an even arc in front of Seth.

"Now child, this will cost you twenty dollars. But let me tell you that money don't have no part in what we are about to do!" she said in an ominous, detached kind of way. Seth sensed something different, but couldn't put his finger on what was happening. Somewhere along the line the

193

Seth Garner: Part One

thing had crossed over from the realm of hoax to that of haunted. He felt it, but didn't understand it. "Proceed," Seth muttered halfheartedly as he placed a gold coin on the table. "Pick one card and turn it over," she said in a tense voice. As Seth slid out a card and turned it face up, the Madame smiled. On the card was the image of a two young lovers holding hands. "More details on your love line," she said. "I see two women, one like yourself from birth to now, one like yourself from now till death," she explained. "I don't believe it," Seth countered. "I am not a man of divided loyalties! My affections are not shared in such matters, Miss Clairveaux!" "Question not! The cards don't lie!" she chastened. "Did I say two loves at once? Hold your peace Mr. Garner, or we will have to part company! Do you understand me?" "Yes ma'am, please continue," said Seth. *"One light...one dark. One born civil gone wild. Another born wild gone civil,"* she divined. "Do you accept the vision?" she asked. "Yes, go on." "Take another card, please." Seth turned up his second selection. The card contained a picture of a blazing sun. Again, a broad smile came across the Madame's face. "This fortune is about your fortune, that is, your wealth, if you follow my meaning," she said cryptically. "I follow," Seth replied. "Very well then, follow this. The vision bodes considerable wealth. I hear these words. Can you discern their meaning? *'Treasure not sought for, twice unexpected; riches not fought for, in gold reflected'.*" "I think I half understand what it means," offered Seth, thinking back on the little brown jug that spilled forth twenty dollar gold pieces. "You may take another card now when you are ready," she instructed. Seth pried up a card halfway, and then looked into the eyes of Clairveaux for direction. As she gave a pensive nod, Seth turned the card face up. A young woman held a balance scale at arms length, as if to thrust the scale into the hands of the onlooker. "You're a man who seeks justice,"

194

Two Madams and a Princess

Clairveaux intoned, "a most elusive thing. One must be careful in its pursuit." As he turned up the next card, Madame Clairveaux's countenance fell. She splayed her fingers flat out upon the table top, the pressure creating light colored wreaths about her finger tips. The card showed an image of a skeleton in full armor riding a horse. "Is something wrong?" queried Seth. "The future is not right or wrong, child. It just is," said she. "You are a violent man...." Before she could finish her thoughts Seth jumped to his feet and shouted, "Not of my own choosing! I don't go looking for a fight, but I don't run from one neither!" "Need I remind you that this is not a debate, sir!" she chided. As Seth sank back into his seat, the tension in the room increased considerably. Trembling, Madame Clairveaux whispered in a strained voice barely audible even in a room of dead silence. "Go ahead... take your time. No need to rush what's coming!" she said. Seth stared at her for a few unsettling moments. He turned a card face up. Madame Clairveaux let out an ear-piercing shriek. As she sprung back from the table, Seth did the same. "What's happened?" he shouted. The card had a picture of a man hanged upside down. Madame Clairveaux was completely undone. Panic and terror filled her every feature. "Stand back! Don't come near!" she commanded. "What's wrong, madam!?" Seth pleaded. "Don't touch me! Don't hurt me!" she shouted. Pushing the gold coin forward, Seth began backing slowly away as if to leave. Grabbing hold of a gnarled walking cane with a snake's head, she poked the coin back with its tip. "Take your money! Don't want your money!" she shrieked. As she backed through the beaded veil she repeated like a mantra, "I see *Him*! I see *Him*!"

Seth retrieved the coin, and made his way for the doorway. Puzzled and unsettled, he stepped through the second beaded curtain onto the boardwalk. Pushing his way through the crowd, he headed back to the *Magnolia*.

195

Seth Garner: Part One

Flopping down on the huge feather bed, he mused, "What a day! Any more like this and I'd prefer a stroll through the British lines unarmed!" For Seth, New Orleans was entertaining for a time, but in the main, the city was an ill fit for him. Shysters and charlatans were on every corner, taking in every wayfarer that was not streetwise. Jean Lafitte's pirates lurked in the shadows planning their next raid and ladies of the night plied their trade unhindered. And all of this was conducted in the shadow St. Louis Cathedral. It was the oldest Catholic cathedral in the New World, Louis XVI being its namesake. The presence of the church and the many clerics waltzing along the red brick avenues seemed to be but one more quaint curio of the city, having no real affect on the conduct of its inhabitants. The incongruities of the place grated on his mind as he shed the finery of Whitbred's and wrapped them in the brown paper they had been delivered in. Pulling on his old and worn buckskins helped settle his nerves. The smell of earth and sweat were strong, but honest, and Seth melded into the leather as if it were part of him. Stuffing all of his trappings into a large leather knap sack he had purchased for this purpose, he tore off a corner of the brown paper and scrawled a quick note,. He then wrapped a $20.00 gold piece within. After a quick look around the room for a memory, Seth walked out of the hotel.

Again the noise and bustle of the city rose up around him. He had had enough and was fighting off the sensation of being smothered by it all. Taking sight of a gruff looking sheriff, Seth hailed him over. "Do you happen to know Princess Mafūsoo?" he called. "Ya' say what, man?!" he growled back. "Do you know a young girl named Honeysuckle?" he continued. "She didn't pinch ya' poke, did she?" not acknowledging the question. "I beg your pardon, sir!" Seth said a bit alarmed. "She didn't pilfer your

Two Madams and a Princess

purse? Filch your living? *Rob* from ya'....*Steal* anything...?" he fired off like a pistol. "I...I....understand now. No, in fact I want to give something to her. Can you pass it on for me?" "Well....I don't know if I can remember. I am busy man, ya' know!" the sheriff hesitated. With regard to memory Seth knew that the sheriff was just another public official on the take, even if one on the lowest rung of the ladder. A politician's memory is either long or short depending upon what side of the scandal he might be on at the time. The sound of jingling coins in his pocket tightened the lines of the sheriff's weather worn face. "Well...I speck I'll see her directly," he offered as Seth pressed some coins into his hand. "Much obliged, and be kindly to her, if you will," he said as he turned away.

In short order the sheriff knew where to hunt for the Princess. "Dat you Honeysuckle?" he yelled as a small figure slipped among some barrels near the wharf. "Leave me be! I dun nuttin' wrong. Ax Madame Clayboo! She tell ya' I bin good!" she protested as she prepared to spring into another hiding place. "Hold on there, yung'un!" he bellowed. "I got nuttin agin ya', not today leastwise. Fact is, I got a gift fur ya'." Edging into the street, Honeysuckle held forth a tentative hand. The sheriff placed Seth's little package into her hand and warned, "Be off with ya' now or else I'll have another kind of gift for ya'." The chuckle of the old lawman was barely out of earshot when Honeysuckle unwrapped her unexpected gift. On the inside of the paper it read, "He who steals, robs his own soul. Signed, Seth Garner." Not being able to read, she cast the note to the ground and made her way to the candy store.

Seth Garner: Part One

Topping a hill, the white canvas of the two covered wagons came into view.

Into Texas

With Raif gone, Seth had to chart his own course now. He entertained the idea of signing on with Jean Laffite and his men, those French privateers who had come in so handy for the Americans in their fight against the British. Word had it that Laffite was heading for the barrier islands off the coast of Texas. From there, he would stage new raids against unsuspecting seamen in the Gulf of Mexico. But apart from receiving letters of mark during times of war, Seth concluded that a pirate was just a thief on a boat, and so quit the idea early on. On the other hand, from what he could gather from fellow soldiers in New Orleans, Lafitte and his men were heading in the right direction. Indeed it seemed as if all of America was pressing its way westward, straining the limits of international boundaries and trying the patience of world leaders from England to Russia. So in short order, Seth found himself moving in the direction of Texas.

199

Seth Garner: Part One

After nearly 300 years of exploration and settlement in Texas, Spain had precious little to show for it. Her lack of success was due to a single factor: Texas lacked that precious metal that had lured Spain to the New World in the first place. Not so much as a thimble full of gold had been found throughout the vast territory. Without the promise of quick riches, Texas had little to attract new settlers. So by 1810, less than 5,000 settlers had gone to Texas. On balance, the Iberian crown was land rich and labor poor when it came to Texas. There were simply not enough people to run the small farms and ranches that huddled about the many missions scattered throughout the land. So even though the constitution banned trade with "Norte Americanos," Spain desperately needed American help to safeguard her investments in Texas. It was for this reason that Americans were granted provisional entry into Texas, so long as they submitted to the laws of Spain and agreed to trade with markets further south in Mexico.

Those Americans who accepted this arrangement effectively became resident aliens in Texas. They were a people without flag or country. Legally, they were in no man's land, not fully coming under the purview of America or Spain. As such they were vulnerable, isolated islands of humanity, exposed to every evil that nature and man might bring against them. They lived at the margins and so developed a survivalist's mentality, willing to do just about anything, whether it be for the good or for ill, to secure their place on the frontier. Into this wild and lawless land stepped Seth Garner.

His trip westward marked a critical turning point for Seth, one that paralleled his flight from Heathshire some four years earlier. Long gone were all of the friendships he had made on the National Road together with the strong bonds he had forged in Pittsburg. Now, too, he had lost

Into Texas

contact with Raif and with all of the deckhands he had worked with on the log raft as it slowly wound its way down the Mississippi. At the end of it all, the violence of the Battle of New Orleans had broken up many things in his life. So in a real sense, he was starting over again.

But this time it was different. In Boston he had fled the school in terror. In Pittsburg, he barely escaped with his life. But now, an odd kind of confidence accompanied Seth as he crossed the Sabine River, that natural boundary that separated Louisiana from Texas. Just now he had reached a place in life where he could stand outside of himself, so to speak, and take stock of his person and of his place in the broad scheme of things. He could certainly read and write, and by the standard of the day, he was well educated. He understood the rudiments of commerce and could make his way in business, if need be. He had seen more of the newly founded nation than most of the Founding Fathers and had traveled its western frontier from top to bottom. And lastly, he knew that the Battle of New Orleans had made a huge mark in his life. He had faced the horrors of war and had survived when many others were not as lucky. So all in all, he judged himself to be well set in the world. He was clearly a man, a young one at that, but a man just the same. His future was as uncertain yet also as promising as the newly formed nation of America. So all of these things... experience....hope ... confidence... traveled along with Seth into Texas.

Once in Texas, Seth soon discovered that his place among the American expatriates was as ill-defined and varied as the movement itself. He simply did what had to be done, and there was a lot that had to be done. He soon gained a reputation as a buffalo hunter providing fresh meat to newly planted homesteaders who were too busy with setting up to harvest their own game. He rode a wide circuit throughout the land, befriending many Indians who taught him woodcraft unknown to the white man. One such skill, one that would serve him well in the future, was how to trap beaver. In time, he gained intimate knowledge of the land, and so became a scout, a kind of frontier guide for those who had newly arrived. In short, he became a settler of settlers, leading small bands deeper and deeper into the Texas territory. On more than one occasion, he could throw a stone into Old Mexico.

His vocation was in step with the times. After the war of 1812, the southeast experienced an economic downturn. People were pulling up stakes overnight and were heading west. Many knew little or nothing about homesteading and had no idea of how to set up and survive the first year on the frontier.

Such was the case of Karl and Elsie Jäger. Being of good German stock they possessed the strength and ingenuity to make a new start. What they lacked was those skills that would have given them a better than even chance of surviving past Christmas. Like Seth, they left New Orleans, meandered deep into Texas and stopped somewhere just north of Laredo. As things went, they had chosen a good location for their first try. Laredo was one of the oldest Spanish settlements in Texas, and as meager as it was, the town boasted some prosperity. Karl was a baker by trade and Elsie could turn a bolt of cloth into serviceable dresses and rugged britches. In time their crafts would provide warm bread and fine clothes for their neighbors in town. But for now, unknown to them, their situation was dire.

Seth came into contact with the Jägers as a matter of course. For two whole years, he had established a regular pattern, more like a great circuit that skirted the territory. He'd hunt buffalo and trap in the fall and winter, meandering up north into New Mexico territory as spring approached. Seth then would begin working his way south and east rounding up the vast herds of mustangs that ranged free in the land. Pushing the herd southward, Seth would cash in at San Antonio, the most prosperous Spanish settlement in all of Texas. It was here, in San Antonio, that a struggling Catholic mission called the Alamo would play a decisive role in the future of the territory.

    He was not so much a molder of the land as the land was a molder of him. The wide expanses of prairie ignored time and so did Seth. He kept no appointments; he was in no hurry. He was a drifter with purpose, a living type of the young country that was his own. He became as rough and wild as the land he rode. He was a Texan now; a real frontiersman. He talked little for there were few to talk to. When the occasion did arise, his speech was coarse and pragmatic. As such, he was perfectly suited for a land where nothing in particular was happening, but where a fate-altering event might come along at any moment. Such was the case when Seth rode into the camp of the Jägers.

    He had seen the smoke of their campfire from afar off. A dark thought passed through his mind. Not all Indians in Texas were friendly, not by a long shot. As the smoke curled lazily upward, Seth wondered how many Apaches and Mexican bandits had seen the smoke as well. Topping a hill, the white canvas of their two covered wagons came into view. As the fertile soil of the Rio Grande valley peeled away from Karl's plowshare, Seth half thought out loud, "That's good." Food for next winter needed to be planted yesterday, so to speak. As Karl hailed him, he slowly rode into camp, casting a learned eye about the place. Seth was just short of 20 years old now, but two years in the wilds of Texas was equal to two lifetimes back east, and maybe a couple of deaths as well. What he saw did not concern him as much as what he didn't see. "Elsie, macht Kaffee!" Karl hollered as he slipped out of the traces. "Mine name isht Karl!" he offered in broken English. Before Seth's boot hit

Seth Garner: Part One

the ground, a warm handshake greeted him. Seth smiled and then briefly set forth the essentials of who he was and what he was up to. "Kinder!" he called out in a jovial tone. "Kum zee a real Texan!" Two beautiful girls and a tow headed boy peeped out of the cook wagon. The girls appeared to be in their mid to late teens and the boy was not yet twelve. Upon seeing them, the smile dropped from Seth's face as he tried to hide a somber mood. He knew that to some about these parts, the girls would be little more than prairie flowers before a buffalo bull, to be devoured or trampled underfoot without so much as a second thought. The boy was simply a walking opportunity to lift a gleaming white scalp, a trophy to be hung from a warrior's belt. As Seth dropped his head and stared at the ground, Karl asked, "Ish zum ding nicht in order?" Seth was a lonely man, not in heart, but in fact. He had very little contact with people as he rode the range, and those that did join him on the trail were much like him. So Seth had no skill in the social graces. When he did speak, he spoke his mind and he spoke it plain. Lifting his head, Seth lit in. "No...nothing's wrong, just that there needs to be a lot more right if you are going to be here this time next year," replied Seth in a deadpan manner. "Vat do you mean? Vir all verking hart!" protested Karl. "No doubt...no doubt about that," said Seth between sips of hot coffee. "Where are you going to spend the winter?" he asked. "In die vaguns, naturlich! Du ask so easy kveschuns, Herr Seth!" laughed Karl as he poured him another cup of steaming coffee. "Not so easy," returned Seth in a grave tone. "That won't do. It gets colder than you might think out here in the winter. The desert wind from the south can whip up in a minute and tear that canvas to shreds. If the fall rains come, and pray that they do, what will you do then?" Seth asked in a stern voice, his brows furrowed with concern. Karl stared back with a blank face and

204

mouth slightly agape. "I know not....I no tink..." "You've got to think, man! You've brought a wife and three young'uns out here!" Seth shouted before he could catch himself. As Karl's eyes widened in alarm, Seth had already apologized for his outburst. He shared that he had seen more grief come to good-hearted, hard-working settlers than he cared to talk about. "Vat kann vee do? Vee kannt go back now. Vill you help us, Herr Seth? Ich hab no money, but Ich promise..." "Save it!" interrupted Seth. "I'll help, but I don't have the patience to say things twice," half smiling. "Vee vill do vat dū says, Ja vee will!" was Karl's hearty reply. "O.K. then. Karl, you start plowing at gray light in the morning, and don't stop till noontime. The older of you two sisters walk directly behind the plow planting seed like this," explained Seth stooping low and hopping like a crow along a freshly cut furrow. Elsie respectfully added, "Her name ish Hanna." "Fine then," he continued without so much as a second's pause. "Now you little sister....." "Dis vun ish called Gabbie," Elsie demurely commented. "Indeed...Gabbie, you work with your maw gathering the summer fruits and berries that I'll show you directly. That for the first half of the day. The second half is for drying them and making preserves," Seth rattled on. "Now son," turning to the boy clinging to his mother's calico and hiding a bit behind...." "Wilhelm ish his name," she continued. "Good, Will, you will go out with me at first light. We will hunt half the morning, then field dress the game and tote it back here by noon. Do you understand?" Seth speaking clearly and directly to the child. His head nodded as fast as a woodpecker after a fat grub. "Now son," he continued, "last month or so you were a kid back east, but now you're a man out here. Do you understand what I'm meanin'?" The boy's head ratcheted even faster than before. Turning away, Seth addressed the whole family, "After a brief lunch, the men folk will get to work on the soddie," Seth said with absolute confidence. "On da vat?" asked Karl. "What did I say about speaking twice?" was Seth's retort. With that a wide grin spread across Karl's face as he pulled the plow harness over each shoulder.

Even though it was early spring, it was a race against time. Enough food for winter and a more permanent form of shelter had to be in place in short order. So early the next morning the regimen Seth had set forth was begun. Elsie, Hanna and Will struck out early while Karl and Gabbie harnessed the plow horse. Seth snapped off berries and wild herbs as he walked along, handing the samples to Elsie. He pointed out that chinquapin, pinion and wild hazel nuts would be ready for harvest in the fall. Taking his leave, he led Will deep into the thicket along the winding creek. He pointed out deer and javelina tracks, while whispering that rabbits and quail must not be overlooked for sustenance. The latter were not worth wasting shot on, but he would get to that later. Having no surplus of time nor powder to practice, Seth hissed out the basics of marksmanship: front and rear sight, hold the breath, pick a spot, squeeze the trigger, so on and so forth. In the dim light of dawn, Will's face revealed puzzled excitement. "Don't worry, it will all fall together when the time comes," assured Seth. As they stealthily worked deeper into the pin oak grove, they picked up more sign, fresh deer droppings lay about the under story of the grove. They settled in behind the upturned roots of a blow down and waited. Soon the graceful shapes of feeding deer emerged from the morning gloom. Priming "Old Terrible," Seth passed the weapon to small unsteady hands. Will pointed to the dominant buck of the herd, but Seth gently hauled the muzzle over toward a fat yearling. "Better suited for our purposes, Will. Take your time now....behind the shoulder." As the boy jerked the trigger, he had already pulled up his head to see the results of the shot, coming to his feet even before the smoke had cleared. The rough trigger pull and lifting up the head had thrown off the shot. The slug went wide to the right, missing the deer's vitals, slamming aft of the killing zone. As the herd flushed in all directions, the stricken prey veered off on its own. Crashing wildly in the mesquite brush, the deer flailed about with its sharp hooves, seeking vainly to regain its footing to escape. Seth rushed forward drawing his blade from the scabbard in mid stride, with Will in tow. Grasping the long ears of the struggling yearling, the knife flashed in a vicious arc across its throat. Hot blood splattered upon the thirsty sand as curls of steam encircled both man and beast. While crimson stream dripped from knife point to ground, Seth looked down into the blanched face of Will as his young face slowly wagged from side to side. A boyish quavering voice barely mouthed, "No!. . . No!" Tenderly laying his free hand upon the boy's shoulder, Seth spoke the harsh words of survival on the frontier. "It's his life for our life out here. For the life of your mother and sisters. There is no way around it, Will." Slowly dropping his head, the boy nodded in grudging agreement to an inflexible truth, to *lex talionis*, a rule he so sorely wished could be broken, but knew that it could not. "What did I do wrong, Mr. Seth?" he pined. "I'm just 'Seth' to you. We're partners now. With regard to shootin', just about everything, but we'll talk later," reflected Seth as his knife tip slipped into the belly of the carcass, point up. "Cut upwards towards the brisket, being careful not to slice into the gut," he instructed, calling for Will to fetch the oilcloth from his pack. "This here's the heart, and further down's the liver," he explained. "We'll have these tonight to celebrate!" Seth offered with a wide grin. Wrapping up the take in the oilcloth, Seth noted, with satisfaction, that Will was coping pretty well with the grisly task of field dressing large game. "We can't eat all of this meat before it spoils, Seth. What can we do?" "We'll roast the saddle in a day or two. The rest we'll make into jerky," he noted as he hoisted the deer up into a post oak by the hind legs. Making quick work of the skinning, he explained that it would be tanned to make him a buckskin shirt. Cutting away the tendon near the hock, he carefully stripped the sinew down the length of the body towards the head. "This is for the rabbits and quail I talked to you about earlier," said Seth to a puzzled youngster. Hafting his tomahawk he had one last job to do. Seth then dealt the most ghastly cut of all. A swift strike behind the ears neatly lifted the skullcap of the fallen deer. Will looked on in horror and disgust as Seth gently emptied the brain into a small membrane pouch he had prepared for this very thing. "Why?!" demanded Will in the strong light of mid-morning. "The brain is for your buckskin shirt," Seth continued. "Tis not disrespect for the beast Will, just the contrary. Use everything the animal has to offer the living. That's how to honor the life it had. If you don't plan to do that, don't take the game in the first place." Having secured these treasures of the field, they began to pack the quartered deer back to camp.

Seth and Will arrived just in time for a hot biscuit and salt pork lunch. Leaving Elsie to preserve the trove of gatherings from the field, Seth introduced Hanna to the rudiments of making venison jerky. That underway, he turned to the task of building the sod cabin.

"Do you have a shovel, Karl," he asked. "Do ish hab a chuvel? Tink a pioneer like me got no chuvel?" Karl exclaimed in mock indignation. Seth's eyes narrowed at Karl's lighthearted reply. "Alright...alright alveady. Ish got zwei chuvels, but Ish no talk about it, jus fetch dem rite qvick!" Seth explained that the scrub post oak and juniper pine were not big enough to make a log cabin. On his last circuit hunting buffalo in northwest Texas, he'd seen some settlers make a house from sod. "Vee vill lib in a house a' mut?!" exclaimed the German. "Just for a season or two. After that, if you're determined to put down roots, with the help of folks in town, you can build an adobe," Seth consoled. "Ah vat?" asked Karl. Seth answered with another deadpan stare. "Alright alvready. Let's begin verking!" "Cut just through the turf one foot wide, then two long," Seth doing the job as he talked. "Then shallow out your spade and cut the block out... grass, roots, dirt and all ... like this!" he said as he hefted the most natural "brick" that one could imagine. Karl caught on quickly. As they dug, Seth patiently explained to Elsie why the structure had to be one room only, and not all that large a room at that. By nightfall they had a knee-high wall of sod some twenty by fifteen feet in area.

As a meager dinner was being prepared, Seth pulled the deerskin over a wagon wheel. He scraped the thin membrane from the hide, and began slowly boiling the slurry in a small kettle over the fire. "Macht dū zum zoop?" asked Karl. "This is for rabbit huntin'," was Seth's puzzling reply. As the family settled into the wagons for the night, Seth stretched out on a bedroll on the ground. A few moments later his keen ears picked up on the idle whispers that often accompany husband and wife before sleep. "Ja...der mann ish hilful, but hart to know vat he will do next!" Karl hissed as Seth fell into a blissful sleep.

The next morning all fell into their routine. Will was anxious to take to the woods for another adventure, as Seth stirred the thickened kettle that had been simmering all night. Getting what Will thought to be a late start, Seth scanned the choked creek bottom. Stopping at a straight trunked tree with thorns protruding menacingly here and there, he said but one word, "Osage." "What?" whispered Will peering through the under story in a vain attempt to see game. "I....I can't see anything." "The tree," he said as he slipped his tomahawk from a belt loop. Hacking away at

Seth Garner: Part One

its base, Seth continued, "Osage orange, hedge apple, *bois d' arc*, or 'wood of the bow' as the French say." "The Osage Indians of east Texas use this wood exclusively for bows, and they taught me a thing or two in this regard," he commented as the bit dug deeper and deeper into the tree. "This one's most dead," said Will. "What we want for now. Should be dried first, and so this one's some dry," Seth remarked. Once felled, he rived the trunk in half lengthwise, and then in half again. "You drag one, and I the other...we'll fetch the other two later. Back to camp!" he being yards on the way before Will lugged his share of the take. Shearing off the bark and squaring up the stave, Seth traced the outline of a bow along the spine of the wood. Chips flew and shavings peeled off as Seth worked wordlessly with hatchet and knife. Final scraping with the edge of the blade and a polishing with fine sand from the creek yielded a magnificent bow by mid-afternoon. Retrieving the sinew taken from the deer, he pounded it with a stone, thus separating the fibers. The hide glue that had been brewing all night now met its purpose. Dipping the sinew in the glue and placing layer upon layer along the length of the bow's back occasioned a lesson from Seth. "The sinew backing will strengthen the bow, keep it from cracking and splintering under strain," he said. As the glue and sinew dry, the bow will bend backwards, but that's O.K. That's what we want. In the meantime, we'll make up a few arrows."

    The arrow making took more time than was spent in fashioning the bow. Split cedar and slow shaving with the long-knife was the ticket here. There was no time for flint knapping, that careful craft of flaking off tiny slivers of rock to hone a razor's edge from stone. Fortunately, Seth had a half dozen metal trade points he could use for Will's arrows. After downing a Great Blue heron for feathers, Will's archery kit came closer to completion. Seth took long, tough Yucca fibers and rolled them between his palm and thigh. Before long a crude string emerged. Seth braced the bow and handed it to Will. The boy was barely able to come to full draw. "Don't worry. You'll grow into it," mused Seth. "This way we double our chances for game; I'll pack the long iron and you'll shoot the bow. I'll take to the higher ground for deer and you'll stick to the creek bottom for small game." Will's eyes widened at the thought of being on his own the next morning, and signaled his willingness to do what was expected.

Progress on the soddie was rapid, with Seth crafting two windows and a door facing southeast to catch the warm morning sun. Employing methods that he had learned from the Caddo Indians, Seth showed Will how to "brain tan" a deer hide. Properties in the tissue softened the stiff hide from the deer that had been killed some days before, making it much more supple. Seth then began to impart a suede finish to the leather by working the soft hide over the iron rim of a wagon wheel. In time they had a product with which Elsie could evidence her special gifts. It wasn't long before Will sported a fine buckskin shirt. "After we fashion some leggings and moccasins, you'll look like a real frontiersman!" announced Seth. In the following days, Seth took a fat doe with "Old Terrible" and Will took a few rabbits with the bow. Things were looking promising.

Seth judged that enough had been plowed and planted for now and that full effort should be devoted to the soddie. Cedar and juniper poles were fashioned in short order for the roof. Over this frame was laid a final thick layer of sod. Within a few days green grass grew on the roof and to Elsie's delight a few wildflowers towered over their heads. "Place blankets over the windows and doors for now, move everything into one wagon, and bring the spare canvas in here!" ordered Seth. He lined the

Seth Garner: Part One

underside of the roof with the canvas, explaining that this will catch some of the dirt that occasionally falls. "It seems like the dirt on the ceiling always wants to return to the floor!" said Seth with a grin. "In time you can white wash the walls to brighten things up a bit. Some even plaster in and out to make a real fine place. Karl will rive off planks of cedar to make a suitable floor as time allows," he rambled as he tucked the canvas tarp tight into the corners. One morning Will failed to return with his usual brace of rabbits, and his mother fretted out loud that he was too young to be on his own in the wild. "If not now then never," Seth counseled. But just before noon, Will's tiny profile could be seen bearing up from the creek bottom, leaning forward struggling under a heavy load. As he got closer, Seth made out the form of a large turkey swaying this way and that as Will trudged toward the soddie. As he breathlessly told the group how he had taken the bird with a single arrow, Seth knew it was time.

"Well, you're on your way!" he said as he saddled his horse. Seth had done all that he could for the Jägers. He needed to head north to catch the buffalo hunt in the fall. "Dū dōn mean to leab bus just now?!" protested Karl. "Da harvest ist vready to take in, und der ist verk..." "You can handle it now. I'll just be in the way," Seth said as he prepared to swing up on his horse. "Vait a minute, Herr Garner!" Karl said with unusual firmness. He hadn't called Seth "Herr Garner" since the first day they had met. Seth knew something serious was afoot. "Dū kann nicht just vride oudda here like nutting!" Karl added. "Vee are Christian volk! Vee should pray or zing or zumting! Vee may be in der vilderness, but vee are schtill human binks!" he said with warmth in his eyes. "Well, I haven't prayed in a long while..." "Dat dōn matta. Da Vater ish schtill dare!" Karl interrupted. "That's for certain," replied Seth with downcast eyes, feeling a bit chastened by the sincerity of

Into Texas

Karl's words. "Alvright den. Let uns pray." As the wind whipped over the land, calico skirts ruffled and hands clasped over hats that threatened to leave their owners. A small circle of brave souls bowed their heads in the midst of a vast and unyielding wilderness. "Dear Vater, vee tank dū fur everting und fur Herr Seth. Bless him and keep him unter dine hant. Amen!" With prolonged "good byes" and a few tears the Jägers bid him farewell as he rode out of camp. That evening as the family retired, Karl found a small leather sack filled with twenty-dollar gold pieces. That night they gave thanks to their Maker for all His provisions. They thanked Him again for Seth Garner.

Word of Seth's courage, commitment to duty and self-sacrifice spread from one humble dwelling to another, until the name of Seth Garner meant something more than a mere person. It meant the presence of hope in the midst of a wilderness that otherwise harbored none. It meant that human cruelty and injustice just might not have the last word. The name of Seth Garner, and persons like him, meant the presence of those civil qualities that pave the way for law and order. And so it was that Seth was drawn into another vocation, one not of his own choosing. He became a lawman in a land without law. He became a ranger, casting the mold for another kind of pioneer to follow after him, the Texas Rangers. He became a righter of wrongs, a frontier judge who often had to pursue, prosecute and punish those who would take advantage of the lonely recesses of a vast and untamed land. He never once relished these occasions, yet shuttered at the thought of such predators roaming unchecked among the people. He simply took care of business. That was what was expected of him. Indeed, on more than one occasion he alone slapped the flank of a horse and watched some rustler, murderer, or abuser of womankind swing in the wind at the end of a taut rope. That rope would be used

213

Seth Garner: Part One

again......and ....again. The more innocent, hardworking settlers poured in from the east, the more Seth began to loathe the lowlifes that he was sent to track, and if called for, to send on to their reward. A seething contempt mixed with frustration grew in his heart. This growing disgust was born of the fact that as soon as the plains were shed of one varmint, two would take its place. No sooner had justice gained a fragile toehold in the land than word would come of one more hate-filled deed. And it galled Seth to the core.

As Seth wandered on throughout the fall and winter of 1816, living a life of peace became harder and harder to find in Texas. Tensions between the Spanish, Mexicans and Americans were rapidly approaching a flashpoint. Already the region between Texas and Mexico had become a killing zone. Desperadoes and bands of Indians would cross over from Mexico and plunder American settlers, only to spirit away into the rugged region just south of the border. Savage as they were, they knew that Americans were barred from pursuing them into Mexico and that any formal appeal to Spain was futile. Such conducted their slaughter with impunity apart from occasionally being caught in the north and suffering swift justice.

It was this kind of business that led him, and a fellow scout, Jim Drury, further and further south towards Mexico. Jim had ridden with Seth nearly the full length of Texas. He was hewn from similar stock as Seth, so it was natural that they would fall in together. He too had found himself drawn into the lives of those first Americans who claimed, albeit prematurely, Texas as their home. Also like Seth, Jim rode a nondescript path around the territory, "mending fences" so to speak when he could, and making a living by whatever was close at hand. What was close at hand, at least most of the time, for both he and Seth were mustangs, thousands of them. They had wrangled these wild horses in late winter, breaking them enough to herd them on to Nachadoches. There the beasts were sold for American cash, bartered for shot and powder, and whatever else furthered their way of life.

It was here, in Nachadoches, that Seth and Jim began hearing of renewed attacks along the border. So they rode ever southward, picking up even darker news as they traveled on. Even to these trail-hardened rangers, the accounts of wanton carnage were more than they had ever heard, much less experienced. The slow, laborious journey gave Seth plenty of time to think and brood about the slaughter of the innocents. He never said a word to Jim, but the Jägers weighed heavy on his heart every minute of the ride toward Mexico.

Seth Garner: Part One

Señor, do you want to see the country?

A Vile Deed Done

Karl had learned well. The first days of spring found him in the field early and staying late. Survival in the future was secured in the present, and to that end Karl wrung out every drop of daylight. He began this day when he could barely see the tack harness, rigging up the plough mule more by feel than by sight. He ran the furrows straight and long as he raced the sun to get the main crop in. In the end, the life-giving orb of the new season sun had excused herself without asking permission of any, taking the light and warmth with her. Soon the gray light of dusk was replaced by the strange but lovely luminescence of the full moon. He was ending the day as he had begun;

217

Seth Garner: Part One

struggling to pick out points of reference to guide the mule on one last pass, even as he anticipated a warm meal with his beloved family. Karl marveled at how the moonlight cast blue shadows before him, even as Elsie's thin high voice carried over the field. On the way in, he amused himself with the ever-changing shapes upon the upturned clay, as if some private shadow play was unfolding before him. Fully drawn into a nameless game born of imagination, one that flourished then faded like the shadows and mists employed, Karl did not notice the dark forms cast before him. Within moments, Karl came to realize that someone had drawn up from behind. Slipping out of the traces, he turned to see three faceless silhouettes against the cold silver light of the moon. As he offered the welcoming hand of hospitality, inviting them to dismount, a long rifle barrel cantilevered upward in the gathering darkness.

At the sound of the blast, Elsie burst through the door into the open field. Moments before she had laid aside her flour sack apron, despairing of calling out her husband's name, now planning to compel Karl to come in from his work. Now with a shriek "Karl!" pierced the evening stillness with a power that rivaled the horror that had disrupted it. Indeed even as the white-hot lead violated the honest flesh of a hard-working man, the name "Elsie" crowded out all else in Karl's mind. As his body grotesquely torqued about only to see his wife's knees sink into the soft upturned soil, her hands rising to cover her face, impulsively struggling to block out the nightmare uninvited, Karl felt more sorrow than pain. Sorrow for trust betrayed and sorrow for senseless hate that never rests until it devours its own self.

The marauders were born on the borderlands of humanity. As fresh river water blends with the salt of the sea, being in no place in particular, but generally a little bit everywhere, having lost the strength of its singular purpose, these three killers belonged to no one human family. They were pariahs, predators, morally bankrupt in their souls, distillates of the worst that coursed through the veins of humankind. The shooter stayed mounted as the two others slogged toward the soddie. Hanna, the elder daughter, ran toward the short squat renegade, not knowing what she was to do when she met him. She didn't need to know, for a vicious backhand knocked her senseless to the ground. Gabbie, the younger, embraced her sobbing mother, not wanting to believe the cruelty unfolding before her eyes. The third villain reached beneath a tattered serape and drew forth a well-used blade. Gathering strength to lift his head, Karl could barely make out the face of one who knew no pity. With his free hand clasped over a bleeding shoulder, he heard the whistling sound of a lasso cutting though the thin night air. As it settled down about his torso, a sinister laugh framed a mocking invitation, "Señor, do you want to see the country?" The bolting horse snapped the rope taught dragging Karl away into the blackness of night. His body tore through the mesquite scrub and the thorny Palo Verde brush. Careening wildly behind a steed driven as much by fear as by the savage lash of his murderous rider, Karl's body drove through cactus thicket and loose rock alike. Mercifully and inexplicably, he felt no pain. An unexpected calm settled over him even as he surged through the night. He had the strange sensation that he was not in himself, as if he were a third other observing the sadistic drama from a distance. A soothing warmth swept over his body.

"What are you going to do with us?!" Hanna demanded. "Tu no worry, señorita. Tu and su hermana, muy bonita! But su madre, she old and no so pretty!" With that Hanna flew into a rage that drove her forward as a lioness as it closes in for the kill. With nails extended, she leaped through the air all the while clawing for the grimy face that uttered contempt for her dear mother. But with a jolt her lunge was arrested in midair as calloused fingers closed about her slender neck. Her toes now barely touching the ground, the thick bodied one slowly squeezed the life from Hanna. Just before going unconscious, she heard him say, "No can breath, señorita?" The impact of the ground shook her to her senses, and her lungs heaved to draw in the cool night air. Gabbie was now at her side, softly stroking her long red hair, even as blood streamed from her own wounded lip.

Complete darkness now spared them the last grizzly scene of this sick and terrible night. Frenzied hoof beats and a clattering of brush and rock signaled that the tall mounted one had returned with their dear father in tow. The knife-wielding killer strode forward as Karl rocked back upon his knees, barely clinging to life in this world. Grasping a tuff of Karl's blood matted hair, with a scraping, slashing arch, the one in the tattered serape lifted the scalp from a proud head unbowed. Falling forward into the good earth that he had plowed only hours before, Karl rehearsed a verse he had learned as a child. "Der Lord isht mine Shepherd....Ich vill fear no ebil" and so he breathed his last in this world.

As the scalper callously yanked the rope from Karl's body, the thick one charged into the soddie. As chairs, utensils and such were cast out of the door, the mule was cut loose from the plough harness. The racket from the ransacking of their little home did not muffle the sound of soft sobbing without. Gabbie looked upon the carefully wrought white-oak splints of the chair, supple ribbons of wood that her mother had so lovingly woven just weeks ago. The knife man bound up the girls' hands with harness leather from the plow. A wicked "hoop" from inside signaled that the gold coins that Seth had left them last fall

A Vile Deed Done

had been found. Grimy fingers fastened upon the trembling hands of Gabbie and with the other hand he rudely thrust her atop the mule. Hanna, always the strong one snarled, "I can help myself!" Of course, with tethered hands, she could not. Ignoring her rebuff, the craven shadow of a real man made his way toward Hanna. No sooner had the hate-filled spittle splashed across his face, a savage backhand knocked the light out of those beautiful eyes, eyes that burned with a fierce love for her family. Heaving her limp body across the withers, the abuser flashed a murderous stare toward Gabbie, promising worse if she offered trouble.

The shooter rode up as the sound of broken glass came from within the soddie. Within minutes orange-yellow flames devilishly licked out from the door and windows. For Elsie, the crying had stopped now. There were no more tears. Only a blank stare into the deepening darkness of the night. The murderous three slowly rode off with Gabbie and Hanna in tow. Illumined by the burning soddie, it was clear that they were wending their way from whence they came. The Rio Grande to the south, border between Mexico and the Texas territory, was the safe haven for them. With Mexico pressing for independence from Spain, and the Americans stirring the pot in Texas, marauders like these lurked in the fog of chaos. They sought out that strange crease in the law that protects malefactors and shields them from what they deserve. So with a confidence born of experience in such vile work, they slowly made their way south. Having no fear from a broken woman, bereft of all that she had lived for, they chortled and joked as they fingered the gold they had stolen. As far as they were concerned, Elsie was dead on her feet, and they figured that they had left no witnesses to their heinous crime.

221

Seth Garner: Part One

    The slats of the corncrib provided little room, but it was enough. Frightened blue eyes of a young boy pierced the gloom. Gripped with fear, Will had not moved a muscle since he had heard the gun blast at the beginning. Yet he had seen it all. The faces of the killers had been permanently etched upon his mind. The creak of hinges sounded his release from a nightmare that he would never fully escape. Stiffly trudging through the dark, he knelt beside his voiceless mother. Slipping his arm about her, they both waited.... for what, they did not know. At that very moment two lone riders crested the hill behind the burning soddie.

Two Rangers, a Scout and a Mission

"We're too late," Jim muttered. The rose-colored glow of the burning soddie meant that they were, indeed, too late, but just barely. Tragically, the Jägers had been hit only a couple of hours before. Seth cast a quick eye about the scene and concluded as much. As the horses sauntered down the hill toward the mayhem, Seth cursed the ill-fated timing of their arrival. As they approached, Will whirled about in fear, expecting more woe to come their way. As he climbed out of the saddle, Seth called out, "It's O.K., Will. It's me, Seth." With his left foot still in the stirrup, Seth found a pitifully small, frightened boy clinging to his thigh. Patting him on the back as he whimpered, Seth instinctively made his way toward Mrs. Jäger. The light from the fire made for a stark silhouette, kneeling stone-still in the dirt, staring toward the river. Wearing the boy like a splint, Seth hobbled his way toward her, not knowing what to say or do. Slowly, almost mechanically, Elsie turned her face until she spied Seth and her son. With a start, she leapt up and lunged toward Seth, wrapping her thin arms about his chest, all the while sobbing with anguish too sad for words. With that every muscle in Seth's body tensed. His lonesome life was not used to such, if anyone could ever be used to such. He found himself involuntarily patting her on the back and stroking her long hair, all the while inexplicably repeating, "It's over now... we're here. It's over now...." After a few awkward and sorrow-filled moments, her crying tapered off, and Seth called to Jim, "Gather up some of this wreckage and make a fire for coffee! Break out some of the hard tack and jerky too!" Seth up righted one of the white oak splint chairs that had been thrown about and gently led Elsie over to it. He motioned to Will to fetch another. If

Seth Garner: Part One

it was not so low down pitiful, the sight of folks sitting on chairs out in a field at night might have been comical. As Elsie buried her face in her hands, Seth wrapped a saddle blanket around her and led Will off a piece.

Will started right. "I wasn't like I thought I should be. I was..." "Afraid," Seth interjected. "Yes. I'm sick about it." "It's smart to be afraid when there's cause for it, Will, and there was plenty fear to go around here," Seth assured. "I'm a cowar..." "Don't even think it!" Seth barked. "Being afraid and being a coward ain't the same thing!" he continued. "But I hid, Mr. Seth!" "There is a time to hide in a fight! I hid plenty when I fought for Jackson in New Orleans. That's cuz' I was a scout. And from what I can see you're a first class scout," Seth said firmly. Will argued on, "But I didn't fight!" "Scouts don't fight. They travel light, toting few weapons. Their job is to prepare for the fight, or more rightly to prepare others for the fight," Seth explained. Shifting to military mode, Seth added, "Their weapon is strategic reconnaissance." "What?" the boy asked, in a bit lighter mood. "For a scout, it is not what they do that is important. It is what they see and remember that can win the war. Did you see anything, Will?" Wagging his head from side to side, the boy lamented, "I seen it all, Seth, all of it." "Then you are a scout, as I said," replied Seth. "I don't know their names," Will said. "Not necessary. The likes of them don't deserve names. Tell me what you *saw*!" Seth said with emphasis.

"It was almost dark, and maw was preparing dinner. I was in the corn crib taking stock of what was left. It was then that I heard a shot." "Who shot?" asked Seth. "A tall, thin man on horseback was holding a long iron, so he must have fired the shot," Will said. "My paw fell to his knees, while another in a tattered serape dismounted. A third..." "So there was three of them..." Seth said. "Yes, the third was fat and already on the ground walking toward the

Two Rangers, a Scout and a Mission

soddie. Maw had already burst through the door, with Hanna and Gabbie right behind." "Keep going," Seth encouraged. "I could barely see now. The tall horseman threw a lariat around paw, and wildly yelled, 'Let's see the country,' or something like that. I turned away to see the fat man strike Hanna, so I don't know what happened. Hanna fought the fat one, but he grabbed her by the throat, and said...said..." "What did he say? Will, can you remember?" asked Seth. "Yes...he said....something about her having trouble breathing, and he called her señorita. It was dark now, and I heard horse hoofs galloping up again, so the tall one must have returned. Not long after, the one in the serape walked up, as the stout one tore up the soddie. He found the money that you gave us. I'm sorry..." "Don't worry about it. You are doing good. Is there more?" Seth asked. "The fat one threw the lantern into the soddie. By the light I could see more. The man in the serape came walking up then. He had a knife. It had blood on it. He must have..." "I'll tend to that, Will," Seth said trying to comfort the boy. "He cut the harness from the mule, and tied up Hanna and Gabbie with the leather. He threw Gabbi onto the mule. And here's the best part. Hanna spit in his face!" "Good for her!" Seth chimed in. "So they are both on the mule, then?" "Yes. They rode that way." Will pointed a trembling finger into the night. "You're a first class scout! I am proud of you!" Seth said, hugging the boy who did more than any man should ever have to do.

"Coffee's ready!" called Jim. The two walked back to the warm fire. Seth thought how odd it was that one fire spoke of greed and hatred, while the other spoke of love and care. Elsie took the cup from Jim, and said, "Danke schön." These were the first words that Elsie had spoken since her life was brutally changed forever. She took a piece of hard tack and clasped Jim's hand in appreciation. A good sign, Seth thought. For some time, they sat silently about the fire, while Elsie held Will closely. Jim prepared two bedrolls for Elsie and her son. Within a few moments they drifted into a blessed sleep that offered some respite from the day's horror.

Seth had Jim watch over them as he planned to have a look about. Taking a torch with him, he walked in the direction that Will had pointed to earlier. As he entered the plowed field, the events Will spoke of became clear. The tracks of men and horses were easy to follow. He backtracked down toward the creek, and there he found Karl's mangled body. Reading sign as clearly as a book, Seth unraveled the bloody scenes of a frightful night. A crimson trail through the brush marked the place where Karl had been drug. Seeing that Karl had been scalped made Seth's blood boil. The German's hands were clasped together as if in prayer.

The eastern sky began to slowly lighten as he worked his way back to the burned-out soddie. As Elsie and Will slept, Seth filled Jim in on the gruesome details. Rummaging around what was left of the Jäger homestead, Seth found one of the spades that they had used the year before to build their little home. His mind flashed back to how eager Karl was to learn and of how hard he worked. Seth was overcome with grief... and anger. Struggling to get feelings under control, he climbed into the back of one of the wagons. There he found a roll of canvas that all settlers kept to make repairs on the trail. Winding up a length of bailing twine, he hopped to the ground to meet Jim.

In the gathering dawn, he needed no explanation of what Seth was up to. While Elsie and Will still slept, Seth confided that he thought it better this way. Better for the family to remember Karl as he was, not as he now lay. Striking out again, Seth spied a grassy knoll topped by a lone pin oak tree. Karl had often remarked of its solitary

Two Rangers, a Scout and a Mission

beauty, and if he could now speak, he would no doubt choose this place for his final resting place. The spot was well above the flood plane of the river, and so Seth began to dig near the base of the tree. The late winter rains had softened the soil, and in short order he was satisfied with its depth. With all the respect he could muster, Seth rolled Karl's body in the canvas, tying it about here and there with some chord. Then gently sliding the corpse into the fresh grave, Seth began to toss the cold sod atop his good-hearted friend. When there was no dirt left, he walked about gathering flat stones to stack on top of the grave. Karl had suffered enough indignity without varmints tearing into the place where he now lay forever.

Picking up the shovel, Seth turned into the warmth of a new sunrise, intending to trudge back to the family. Yet a strange feeling overcame him, as if he had left something undone, that vague kind of feeling that you have forgotten something, but can't quite tease it out. Turning about, his figure cast a long shadow over the mound where his friend lay. Of all the roles that Seth had been forced to play since he had left his own home in Ohio, there was one responsibility that he dared not take on. Yet as the morning breeze coursed through the spring grass, he was alone in that place. There was no pastor to praise the life and bless the death of this good man. There were no distant family members or friends that could take on the mantle of this hour. Only Seth Garner was present now. He had been raised in a godly home by good parents. Yet like a wild river that had overrun its banks, his life had taken another path, often against his will, but different nonetheless. It had been years since Seth had prayed, really prayed, but for Karl's sake, he couldn't bring himself to walk away. Looking about as if to hail some other human who could free him from this awkward moment, Seth accepted what he knew all too well. Swallowing hard,

227

Seth Garner: Part One

while removing his hat, Seth bowed his head: "Heavenly Father, I should start by saying that I'am a sinner, and that's for sure. And I am telling you right now, that most likely I am gonna' sin a lot more before this day's done. So... I am ashamed...." Seth's voice broke as hot tears began to stream down his wind-burned face. "What I mean is, I'm not prayin' for myself, but for Karl. He loved you, and you know that. Please take care of his dear wife, Elsie, and her fine son, Will. And as for Hanna and Gabbie, I'm asking for them... you understand, please protect them from them vermin until I can get there. For I must tell you .... if that's permitted... that I aim to fetch them back. And ... you should know too...I aim to do what must needs be done...and ... if that's wrong, and you can see your way through on this, I do ask one thing for myself. Have mercy on one who don't rightly know anymore.... Amen."

As he walked back into the camp, Elsie and Will were already up and about. Jim kindled up the fire again, and was brewing something warm to eat and drink. Some of the strain of the previous night had drained away from Elsie's face, and Seth was glad of that. He explained that he had taken care of Karl's body, and with this Elsie began to cry softly again. He didn't try to stop her, for he too had tasted a bit of her pain. He described the place, adding that he was sure that Karl would have liked it. He noted that Karl had remarked on the simple beauty of the place while he was still with them. Continuing, Seth said that if she and Will felt up to it, Jim would take them up to the grave site, but that was completely up to them. The time was not important now. He told Elsie that, as far as he was concerned, the spot was a monument to one of the best and bravest men he ever knew.

Having said this, Seth drew Jim aside, instructing him to take Elsie and the boy further north to San Antonio, and see to it that they get settled in. As he talked he strode over to his horse and hefted the saddlebag, and flung it across the rump of Jim's mount. The clear ring of coinage sounded out in the cool morning air. "Make sure that she gets this," Seth said as he turned back again. "What are you up to Seth?" knowing all along what his partner had in mind. "I'm crossing over. Going into Mexico," he replied as a matter of fact. "That's against the law, Seth." Whirling about Seth roared, "What law?! The law that protected the Jägers?!" Seth bore a dark and grim face, one that Jim had never seen in all the days they had ridden together. Seth charged on, striding up to within a hand's breath of Jim's nose. "Wake up, man! Look around you! Do you see the law? *We're* the law if there be any within a hundred miles. *We're* the only thing, blessed or cursed, that stands between unbridled killing and some semblance of order out here! Between these plains being soaked with innocent blood and something good happening here, there's nothing, not a single thing, except you and me." Pivoting again, Seth loosed his rifle from the saddle and then led his horse over to Jim. "Keep the horse, Seth, we'll double up and make it up to San Antonio some how." "No, Jim. You take don't her. When I'm done, I'll have more than enough mounts for the trip back to Texas." "Well, I'll be tied if I go with you!" piped in the high pure voice of Will Jäger.

"My scoutin' days are over! If there's going to be fighting, I want to be the first to tear into those lowlifes." "Not quite over, yet," Seth's voice softening at the approach of the boy. "Your sharp ears have heard all my hasty words. But you are needed more here with you maw now," Seth admonished. "Jim knows what to do, so team up with him and lend a hand." As he gathered up his gear and headed for the Rio Grande, Seth yelled over his shoulder to Jim, "Count me dead by this time tomorrow if I don't bring the girls back alive and unharmed!" And with that he was

Seth Garner: Part One

gone. He had given all of his worldly wealth to Elsie. But most importantly, in this dark hour, he had given her something more precious than gold. He had given her hope.

Judgment in Mexico

There is a kind of intelligence that merits no praise. It is that craven craftiness, bent on survival, totally bound up with the self, having no regard for others. It is that sick wisdom that knows when the helpless are the most helpless so that with measured timing, it might wreak havoc.

The killers that hit the Jäger homestead were of this kind. They no doubt had been watching the family for some time and concluded that the only real resistance they might encounter was a good-natured farmer behind a sleepy mule. After an attack, their "flight instinct" was strong, having evolved from the many raids they made on border folk. They had carefully planned their escape across the Rio Grande into Mexico, covering their trail as much as possible. Pursuit would be difficult, even for one who knew how.

Seth Garner knew how, and then some. His scouting for General Jackson in the Louisiana bayou was his baptism of fire in this regard. From that service he learned that failure had consequences, and Seth had respect for consequences. The big lesson here: when there is absolutely nothing to see, look closer. Trading with the Indians in Texas had helped Seth even more in this regard. Befriending the friendly, he had often spent time with small bands learning the wood's lore they had gleaned throughout the centuries. In short order, he came to understand that as a white man, at any given time, he was more or less out of touch with his world. Eons of domestication had dulled his senses. On the contrary, the Indians were in nowise domestic. For them, every trail was a book legible to those who knew how to "read" the sign. A blade of grass laying in an odd direction, an overturned pebble, all "spoke" a language easy to follow if one knew

231

Seth Garner: Part One

the code. It was with this kind of mindset, this eye for detail, that Seth now took up the trail.

Seth ran through the plowed field and quickly unraveled the maze of human tracks and horse prints. His first task was to determine how far ahead his adversaries were. In short order he reckoned that all was not as bad as it seemed. Four horses and the plough mule make for slow passage through the mesquite. Also, once the band crossed the river, Seth knew that they would proceed at a leisurely pace, figuring that they were safe in Old Mexico. Finally, as the killers pressed into the desert, the heat would be unbearable by mid-morning. They would have to find some shade early and stay put until late afternoon, then trek on for a couple of hours more until dark. Seth's plan was to meet up with them just before nightfall as they made camp.

Once the bandits left the Jäger field, they immediately sought out rocky areas to mask their path. Again, scuff marks on the flat stone from shod hooves and flakes chipped up from the crumbly sandstone told the story. This stratagem would come to an end once they met the muddy soil of the riverbank. Seth clipped along at a fast pace, picking up sign at a trot. As the group broke out near the river, the trace looked like a veritable stampede. The bulbous prints of the slow, but sure-footed mule practically shouted, "This way! We're over here!"

The Rio Grande, mighty at its source, fairly well pans out as it winds through Mexico. Even with spring rains to the north, islands of mud and sand dotted the course of the shallow river in its lower stretches. Fording this natural boundary between this tenuous possession of Spain and the "Americanos" to the north would be no problem. Determining which direction they went once they entered the river would seem to be a matter of even odds, that is, either up stream or down. But Seth knew that they would

Judgment in Mexico

walk their animals a good piece up stream, against the current, in an effort to conceal their path. The current, though slow moving, would wash away the silt from their tracks. So after gathering up his powder and tinder above his head to keep them dry, Seth simply cut a straight route to the far bank. He then strode up river to intercept the trail of the raiders as they emerged on the other side. Just as he had thought, after less than a quarter mile, fresh tracks clambered up the bank and into the scrub of Mexico.

The sun was getting hotter, and Seth knew that his prey would pause soon. He could not. He pressed on, gashing open a barrel cactus to slake his thirst when he could bear no more. Reflecting upon the carnage at the Jägers, Seth muttered, "Uncalled for. Unnecessary." His wrath grew hotter as did the noonday sun. "Robbery is one thing, but.... that...that..." he grumbled as he searched the ground like a hawk looking for prey. From the start he was gripped with that dark spirit which drove him to pursue outlaws. It was a grim obsession, a relentless compulsion to run them down and be rid of them for good. Foul words and curses coursed through his mind. The red-eyed demon of vengeance took hold of his heart as his pace quickened. Seth came upon a place where they had stopped for a siesta, just as he had imagined they would. Looking about the ruffled ground he could make out the footprints of the two girls. "Good. They are fit enough to get about on their own power" Seth mused. Following the small and delicate tracts of the girls, he could see where they had once again been lifted on to the back of the mule for the last leg of the day's journey. Amid the rubble and disturbed soil Seth made out a clearly marked "arrow" gouged in the dirt by a small foot. He thought, "I don't know which of the girls made this sign, but I bet it was Hanna!"

Seth was closing in on the captors. The upturned earth of the horse prints freshened, being a faint shade darker

233

than the prints crossed an hour ago. His heart lightened for the first time since he started this dreaded journey. As Seth rounded a bend, a broad grin spread across his face. A fine white handkerchief was snagged at the tip of a Palo Verde tree. "Hanna...still fighting and resisting her captors! Brave woman is she!" The secretly dropped sign was welcomed, but hardly needed. Seth was hot on the trail, and the marauders had long since stopped efforts to conceal their journey, feeling secure on their home turf. But the handkerchief was a sign of a strong spirit, of good morale, and Seth was encouraged by it. He continued on with renewed intensity.

Wood smoke! Seth definitely smelled the smoke of a campfire. He slowed his tracking, and did more looking than walking. A horse whinnied far off, but clear enough for Seth to estimate range. Very close. He dropped to the ground, remaining motionless for some time. Duck-walking along in a low crouch, he inched from one clump of brush to the next. Watching and waiting like a cougar on the hunt. Voices. "Silentio! Las senioritas are mine! Da horses are yours!" Seth could tell that they were just making their second camp of the day, settling in for the night. He bided his time, peering through the soft evening light. It wouldn't be long now. Throughout what was left of the day, he heard fights and scuffles coming from the camp. It sounded more like a pack of wolves than a place of human habitation. At one point a sinister laugh seeped through the desert scrub, followed by the whip like crack of a woman's palm across a swarthy face. That lightened Seth mood for a moment, but just that, for he then heard a dull thud, followed by Hanna's voice moaning in pain. Seth bit his lip; it took all of his strength just to do nothing; to stay put. For now, his only company was his thoughts. They proved to be dark humored guests. Every time his thoughts would turn to Hanna and Gabbie, his heart would ache. When he thought of Elsie and Will, he fought back tears. When he thought of Karl, and what the killers had done to him, his blood boiled. As shadows swept in from the west, Seth steeled himself for what lay ahead. It wouldn't be long now.

Night fell over the camp like a pall. Apart from the mumbling and shuffling of the camp, it was completely silent. For Seth, the time had finally come. He cinched up the long-knife, checked his weapons and coolly walked toward camp.

Gabbie watched as one of her tormentors carried a firebrand through the camp. Following the patch of light as it passed on, she suddenly let out a gasp. From the leading edge of the light to its trailing glimmer, the buckskin-clad figure of Seth Garner passed before her eyes. "Something wrong, Señiorita?" growled the knifeman, whirling this way and that, holding the torch high and glaring into the darkness. "No...no...nothing's wrong. Just stepped on a cactus spine, that's all," she offered. Hanna looked wide-eyed at Gabbie, knowing her sister well and thus not believing a word she had said. A single wink from Gabbie followed by a slow deliberate nod let Hanna know that something was up.

The Devil's Club cactus is aptly named. It is a wicked combination of spines and toughness. Wrapping his hand in a fold of rawhide and cutting off a shank of the menace, Seth eased through the darkness. His knife made short work of the hobbling on the mule as well. When the Devil's Club came down hard on the beast's flank, it let out a bray to wake the dead and then set out for parts unknown.

Everyone bolted to their feet as the stricken animal tore through the brush, bawling pitifully in an attempt to dislodge fiery needles stuck in its rump. "Santos!" yelled the shooter. "Que pasa, hermano?!" he shouted to no one in particular, looking a bit frightened as he tried in vain to

Seth Garner: Part One

make out what the racket was all about. "Gordo! Go check the horses! Ride out and reign in that fool-headed mule too!" "Gordo" means "fat one" so Seth now had advanced notice that the strangler was coming his way. Plodding through the darkness the raider found the other livestock all in order. Rigging up his horse for a harebrained ride in the dark, the choker hauled himself onto the back of a sleepy steed. Not really knowing what to do, but not wanting to invite the wrath of the gang's leader, he'd ride a few steps, listen, and then move on a pace or two more.

A split second can seem like an eternity when it's your last. As the fat one's eyes opened wide in the moonlight, he realized, more by way of impulse than thought, that this was indeed his last. Like a panther springing in the dark, Seth had timed his move perfectly. Both hands had come down hard on the horse's rear, just behind the saddle, lofting him above its flanks. Even before his legs settled down about the horse, a whirring sound ringed about the strangler's ears. As Seth secured his place on the mount's rear, the soft supple rawhide garret settled under a double chin. "Mi madre!" he wheezed as filthy fingers clawed at the leather strap sinking into his throat. Seth clinched his teeth as he ratcheted up the tension on the hide chord. All the pent up hatred he had been harboring against this group of killers, all of the white-hot rage, flowed into his hands and telegraphed into the deadly leather as it dug deeper and deeper into the folds of sweating flesh. As Seth jammed a knee into the back of his victim, the fat man writhed about struggling to get a glimpse of the night demon that had fallen upon him. Sensing he was trying to say something, Seth eased up on the tension, only to hear the choking whisper, "Quien eres?! Who are you? Porque...Why are you...?" Violently crushing his knee forward again while at the same time hauling back with a vicious jerk, Seth hissed a hate-filled message into the dying man's ear: "*Are you having trouble breathing, Señior?!*" "Ajudame, Dios! No! No!" he wheezed as a terrifying moment of recognition pushed through a dying brain. Then it was over. Limp arms lay quivering at the side of the mounted dead. Seth was not done with him yet.

Tense-filled minutes passed in complete silence. The two remaining killers became increasingly nervous. They talked to each other in muted tones, eyes flashing wildly in the firelight. "Gordo! Hermano! Donde estas?!" the leader shouted out into the night. Soon there was the shuffling of an approaching horse easing into the edge of the encampment. The animal halted just outside the range of the campfire, the mounted figure backlit by the rising moon. "Gordo! Esta tu?!" The shooter and the scalper stared trembling at the specter as the horse took a step or two closer. As the ring of light crept up the approaching horse, all in the camp gasped in horror, Gabbie nearly fainting at the sight. A purplish bloated face came into view. A hideous crazed smile lay frozen across a mass of lifeless flesh; terror stricken eyes bulged from swollen sockets. The corpulent victim's hands and feet were lashed to the saddle horn and stirrups. "Sangre de Christo!" shrieked the shooter. "Cut him down, quickly!" he shouted to the one in the dingy serape. Drawing his knife, and running to the far side of the horse, he cut with one hand while grasping the bridle with the other. As he hacked a dead hand loose from the horn, a sharp air-splitting sound, followed by a sickening thud, was heard above the clamor. Now the scalper wielded two blades, one in his hand and another sunk deep in the center of his back. The death spasm caused the scalper's hand to clamp down on the horse's bridle like a vice, even while the rest of his body slumped to the ground. Terror stricken, the horse began to wheel in tight circles, dragging the scalper round and round as it turned. Even so the freed arm of the dead rider

237

Seth Garner: Part One

flopped wildly in the air like a grim parody of a rodeo from hell, his bizarre face not changing amidst the dark gyrations of the steed. All the while the shooter was wagging his head back and forth in disbelief, senselessly shouting out, "Santos! O' Santos!" The flickering campfire made a freeze frame effect at each circuit of the animal, the women screaming at every exposure of the nightmare before them. Hanna swept Gabbie into her arms, carrying her to the ground, shielding her eyes from the gore that whirled before them. Sinking to the earth, Gabbie whispered, "It's Mr. Seth! It's him!" as fast as a breath can breathe. The stricken beast finally broke loose from its spin, charging out of the camp into the night, bearing the two bodies away.

All went silent. The crackling of the fire was all that dared break the deadly quiet. And then.... it started. A slow but steady loping of an unseen horse sounded out in the dark. The shooter ran over to his saddle and yanked a long iron from the scabbard. Turning in time with the pacing horse, he yelled out to the unseen menace, "Who are you! What do you want? Dinero?! I have money!" he bawled as he snatched up the stolen money of the Jägers. Still turning in one place, he waited for an answer that never came. The steady sound of the horse's hooves, circling about, was all that he heard. "The *señioritas*? You want the girls?" he shouted, still spinning in place as he chambered a shell. Again, nothing but heavy footfalls met his ears. Sweeping the muzzle in time with the sound, he fired a shot, and then another. At that, the horse's pace quickened, as the shooter fired off two more rounds, all the while pirouetting in a tight circle. "The girls? Muerto! Digame! I kill the girls!" he said as he locked his feet into the sand and shouldered his rifle, pointing in the direction of Hanna and Gabbie as they hunkered down on the ground. In an instant, a shot rang out from the darkness. Hot burning lead tore through the

Judgment in Mexico

left shoulder of the shooter. As a reflex, he squeezed the trigger, but this time only a metallic click emerged from the weapon. Slumping to his knees, the rifle slowly slipped from his hands. Blood streamed from a gapping wound in his shoulder as he hung his head and wept pitifully.

Hanna and Gabbie stared at their stricken tormentor from across the fire. Hoof falls slowly drew closer. The profile of a mounted ranger, like the Angel of Death himself, loomed up from the night directly behind the beaten desperado. A whirring sound directed their eyes upward, and the girls could barely make out a twirling lasso by the moonlight. Like a viper's strike, the rope shot forward, reaching just enough girth to slip over trembling shoulders before it was snatched taught. With a groan, the vanquished killer made short choppy movements with his knees, eventually wrenching about to face his unknown attacker. "Porque? What you want from me? Who... who..." His voice trailed off as his head sunk back toward the ground. A few moments of silence, then a steely voice said, "*Do you want to see the country, Señior?!*" The eyes of the stricken men gleamed white in the night. As Seth's horse reared up and twisted in midair, Gabbie screamed, "No, Mr. Seth! No!"

The rope snapped so tight that the shooter's body went airborne, launched forward through the night at terrific force. The women screamed aloud, clasping their hands over their ears to blot out the wails of pain and the sound of breaking brush as the two ploughed on through the darkness, all the while clinching their eyes shut in an effort to erase all trace of a night gone mad.

Seth stretched low over the mane, driving hard to eke out every bit of speed the horse had in him, viciously lashing the forequarters with leather reins. As the shooter crashed through thorny mesquite brush and cactus, his unearthly howls goaded the beast to a heightened frenzy.

239

Seth Garner: Part One

Then one massive gut-wrenching thud signaled that the half-flailed man had slammed into a boulder. With that Seth hauled in on the reins, as a mangled body slid to a halt in the desert sand. Seth turned to spy the broken heap that lay behind him. Ever so slowly, battered legs pulled up and folded beneath a heaving chest. The shooter rocked back and barely lolled a bleeding head off to one side. With effort he was able to angle up in time to see Seth's gloved hand steadily rising in the air, prepared to strike the horse on its flank again. "In del nombre de Patri, have mercy on me!" the marauder pleaded in a voice that was barely audible in the stillness of the desert night. With hand still raised, Seth growled, "Karl Jäger would have had mercy on you. But *he's*....not....HERE!" The hand came down like a hatchet and the gruesome trek began anew. Seth blazed on with increased intensity now, as the rim rock of the canyon drew ever closer. Slipping his knife out of its scabbard and fingering the reigns with his free hand, Seth suddenly cut to the left. The horse whinnied in alarm as the shooter's body fishtailed through the scrub. In tumbleweed fashion it careened toward the precipice even as Seth's knife sliced through the rope's taught fibers. The last cry of a ruthless man trailed off in the ears of one who had become as ruthless as he, if not more so. Staring down into the abyss, Seth gasped for breath; his parched lips cleaving together, as he listened to his own pulse slacken and fade to normal. Surprised by tears welling up in his eyes, he blinked a couple of times, looked about and took an odd glance at the severed rope as if it was something foreign. He felt as if he was waking from a bad dream, as if the previous hour had never really happened. But he knew that it did happen. It was not someone else who had committed wanton slaughter against his fellow man, regardless of how vile they might have been. It was Seth Garner. A wave of nausea swept over him and he fought to swallow again trying desperately to get a grip on himself.

The ride back to camp was like a bad dream, as if he was looking down upon himself, yet removed from it all. As he dully plodded along in the dark, he soon saw the flames of the campfire licking blurrily in the night. And then he could hear the two sisters crying softly as he approached. He had no idea of what to say the two terror-stricken girls he had come to save. No doubt they were as afraid of him now as they were of their kidnappers. He slipped to the ground and tied the reins of the horse a short distance outside of the camp, softly walking in on foot. As he approached the girls he held his arms open, and in an instant they leaped up reaching out in similar fashion toward him. Yet almost at once they waved him away, burying their face in their hands, heaving with uncontrollable sobs. Seth drew up short and pleaded, "It's me, Seth Garner. I came to help. Your maw and Will, they are fine, and..." With that Hanna straightened up and smoothed back her hair and straightened her rumpled clothes. Emboldened by her older sister, Gabbie managed to pull down her hands, and gain control of herself, yet remained partially behind Hanna. Hanna spoke softly but firmly. "We know who you are, Mr. Garner. We are thankful that you've come. It just that ..." Seth looked about to see what was wrong. His hands were encrusted with dried blood and his buckskins were splattered as well. His worn out boots cut furrows in the blood-soaked soil. The camp reeked of carnage. Looking into their eyes, for the first time since the ordeal began, Seth got a glimpse of who he had become. He did not like what he saw. There was worry and fear and doubt. They were indeed thankful *for* him, but they were clearly afraid *of* him. Seth stood silently in the dark for a few awkward moments. Finally he spoke. "We need to get across the river right quick. It's

Seth Garner: Part One

against the law..." His voice trailed off as Gabbie drew closer to her sister. Seth didn't exactly know what to do right then. He had accomplished what he had set out to do, but didn't exactly know how to proceed from here. The girls had been traumatized for sure and Seth's rescue, for the moment anyway, was no help in this regard. He didn't regret the end of the killers, but he was soul sick at what he sensed from the girls. The air was tense. He took a deep breath and started in again. "The moon is out and bright. Can you manage to move off a piece toward the river, and make a new camp northward?" Hanna replied, "I'd say that would be good, Mr. Garner. We shan't stay *here* tonight. Please, guide us away from this dreadful place!." Without talking, Seth gathered up a few items from the camp, grabbed a torch from the fire and retrieved his horse. The women followed as Seth struck the main trail toward the border. They walked in complete silence the better part of an hour. Seth was bursting inside to give some kind of explanation, some kind of newly kindled apology for what he did, but he didn't know how. Reaching a soft sandy spot, he spread out some bedrolls he had salvaged and laid two wool blankets at their feet. Instinctively the two sisters descended on the spots and nestled in for the night to rest as best they could. They held hands beneath the blankets. Striking flint to steel, Seth lit tinder and started a small fire. "It's amazing what a fire will do for spirits!" he said with all the cheer he could muster under the circumstances. The girls made no answer, but lapsed into an uneasy slumber.

Well before dawn Seth slipped back to the camp of the highjackers to retrieve the livestock and any provisions that would help them on their way. The two remaining horses were nearby, but the one with the fat man atop was no place to be seen. Seth ranged out in a zigzag pattern and after a time, he spotted him. The beast had managed to give the scalper the slip somewhere out in the desert, and Seth reckoned that was no concern of his. But the strangler was still lashed to the saddle, yet listing grotesquely to one side due to the one arm that had been freed the night before. Again Seth viewed the deadly work of his own hands as if it had been done by a stranger. It was difficult to believe that he was the same person who had killed so savagely. But he was, and it troubled him greatly. Taking out his knife he cut the other limb free, sliced the boots from the stirrups and shoved the bloated body to the ground like so much unwanted lumber. He drew the horse away a bit and softly spoke to it as if it were human. "None of this is your doin'. I drug you in on all this.." The horse snorted and nuzzled Seth in the shoulder as if he understood. After packing some provisions onto the horses, he made a train of the beasts and headed back to the girl's camp just at gray light.

Seth stoked the fire back to life and made a pot of coffee. Spreading an oilcloth over a flat stone near the waking girls, he set forth some hardtack and jerky. He then stood back a few paces, folded his arms and looked down upon the girls waiting for them to come to, all the while feeling a bit silly. It was like making a tea party in the desert. But he had to find a way to communicate that he appreciated the difference. He had to let them know that he knew of that gentle power held only by a woman, and that he believed in it. Theirs was a presence that somehow brought a degree of civility and beauty and decency. He was determined to make a new start of it.

Hanna opened her eyes only to see the dark figure of a man towering over her. She drew her hand to her mouth in an attempt to stifle a scream. Leaning a bit forward, Seth said loudly, "Good mornin'!" Seth had lived a lonely life on the trail. When he did have company it was with men so like himself that it was as if he was still alone. That is, there was never any need to use language or express ideas that were not part and parcel with the dusty, simple life they lived. He didn't really know how to talk to *other* people, much less speak with a female.

Gabbie soon arose and instinctively wrapped her arms around her older sister. Awkwardly Seth started in, "Well...we got horses! I went back to *the other* place last night," he said, thinking that using different words for the dreaded camp might ease their minds in some way. "And I fetched the horses. But that mule was nowhere to be found. Probably running through the streets of Mexico City by now with that cactus in his hind end!" he said with a hardy chuckle and a slap on the knee. There was not the slightest response from the girls.

Bumbling on he said, "I found this one right off. Now that other horse... now that was a chore... having to cut off a dead man, he being all stiff and all..." Just then Seth noticed that Gabbie's eyes had once again grown wide with terror. Hanna lock eyes on Seth and with a wry smile slightly wagged her head from side to side, trying to get Seth to leave off his gory tale. "Oh! Then again, Gabbie can ride my horse. He's all clean and gentle...most times." "That will be fine, Mr. Garner." "Oh...and...I been wanting to tell ya' from the start. 'Seth' or 'Boy' or even 'Hey you!' will do. I'll know that you're meaning me, seeing that I'm the only one around way out here...least wise." "Thank you, Mr. Seth," was Hanna's polite reply. "'Mr. Seth'...well...Alrighty then! We best be getting down the trail. We can't ride when the sun's high. But that's o.k. too because the horses can't take the heat neither." "That sounds like a fine plan, Mr. Seth." "It has to be cool for travel out here. First thing in the morning, and really, just before dark. The desert critters will let us know. When the tarantulas and rattle snakes move...that's when we move..." Just then, Gabbie buried her face in her older sister's side even as she gently stroked her hair in an attempt to ease her nerves. "Maybe we should help you break camp, Mr. Seth." "No! No, ladies. Ya'll just take your time. I made you some breakfast...and you both...you just eat your fill. I'll go saddle up the horses." Seth dropped his head, looked long at the desert sand while slowly stroking a heavily stubbled beard, trying hard to think of what to say next, something to make up for the gaffs he had just made in one of the few conversations he had ever had with a mature woman.

Hanna broke the long silence. "All of this is very thoughtful of you, Mr. Garner." "*My* pleasure," Seth said even more happily for he had stumbled onto something that pleased her. "Now that cup...you're gonna have to share it," he explained with as much care in his voice as he knew how. "That's quite alright, Mr. Garner..." Interjecting, Seth continued, "Now this one here's mine. I'd let you use it too, but betimes I chew tabakki...and a cup like this...." "I'm sure that it has many interesting uses," Hanna opined. "We'll manage fine with this one cup," she said assuring him with the hint of a smile on her lips. "Well...*of course* you will! What *am* I thinking!" he said thrusting both arms up in the air, then slapping two over-sized palms on trail-worn thighs. As two puffs of dust slowly drifted away, he turned about and strode across the camp toward the horses. For some reason, about halfway across the clearing, Seth weakly waved over his left shoulder without looking back, and for some reason Hanna felt obliged to wave back too.

Seth took his time with the horses for he was really in hiding; kicking himself for his lack of social graces. "Betimes, I chew tabackki...!" he growled. "What a talker you are!" he moaned. Kicking a blotch of sand from the creek, he muttered, "I cutta' dead man down!" he groaned. "Goes good with breakfast, I'd say!" As he ruminated in the

Seth Garner: Part One

brush, trying to steel enough nerve to return to camp, Hanna cherished a moment alone with her beloved Gabbie in the warmth of a new day.

Before they pulled out, he handed over the leather pouch of coins that the strangler had filched from their soddie. He had learned this much...not to go into detail of how he got it back from the killer. Explaining again, that they had to get over the river as soon as possible, he shared that there would be no midday siesta. The sisters said that bearing the noonday sun would be worth the price of seeing their beloved mother and brother.

Seth led the group, he riding the horse that had been stolen from the Jägers. He thought that keeping something familiar in sight would help the girls on the way back home. Hanna and Gabbie followed on their own mounts, side by side, for they talked almost constantly all the way to Texas. Another saddle horse, the one he had cut the fat one from, trailed the group. "Out of sight, out of mind," he reckoned in his heart as he rode slowly on. Seth spoke not a word, yet strained his ears to pick up anything from the girls' conversation. Hanna's occasional, "He's a good man....on the inside...I think" and "It's going to get better," was like healing to Seth's soul. Grinning like a possum for miles, he was grateful for any phrase or snippet he could glean out of the air.

A few miles from the river Seth saw a familiar track emerge from the bush. It joined the trail that they were on, leading due north toward the Rio Grand. "Looks like your mule is part blood hound, or homin' pigeon or sumptin' like that," Seth hollered over his shoulder. Hanna rode up along side of Seth as he pointed down to the ground. The nearly circular tracks were unmistakable. Through the night the mule had wandered its way toward the river on its own accord. "Looks like he'll make it home before we will!" Seth said cheerily. A broad smile spread across

Judgment in Mexico

Hanna's face as she turned back to share the good news with Gabbie. Things were coming together again.

As they approached the river, indeed, Seth spotted something out of place a bit out from shore. "What do we have here?" he barked over his shoulder again. The girls rode up and as they got closer they spied a comical sight. There was their mule, sitting with the sore end of his living in the cooling river water. Tail down, front legs propped stiff, flopping his big ears to and fro, the beast framed a silly picture. For the first time since the attack happened, the girls began to laugh. The mere sound of their joy was like the breath of life to Seth. An exhilarating tingle coursed through his body. Retrieving the mule could only help. As Seth dismounted, the mule stood up with a start, laid back his ears, and side-jumped a few times, kicking up an awful froth in the shallows. To him, anything that looked and smelled like Seth Garner was trouble. "Whoa boy!" he said as he back peddled, realizing the problem. Mules are slow on thinking but long on memory and this mule remembered Seth in a bad way. "Poor baby!" Gabbie crooned as Seth tried to figure out how a half-ton of mule could be a "baby." The mules' ears pricked up at the sound of Gabbie's voice, even as she snatched up a big shank of spring grass before wading into the river. Accepting the juicy offering, the beast nuzzled Gabbie with tender affection. At that, Seth could see that the Devil's Club was still deeply embedded in his trailer, the surrounding area a bit reddened and swollen. Seth said that they would have to get a blanket over his head, and then they might be able to do some good. Taking the blanket and shrouding its head, Gabbie tried to calm the animal down even as Hanna did her part. She slipped a stout stick through a gap between the cactus branch and the mule's hide, giving it a quick flip. With that the mule let out a bray and several vicious kicks, but the thorny torment was gone. Still shrouded, Hanna gently picked out all the spines that stayed behind, and so the job was done.

"Let the animals eat a little grass before we ford!" Seth shouted from a distance. Each time the mule saw Seth its eyes would flair with fear. Wagging his index finger in the air and musing philosophically, he said, "Not to blame. Not one bit. I would feel the same way toward any one who tagged me with a cactus club!" As the animals grazed Hanna continued to care for Gabbie. Sitting in the soft grass she said, "Girl your hair's a mess!" Using her long delicate fingers as a comb, Hanna began to work out some of the tangles. Gabbie let out a good natured wail or two when Hanna met a snag here and there, the kind of banter that is common to small talk among loving sisters. Seth smiled as he gazed upon this cameo of family life. "Have a look at what I pulled out of that mop!" joked Hanna as she held up a ball of golden strands. "I don't have to look! I felt every one of those when you so rudely relieved me of them!" Gabbie said feigning displeasure. "Well at least you look more human now," chirped Hanna as she let the golden stands fly loose in the wind. As the small cluster scampered away, it caught on a bush and held fast. In a moment a small bird descended and took up the offering in its beak. "Hey! That's my hai...!" "Look Gabbie, she's building a nest!" noted Hanna as they followed the bird into a mesquite bush along the shore. Sure enough, in this wild and harsh land, the frail bird was making a new home. Against all odds, this tiny thing was working toward the future. As Seth wistfully took in the scene, he said resolutely, "Let's cross over."

The ride to San Antonio was uneventful; not so his arrival. Word of the massacre had heightened emotions, making the reception of Jim and the Jägers that more sensational. By the time Seth and the two girls rode into town, he was already a local hero. The folks smiled and waved, while others strode up and shook his hand. Seth was nonplussed by the whole thing.

Jim had done his job well. Within hours after arriving in town, the Miranda widow took in Elsie and Will. She had been the wife of one of the wealthiest men in town, and had been widowed for a long time. She craved the company and the chance to look after someone other than herself. After the tearful reunion of Hanna and Gabbie with her mother and little brother, Señora Miranda was overjoyed to have a full house. Ordering food to be prepared, she got a hot bath ready for the sisters.

While in town, Seth had taken time to get bathed and groomed. He shined up real nicely. "Well, I guess it's time I be moving on!" he announced after one of his brief visits with the family. Will ran up and gave him a hearty hug. Patting him on the head Seth said, "Now here's the real hero! It was the eyes and ears of this scout that got the family back together! Why I knew exactly what I was up against because of Will's report. Well done son!" Señora Miranda told Seth that a horse would be saddled up and made ready for him to go. "No...no...I get my horses like I pick up firewood. There are a lot of mustangs out there, and the good Lord will grant me the pick of the litter, I'll wager." That was the first time that Seth freely spoke of his Maker in a long while. But the whole ordeal had brought Him to mind a time or two. "Und der Herr vill bless you fur dat!" Elsie affirmed. Will stepped forward and looked Seth full in the face. "With me being a scout and all, I been thinking that I will be in sore need of a horse too!" his eyes pleading for a departing gift from Seth. "Well I've commissioned Hanna to be in charge of all the livestock. It's up to her now what to do with the family herd," explained Seth. "Take one of your choosing, little brother," she said patting him on the back as he sped past her on his way to the stables. As Seth turned to leave, Elsie boomed,

Seth Garner: Part One

"Now, vait vun minute! No vun leebs mine hause wit' dout a prair!" With that everyone bowed their head out of reverence to the matriarch. Seth slipped off his hat and stared at the floor. "Herr, bless Mr. Seth. Protect him, and prosper him. Most of all, dear Herr, show him your lub und kraft! Amen!" As Seth raised his head slowly he looked into the limpid blue eyes of Hanna. She slipped her lithe hand behind his head and gave him a warm, honest-to-God kiss right on the lips. For a moment, Wesley Seth Garner felt peace inside. He had feelings for Hanna, but had no idea what to make of them. As his face turned red, Seth fumbled through a farewell and crawfished out the door.

As he strode out of town, Seth was deeply troubled, but shared his thoughts with no one. The terror he had seen in the faces of the women when he first entered the camp after waylaying the bandits still haunted him. For the first time he had gained a glimpse of himself from the outside, so to speak, and he was repulsed by it. In riding hard after the law, he ridden rough shod over it. He had crossed the fine line that divided justice from punishment. He had taken upon himself things he should not have. He had acted like judge, jury and executioner, all in one. Deep down inside he felt that something was out of place. From the start, he had no intention of capturing the bandits. He had planned to kill them all along. And he did. He had not the slightest bit of remorse at the violent deaths he had meted out that night. On the contrary, as he held their life in his hands, he harbored a twisted sense of satisfaction. He recoiled at that thought but it was there, and there was no denying it. The wild lands of Texas had changed him, and not for the good. As he marched northward into the evening, a voice from long past welled up in his soul: "Vengeance is mine says the Lord. I will repay." With that, Seth determined that he would ride the fair plains of Texas no more.

Timeline

Seth Garner - Born May 1, 1795

Abandoned Heathshire Boarding School, Boston, MA- Sept. 1810, (Seth =15 years old)

On the Boston Post and Pennsylvania Roads- Fall and early Winter of 1810

Over Winter in Pittsburg – Winter of 1810

On the Ohio (Pittsburgh to confluence of the Ohio and Mississippi Rivers) - Early Spring of 1811 to early Summer of 1811 (Seth = 16 yrs. old)

Summer in St. Louis – Summer of 1811

Log raft float down the Mississippi River – Begins late Summer of 1811 and ends in New Orleans in Dec. 1812

Rides out the New Madrid earthquake on the Mississippi River – Dec. 16, 1811 and Jan. 23, 1812 and Feb. 7, 1812

Seth turns 17 yrs. old on the Mississippi River

Fights in the Battle of New Orleans- Winter of 1812 (Seth = 17 ½ yrs. old)

Life in Texas- Mid-Spring of 1813 through Early Spring of 1817 (Seth = 22 years old)

Into the Colorado and Wyoming Territories – Summer and Fall of 1817 (Seth = 23 years old)

Capture by the Lakota and Rescued by Bright Eagle- Late Fall of 1817 (still 23 years old)

Healing and Recovery in the Mandan Village – Winter of 1817

Courtship and Marriage to Abigail – Spring of 1818 (Seth just turned 24 years old)

Homestead and First Year in the Soddie – Late Spring through Winter of 1818 (still 24 years old)

Start of "Garner's Station" and the Snow Storm – Early Spring 1819 through Winter of 1820 (Seth = 25 years old)

The Prospering Time: Expansion of "Garner's Station" and "The Announcement"- Spring and Summer of 1821 (Seth = 26 years old)

Great Expectations...Birth of Blue Wolf.... All Lost—Fall and Winter of 1821 (Seth = 26 yrs old).

The Barren Years – Early Spring of 1822 through early Spring of 1824 (Seth turns 29 yrs. old)

Saved by Raven – Spring of 1824

Life with Raven until the last rendezvous- 5 years = 1827-29 (Seth is 34 yrs. old)

Building the dream – 5 years – 1830-34 (Seth is 39 yrs. old)

Seth, Raven and his father together – 5 yrs. – 1835-39 (Seth is 44 yrs. old)

The last trouble – 1839; Blue Wolf turns 19 yrs. old.

Young Seth Garner

About the Author

Bill Simmons, a life-long educator and writer, draws heavily on his own experience in *Seth Garner*. Born and raised in New Orleans, Louisiana Simmons soaked up the many cultures and experiences of that great city. Its history, cuisine and love of nature drove home a central truth: all of life is interconnected. The joy is seeing the parts and realizing what holds them all together. So what made his home town great is what made the nation great, and what made the nation great, helped make sense of the rest of the world.

His commitment to faith and study led to a five-year stint in Europe and the reception of his Ph.D. from the University of St. Andrews in Scotland. Again, the individual stories of Europe only served to highlight the beauty and power of the American story. All of these experiences birthed a passion in Simmons to convey that story in an exciting and novel way. That passion is what birthed *Seth Garner*.

It comes as no surprise that the author loves history, travel, cooking, and outdoor sports. For him, God is at work in nature and in human nature and is the One who holds all things together.

Bill resides in Cleveland, Tennessee with his wife, Lenae. They have three children, David, Nathaniel and Laura. He is Professor of New Testament and Greek at the local university and is well-received as a speaker and writer, not only at home but also abroad.